JUST ONE KISS

CHELSEA M. CAMERON

Get a Free Book and Stories!

Tropetastic romance with a twist, Happily Ever Afters guaranteed! You can expect humor and heart in every Chelsea M. Cameron romance.

Get access to a free book, free stories, and free bonus chapters! Join Chelsea's Newsletter for bonus content, receive a free ebook, get access to future exclusive bonus material, news, and discounts.

About Just One Kiss

Sasha Klein couldn't be less happy to be living in Castleton, Maine. If only her sister hadn't fallen in love with a Castleton guy nicknamed Skippy who got her pregnant and then bailed on her and her little girl and gone to Las Vegas. Sasha plans to get out of the tiny town just as soon as her sister, Lizzie, is back on her feet.

Looking for any kind of excitement, Sasha escapes Castleton and ends up at a lesbian bar. Things get out of hand when she spills a drink on, almost gets in a fight with, and then kisses a gorgeous mystery woman. Much to her surprise, she sees that woman the following week at her niece's parent-teacher conference. Awkward.

Jaqueline "Jax" Hardy is everything that Sasha is not, and it's annoying as hell. Jax just can't stop rubbing her perfection in Sasha's face, and Sasha can't stop being attracted to it. No matter how hard she tries to resist, Sasha keeps finding herself waking up in Jax's bed under her Egyptian cotton designer sheet set.

Against her better judgement, Sasha starts getting to know Jax, and the more she learns, the more she likes. It also doesn't hurt that Jax clearly has money and doesn't mind spending it on Sasha.

Will Sasha finally give in to her heart and stop fighting her feelings for Jax? Or will she cut and run, leaving Castleton for good?

Chapter One

THE EVENING STARTED out less than auspicious. First of all, my car did not want to start, but then finally kicked into gear after a lot of begging and cursing. I knew I had to take it in to get serviced, but that would have to wait. Tonight, I needed to get out.

I'd been watching my niece, Luna, all day, and she'd been a handful. I needed to be somewhere adults only. Somewhere I could disappear, but somewhere I could still be among people. By some miracle, there was an actual lesbian bar about forty minutes from Castleton, and that's where I set my sights, as well as my GPS.

I parallel parked on the street and fed the meter before heading down the sidewalk toward the sound of pounding music and raucous laughter.

The bar was just what I'd hoped it would be: somewhat dingy, but with a clean floor, and full of all kinds of queer people. I breathed a sigh of relief as I handed my ID to the woman watching the door, tattoos roping around both of her arms. It was too dark to make them out.

Inside was loud, and somehow smoky, even though cigarettes had been banned in public for decades. I pushed my way to the bar and ordered an Old Fashioned that I planned to drink slowly, so I would be sober enough to drive myself home.

I'd just picked up my drink from the sexy bartender with orange hair wearing a black corset top when I felt someone staring at me. I surveyed the smoky bar, trying to find who it was when I locked eyes with someone standing in the center of a large group. They were all dressed differently, some in cute dresses, some in flannel shirts and boots that had seen some dirt, but they all had an energy about them that made you stop and take notice.

The stranger at the center wore a low-cut black dress that hugged every curve and almost made my mouth water. Her hair was long and dark, hanging down her back. Our eyes met and I felt jolted, as if I'd grabbed an electric fence, like that one time when I'd done it on a dare.

I quickly looked away and tried to find a dark corner to lurk in. I wanted to be surrounded by people, but not have to interact with them.

As I shuffled through the crowd, I felt her eyes still on me and I was starting to get annoyed. What was she staring at?

I looked down at my outfit. So my jeans had holes in them that weren't put there by a machine. My shirt had been washed so many times it was soft and faded and you could barely see the print of two little cartoon marshmallows hugging anymore.

There was nothing wrong with my outfit, but if stranger wanted to judge, then go ahead. I'd sit in my corner and judge her right back.

I tucked myself against a wall in the corner. I could see, but not be seen. Ideal.

My drink was perfect and I felt myself falling into the noises around me. The music, the yelled conversations, the laughter, the flirting from first dates and committed couples alike.

I tried to avoid the stranger and her group, but they were literally in my line of sight. They'd taken over two high top tables and were all talking over each other at once as they sipped bottles of beer and bright drinks the color of candy.

Our eyes met again and hers narrowed ever so slightly.

What do you want? I thought to myself. It didn't matter. I wasn't here for anything but an escape for a few hours.

I finished my first drink and realized I needed a second. I went to the bar and this time was served by a bartender with an undercut and a pierced septum, and when she gave me a wink with my drink I got weak in the knees.

I turned around to head back to my corner and BAM! Slammed right into someone behind me, spilling my drink all down the front of her very tiny black dress.

"What the fuck?!"

"Oh, shit!"

I looked up into the eyes of the stranger, which were narrowed in rage.

"I'm sorry," I said, just standing there holding the now empty glass and staring at her, standing there in her wet dress.

"Well, as long as you're sorry, then it's all good. I'm dry!" She threw her hands up in the air and I gaped at her.

"It was an accident."

"You should be more careful," she said as someone handed her a paper towel. She snatched it and started dabbing at her front and I couldn't stop staring at her tits.

Stop staring at her tits, Sasha. It's fucking rude.

"I'm sorry," I said again, because what else was I going to say?

"Fuck," she said.

"Do you want to go to the bathroom?" one of the stranger's friends said.

There wasn't much I could do, honestly, as her friends

dragged her toward the bathroom in the back. She glanced once over her shoulder at me, and I just stood there.

Oops?

"Let's try that again," a voice said behind me, and the nice bartender with the undercut pushed another drink at me. "This one's on the house."

"Thanks," I said. Someone else came by and started mopping up the floor, and I slunk back to my corner, which took forever because of how careful I was trying to be with my drink.

I made it in one piece and couldn't stop feeling like people were staring at me.

The stranger emerged from the bathroom, but this time she was wearing a completely new dress. Dark blue this time.

Was she some kind of magician? Or was I losing my mind? This was like that time when the internet went wild over a dress that looked blue and black to some and gold and white to others.

But this stranger was real, and I couldn't figure her out.

She still seemed annoyed in the way walked as she crossed the floor back to her group. Like she was some angry goddess, people seemed to part and let her through. Maybe she was someone famous? It wouldn't be completely unheard of for some actress to have a summer place in Maine. Perhaps some kind of influencer or something?

Why was I thinking so much about this? It was silly.

I finished my second drink and was feeling warm and cozy and comfortable. Sure, I wished I had someone to talk to every now and then, but I was pretty happy in my little corner.

I did start to get warm, so I headed outside for a quick breather.

Several people smoked near the entrance or vaped into the warm late summer air.

I stood on the street and looked up into the sky, struggling to see the stars.

"That was an expensive dress, you know," a voice said, and I turned to find the stranger glaring at me.

She wobbled a little on her feet. Oh. Maybe she was one of those people who got pissy when she drank. That would explain it.

"I'm sorry," I said. "It was an accident. I can pay for it to be dry cleaned." I didn't want to, but if it would get her to accept my apology, I'd scrape up the money.

"It's not about the money, it's about the principle," she said, pointing at me.

"Did you change your dress?" I asked, because I was dying to know.

"Yes," she said, looking down at the blue dress that wasn't as low-cut as the black one had been, but it was still tight enough for me to appreciate her body.

"That's really smart," I said, and she blinked at me. Clearly, I'd surprised her.

"I don't like being wet," she said, tugging at the hem of the dress.

I couldn't help but snort with laughter and then pretend I hadn't.

"Perv," she said, realizing that I'd taken her comment in a dirty way.

"It's okay. I'm fully aware of my dirty mind, and I'm not ashamed of it," I said.

The stranger chuckled and shook her head.

"No, you ruined my dress, I'm not talking to you anymore."

"Okay?" I said, but she didn't move.

I took a step closer to her, and I realized that her dark hair was a wig, and not a very good one. Was she trying to disguise herself, or just playing around with a different style?

What was her story?

Why did I even care?

She took a step toward me and we locked eyes in the dark.

"I'm really sorry about the dress. I will pay to clean it," I said.

"It's fine," she said.

"Is it?"

She closed her eyes and licked her lips.

My fingers ached to reach for her. To pull her body against mine and feel how all her warm curves fit against me.

"Can I just…" she reached up and tucked wisp of hair behind my ear. My heart hammered erratically in my chest.

What was she doing?

I didn't realize what was happening until her lips were on mine.

She tasted like mint and gin and soft warmth.

Before I knew what I was doing, I was kissing her back.

Just as I was about to see if she'd let me slide my tongue into her mouth, she pulled back and stared at me.

"I shouldn't have done that," she said.

I didn't know what to say, so I didn't say anything.

Someone yelled a name that I didn't catch, and then she was turning her head and walking back to her friends, who waited at the entrance. There was a short conversation, and a few of them gave me dirty looks that made me want to roll my eyes. They really were making a big deal about the dress.

Before I could do anything, they headed down the sidewalk and got into two cars.

I hadn't even gotten her name.

Chapter Two

"AND THEN SHE KISSED ME. It was wild," I told Paige the following Monday as we sat together at a table and worked at the Castleton Cafe. We'd met less than a year ago online in a support group for freelancers, and then she'd introduced me to some of her friends and I'd joined her little circle. I'd been talking to her for weeks when I realized that she and my sister lived in the same town. Small world.

"Wow, what did you do?" she asked, leaning forward. Her eyes were wide with interest under the fringe of her light brown bangs.

"I mean, what could I do? She was hot and I'd had two drinks." I shrugged.

"And then what?"

I told her that the stranger had disappeared into a car with her friends, never to be seen again.

"I mean, I'm happy I don't have to foot a dry-cleaning bill, but I also wish I could have figured out who she was."

I couldn't stop thinking about the stranger. What had possessed her to yell at me and then kiss me? Who did that? What kind of woman was she? I was fascinated.

"But I'll probably never see her again and live out my years old and cranky and alone," I said, sighing and sucking back the last of my lukewarm white mocha latte. I needed another ASAP.

Paige laughed and then looked down as a message came in on her phone. From her smile, I knew it was from her fiancée, Esme, who worked at the bar attached to the Pine State Bar and Grille, located conveniently just down the street.

Everything in Castleton was concentrated in the small downtown area, which was also near the beach and the light-house. It made sense, but it annoyed the shit out of me, like everything else in this town. Everything here was just so damn *cute*.

"How's Esme?" I asked.

"Good," Paige said, letting out a little giggle.

They'd only been engaged for about a month, but I didn't see the honeymoon wearing off anytime soon. They were just one of those couples that was always painfully and disgustingly in love.

Good thing I adored both of them or else I wouldn't have been able to deal with being friends with them.

"I need a refill. You need anything?" I asked Paige, and she asked for a cup of herbal tea.

"Tea?" I asked in shock.

"Yeah, Esme is trying to get me to cut back on caffeine," she said.

"Why?" I asked, horrified.

"Because she doesn't like taking care of me when I get on my caffeine binges and then buy too many puzzles online. We're running out of room for them."

That made me laugh.

"Okay, I can see her point. Sort of," I said.

Paige had a serious puzzle hobby, and even had a spare table in her living room dedicated to her hobby. She also collected odd and rare puzzles and was strict about who got to touch her collection so they didn't get damaged.

I ordered another white mocha latte and a cup of mint tea for Paige from Blue, who was one of the only a few people I actually liked in Castleton.

They leaned closer to me over the counter and gave me a conspiratorial look.

"I've been giving all the rude people fake wi-fi passwords," they said, winking under a mop of electric blue hair.

"Oh my god, I love that," I said, putting a few bucks in the tip jar, even though they told me not to.

"It's all about the little things," they said before going to make our orders.

Speaking of tourists, a whole gaggle of them walked in as I was waiting for my drinks. I'd learned how to spot them by now.

They were just so loud about everything, acting like they owned the place.

Sure, I wasn't from Castleton, and I had no intention of staying here, but at least I wasn't an asshole about it to service workers.

"I hope they have oat milk," one woman wondered loudly. Yes, we did have oat milk in Castleton. We had electricity too.

God, now I was mentally defending the town I couldn't wait to get out of.

Blue handed me the drinks and I took them back to my table.

"Thank you," Paige said, taking her tea and sipping it.

A text message came in on my phone before I could taste my drink.

I opened it to find a funny dancing video my friend, Hollis, had sent me.

She was my other random Maine connection. She and I

had met in Boston when we'd both signed up for the same workout class and had bonded by wanting to be in the back.

Her mom and sister still lived an hour north of me and were trying to get her to come back to Maine, but she was refusing. Plus, she had an apartment and a dog, so why would she give that up for a rural town that barely had working wi-fi? At least Castleton was good in that department.

I sent Hollis a funny video back and looked up at Paige, but she'd put her noise-canceling headphones on and was back in work mode.

There were days we worked together that we barely spoke at all, but it was nice to just be with another human. Back in Boston I'd had a desk at a co-working space, but this was the best I could do in Castleton.

Hollis was actually the one who had hooked me up with my current job as a virtual assistant for several authors. She worked as a freelance book cover designer, so when I'd needed a job fast, she had been right there singing my praises and making introductions. Some days were more boring, tracking ad spend and playing with spreadsheets, other days were looking through stock images of hot people, and some were mailing out hundreds of signed book copies at the tiny Castleton post office and hoping no one murdered me for taking so long to ship so many books all over the world.

"Hey, you're coming over on Thursday, right?" Paige asked, startling me out of my inbox.

"Uh, yes. I will be there." I loved going over to Paige and Esme's because the food and drinks were always top notch. Plus, my little niece wasn't trying to steal the food right off my plate and I could curse without worrying about little ears hearing and repeating.

"Good. Em and Natalie are coming, and so are Charli and Alivia. Linley and Gray have a work thing for him."

When Paige had initially told me that she wanted to bring

me into her little circle of friends, I was wary, but then I'd met everyone and I'd happily let myself be assimilated. It was so nice to have a group of adults I could hang with, and one of the things I'd been worried about when I'd moved here originally. Not that I was saying I was happy to be here. I wasn't. Right now, it was tolerable, and that was about it.

"Sounds great," I said, and then we both went back to our respective work. I got so immersed, that it wasn't until Paige was literally tapping me on the shoulder that I looked up again.

"Time to clock out, Sasha," she said.

"Huh?" I'd been updating one of my author's calendars and had gotten completely lost.

Paige laughed. "Time to be done."

That was one of the things I liked working with Paige. She told me when I needed to stop. Both of us had the tendency to work too much, and having another person give you permission to close the computer was a gift.

I made sure to save my work and back up my files before I shut down my laptop and shoved it in my bag.

"What are you doing for dinner?" Paige asked. "I'm heading over to bug my fiancée and eat some wings." She smiled extra big when she talked about Esme. It was so cute.

"I have to hit the grocery store, so probably frozen pizza, since it's one of the only things that Luna is eating right now, and she has a fit if we eat something different than she does." I rolled my eyes. Being an aunt wasn't as easy as people thought.

"Lizzie is hostessing tonight, so say hi if I see her," I said. My sister had bounced around at different jobs when she'd moved here, and I was so glad she'd gotten steady work at the Pine State Bar and Grille. I was on Luna duty at least two days a week so she didn't have to pay for daycare, and then the rest of the time she worked nights or sent Luna to daycare. It was a patchwork solution, but in just two more weeks, Luna would be going to kindergarten, and we would both be free during the days.

If I said I wasn't counting down the hours, I would be lying. My niece was the cutest and sweetest, but it was hard to watch a five-year-old and do my job. Once she was in school, I could probably take on another client, which meant saving more money to get the fuck out of this one-stoplight town.

Actually, scratch that, Castleton didn't even have one stoplight. There had been debates about putting one in, but the issue had never been resolved. People just yelled at each other about it at town meetings and wrote long editorials that they published in the paper. High drama.

People in this town cared about the most random shit.

"I'll say hi when I see her," Paige said as we headed out the door of the café. She headed down the street toward the Grille, and I headed down the street to the little organic grocery store that was owned and run by Paige's future father-in-law, Butch.

He was in the produce section, arranging some apples and saying hello to everyone who walked in, so I got my cart and decided to buzz past him and come back for produce later. That man could talk your ear off if you let him, and I was in a hurry because I had to pick up Luna from daycare, and I couldn't be late.

By now I knew exactly what I needed in every aisle when I shopped, so I'd made my list in order of where everything was, so I could go down each aisle and chuck everything in the cart as quickly as possible. Sometimes I even raced myself to see how fast I could go.

Butch wasn't at the checkout when I got there, it was one of the teens he'd hired for the summer. She was so swift with scanning everything, I was out of there with minutes to spare.

"How was your day?" I asked Luna when I picked her up at daycare.

"I drew you a skeleton!" she said, holding up a gruesome drawing of what might be a grinning skeleton.

"Oh, very nice," I said meeting the eyes of Linda, who ran the daycare.

"She couldn't wait to show it to you," Linda said as I gathered up Luna's bag and lunch box.

"Well thank you, I'm going to put it up on my wall." At this point there was going to be no visible paint left in my room, because it was covered in Luna's drawings of skeletons and eyeballs with legs and ghosts and snakes.

"See you on Friday, Luna," Linda called as we headed out the door.

"Did you get pizza?" Luna asked as I buckled in her into her car seat in my car.

"Yes, I did, but I got the kind with veggies on it, okay?"

I met her eyes in the rear view and was treated to a glare.

"You gotta eat some vegetables, kid. They make your bones strong."

"Really?" she asked.

"Yeah," I said. I mean, surely vegetables had vitamins and minerals that were good for growing kids?

"I guess," she said, but I could tell that I was wearing her down.

When I had more time, my plan was to start cooking more, and getting her to try some new things. My sister was so stressed with work and everything else, she didn't have time to make elaborate meals to expand Luna's palate. The least I could do was help while I was here.

Luna helped me bring in the groceries with her little arms and I got the pizza in the oven as soon as possible, as well as making a small chopped salad for myself, and cutting up some carrots and broccoli for Luna. If she peeled the veggies off the pizza, I wanted to give her a second option.

Dinner wasn't a huge fight, so that was good, and I let

her watch her favorite show while I cleaned up and tried to gain a little bit of sanity back. I still definitely had work I could be doing, but I'd promised Paige that I'd clocked out. The siren song of my inbox was just so intense, so I busied myself with chores, getting Luna to take a bath, and putting her to bed.

I didn't breathe a sigh of relief until she was breathing deeply, cuddled up in her pjs with her stuffed skeleton in one hand and her monster in the other.

The house was quiet, so I put on some TV and sat on the couch. Different thoughts spiraled through my mind, but what came up clearly, like she was emerging from the mist of my mind, was the face of the stranger I'd kissed.

I still didn't know her name, or how to find her. I mean, did I really want to?

Sure, the kiss had completely blown my mind and catapulted me into another dimension, but also, she was a stranger who had yelled at me. On another hand, she was extremely hot.

I groaned and closed my eyes. What did it matter? I wasn't going to date someone from Maine, anyway. As soon as my sister got things stable, I was headed back to Boston. If I saved up enough money, I might be able to afford my own place with no roommates. The dream, really. I'd been stalking the rental sites for hours, mentally decorating my new place. Once Luna was in school and I had more hours for work, my income would go up so I could qualify for an apartment that wasn't a shoebox infested with roaches.

Gross. I didn't want to think about roaches. Thinking about the kiss with the stranger was much more pleasant.

She'd probably just become a story that I told in my older years about my wild youth.

Yeah, pretty wild youth I was living right now. Getting excited about getting through the grocery store as fast as I could, and making my niece eat a vegetable. I was really living the dream.

I went to the fridge and grabbed myself a little bit of wine and some seltzer to make myself a little spritzer. Made me feel a little fancy.

I was half-asleep by the time my sister got home from work, smelling of fried food and exhaustion.

"She's down," I said as she flopped on the couch. "You want a drink?"

"Please," she said, stretching her legs out in front of her.

I made Lizzie a drink like mine and handed it to her.

"Thanks."

She told me about the night, how sore her feet were, and how much she loathed her ex. I let her vent, because that was what I'd signed up for when I'd agreed to come here and help her after Skippy (yes, that was his nickname) skipped out on her and Luna to marry a woman in Las Vegas that he'd met online. I mean, I could have told her that a man who called himself Skippy was up to some shady shit, but she'd been in love with him, and then she'd gotten pregnant with Luna and he'd been around, at least in the beginning.

Honestly, I was tired of hearing about his deadbeat ass, but I knew Lizzie was still completely heartbroken, not just for herself, but for her daughter. That was the thing that pissed me off most of all, and I had entertained many fantasies of heading to Vegas and giving him a piece of my mind.

"Just a few more weeks and she'll be in school," I reminded Lizzie.

"I know. I can't wait. That probably sounds horrible, but it's true," she said.

"You're not horrible. You're an amazing mom." She absolutely was. Lizzie had kind of been aimless after high school, but the minute she knew she was going to be a mom, she had focus. She had someone who needed her to be responsible. It was amazing to see how she got herself together for Luna. She'd bought this little house on her own, was making ends meet, and making sure Luna didn't want for much.

"I'm really proud of you," I said, and she gave me a look. "What, I can't give you a compliment?"

"No, you can. It's just weird."

"I give compliments all the time!"

"You do not," she said, getting up and wincing.

"Okay, I don't. Maybe I'm trying to be better at giving compliments," I said.

"Well, you suck at it," she called, and I tried to throw a pillow at her and missed completely.

"What the hell was that?" She came back with her drink and sat down.

"Listen, I'm tired," I said.

"Oh, you're tired? Join the fucking club." She closed her eyes and pinched the bridge of her nose.

"I am going to take a shower."

"Are you taking your wine with you?" I asked.

"Yup," she called over her shoulder.

That didn't sound like a bad idea.

Chapter Three

THE REST of the week was normal chaos. Trying to entertain my niece, keep her fed and bathed, and not drop any balls at work.

I needed a fucking vacation.

My sister was on her way out the door on Friday and I was deep in my inbox when she said, "Oh my fuck, I forgot that we have to meet Luna's teacher on Monday night. I already agreed to cover for Brooke. Fuck." Lizzie only swore like a sailor when Luna wasn't around. I'd dropped her off at daycare already.

"I can take her," I said.

"I mean, I guess. I really should be there. Let me see what I can do. I'll let you know." And then she was out the door and the house was mine for the day. Fridays really were the best.

I put on music and drank too much coffee and got to wear my rattiest clothes that I never wanted anyone to see. Plus, I didn't have to look cute, so I just put my red hair up in a messy bun on the top of my head without even bothering to brush it out.

When are you coming to visit?

Hollis and I texted constantly throughout the day.

Soon. After Luna is in school, I'll have some more free time.

I'd been planning to visit Hollis for the weekend for ages. I missed the city so much. Castleton was too fucking quiet. It freaked me out. And what was with all the trees? Paige was always trying to get to me to go walking or hiking with her and I always turned her down. People got lost or eaten by bears or murdered in the woods. I would stick to the populated areas, thank you very much. I didn't do nature.

I miss you.

I really missed her too. I missed everything about my old life. Sometimes it would hit me in the chest and I couldn't breathe. I would never tell my sister about those times when I'd cried in the shower because I didn't want to be here. Sure, I had grown up in a place like this in another part of Maine, but I had done everything in my power to get away from that place and to be somewhere else.

You could always visit me I told Hollis.

NO THANK YOU, I'm in Maine for Christmas and that's enough. That was another thing Hollis and I had bonded over. I actually had visited her mom and sister pretty frequently since I got back. I was excited for her to come back for Christmas. It would make this place more bearable. My parents had moved to Florida, and had never been super big on holidays, so I'd be celebrating big in Castleton with Lizzie and Luna.

I took a break for a lunch of an almond butter and strawberry jam sandwich, and then it was back to work. I had to head to the post office on Monday to do a huge shipment of book swag including bookmarks and stickers, so I was mentally preparing myself for that. I made sure all the labels were printed and the shipping was correct with my little postal scale. When I'd lived in the city, I'd been able to schedule pickup, but they didn't do things like that in Castleton. Oh no, I had to brave the post office and the ancient postal worker, Hilda, who I'm pretty sure hated my guts. Her eyes narrowed every time she saw me walk in. You'd think she'd be glad for the business, but no. Hilda wanted to spend her days shooting the shit with the Castleton locals and petting everyone's dogs. I guess I couldn't blame her. I'd love to get paid to gossip and pet dogs too.

My sister texted me that she couldn't get out of work on Monday to get to the teacher night, so it was my job to take Luna and meet her teacher and some of the other parents. The idea of doing that made me want to crawl under the house and never emerge, but I had to suck it up because there was no one else.

You got it. I'll take her.

Lizzie made sure to tell me all the questions I was supposed to ask. I made sure to write them down on a list, because I was bound to forget. When it came to keeping my niece alive, and doing my job, I was great. When it came to everything else, I was a disaster. My room was filled with laundry I was too tired to do, and cups that I was too tired to bring back to the kitchen. I didn't let Lizzie or Luna come in my room and see what a state it was in if I could help it. Once Luna was in school, I was due for a deep clean.

I forced myself to get up and out of the house and take a short walk. Lizzie's house was on a side road near the edge of the downtown area of Castleton, which was nice. I had to admit, it was nice having a beautiful white-sand beach within walking distance of the house. Sometimes I'd go later at night and watch the sun set over the water as I walked barefoot in the sand.

My legs were stiff after sitting for so long, so I made sure to loosen up. I'd put on a podcast to keep me company and distract me from the cars driving by. One of the downsides of walking on the side of the road is that people always wanted to stop and chat, even if you didn't know them. It made my walk last three times as long, and I despised small talk, so it was like pure torture. What was in the water that made everyone love to chat here? They'd start yammering about their cousin Joe, even though you had no idea who Joe was, but you didn't want to ask, so you'd just stand there nodding like a dumbass until they had to keep driving because they were stopping traffic.

Weird place. Weird, weird place.

I kept my eyes in front of me and tried to make my expression surly enough that no one would want to approach me, and it seemed to work. I did get a few honks and waves that I ignored. I didn't want to be part of your little community, thank you. I'm not one of you.

I gave Hollis updates as I walked, and she kept me laughing with sarcastic comments. Paige asked me if I wanted to head to the beach this weekend and I agreed, because what else was I going to do? The beach was one of the only decent places here.

Paige and Esme always brought drinks, Linley and Gray brought desserts, and Natalie and Em usually brought some kind of food, so we were all covered. Charli and Alivia stole a bunch of beach chairs and towels from the inn where Alivia worked, so that was covered. I always felt like I should contribute, so I made sure that I had tons of sunblock, a full first aid kit, and any other little things someone might need. I had to do something or else feel like a complete mooch.

Luna was going to be upset I was going to the beach without her, so that wasn't going to be a fun conversation. I'd have to give my sister some money to take her to the movies to cheer her up.

I'd deal with that later.

"Oh, shit," I said, realizing that it was almost time to leave to pick Luna up from daycare. I speed walked my butt back to the house and got in the car.

"OUCH!" Em said as she dropped the shell she'd been holding.

"What's wrong?" Natalie, her girlfriend, was immediately by her side.

"Just cut myself on a sharp edge. Occupational hazard," Em said, looking at her hand that had started to bleed.

"Hold on, I have a first aid kit," I said, and dashed back to our spot on the sand and retrieved the kit. Our group had ventured to one end of the beach that was bordered by huge rocks covered in seaweed. Kids liked to climb on the rocks or find crabs or watch the little ecosystems in the tide pools. Luna loved coming here, and it would entertain her for hours.

I handed Natalie some antiseptic spray, some antibacterial ointment, and a bandage.

Natalie cleaned Em's wound with care, fussing over her the whole time. Paige was in swimming laps with Alivia, as Esme and Charli watched them as they waded in the shallow water. Gray and Linley were absorbed making a little sandcastle, their heads bent together, hers blonde, his dark.

Sometimes being with this group made me feel like the odd girl out, and it was never more apparent in moments like these.

"Thanks, Sasha," Natalie said as I packed up the kit again. Honestly, it was shocking that I wasn't the one with the injury. I couldn't count how many cuts and scars I had on my body from silly injuries.

"No problem," I said.

"I think that's enough shells for one day," Natalie said to Em, kissing her hand.

Em had a thriving business called Low Tide Designs where she collected shells from various Maine beaches and made them into ornaments or lampshades or crushed them up and made coasters. She'd managed to make the business so successful that she was able to quit her job at her uncle's insurance agency in downtown Castleton, and now she was in the freelancer club with me and Paige. Natalie helped out when she wasn't working for her boss, Piper, a brand strategist that I hadn't met yet, but whose son went to the same daycare as Luna. Everyone in Castleton was connected, and it would be impossible trying to figure out all of those connections.

Paige and Alivia got out of the water, laughing as they sloshed toward their girlfriends. Kisses were exchanged and towels were held out to warm the swimmers.

I looked away.

"I'm starving," Paige announced. "Should we have lunch?"

All of us headed back to our towels and coolers and chairs, and I sat by myself and ate my sandwich. It was made with thick and soft brioche from Linley's family's bakery, Sweet's Sweets. Charli, Linley's cousin with the pink hair, also worked at the bakery doing social media and customer service. I had to admit, having friends who worked for a bakery was something I was going to miss when I left. You couldn't top free bread and pastries.

"How's construction going?" Paige asked Linley and Charli.

"My dad has been having a ball with a sledgehammer," Linley said with a laugh and then showed us a video of her dad, Mitch, swinging a giant hammer into a wall and leaving a huge hole. He raised the hammer over his head and roared.

"Oh my god, I love it," Paige said.

"Mom has been trying to get him to slow down so he doesn't throw out his back again," Linley said with a sigh. Her family was expanding the bakery and had just purchased a building just outside of downtown Castleton that needed a lot of remodeling work, which they were taking on mostly themselves.

"Oh, Mitch," Paige said, shaking her head. "He's a character."

"That he is," Linley said. "Oh, Sasha, I have something for you."

I jumped at the mention of my name.

"Huh?" I asked.

"Well, since you're new to the group, we made you up a little welcome gift," Linley said, her face going red. She pushed her purple-framed glasses up her nose and pulled something else from her giant beach bag. It was a basket wrapped in clear cellophane with a big white bow on it.

"Wow, this is intense," I said, taking it from her. All eyes were on me.

"Am I supposed to open it now?" I asked.

"If you want to," Paige said.

I pulled off the cellophane and found various items including some ground coffee from the Castleton Cafe, a mug from the Pine State Bar and Grille, some coupons for various businesses, a Sweet's Sweets t-shirt in a soft pink color, a shell ornament with a beach scene painted in it, a gift card for a free one-night stay at The Honeysuckle Inn, and a little carved animal that turned out to be a raccoon on closer inspection.

"A raccoon?" I asked. Gray smiled.

"It just seemed like you," he said. Gray was a master wood carver and made all kinds of sweet little animals that he sold and posted online in his spare time, when he wasn't working as a phlebotomist. Linley beamed at him.

"You saw our wedding cake topper, right?" She showed me a picture of her cake topper with two little creatures, one with a veil and one with a top hat to represent the bride and groom.

"What are they?" I asked.

"Pangolins, of course," Gray said, putting his arm around Linley and kissing her temple.

"Right," I said, missing the inside joke. "Well, thank you everyone. This is seriously so nice."

I could feel how red my face was. I wasn't used to stuff like this.

"We just wanted you to know we're glad you're here," Paige said, popping a grape in her mouth.

"Thanks," I said. I pressed my lips together so I didn't tell them, again, that this was temporary. I wasn't staying. They'd have to find someone else to join their friend group on a permanent basis.

After we ate, Gray produced a frisbee and tried to get everyone to form teams, but it didn't go over well. Linley agreed to play, as did Paige and Alivia.

"I'll play," I said, getting up.

"Okay, fine," Em said. "Nat?"

Natalie shook her head. "You go ahead, dear." She put her earbuds back in her ear and laid back on her chair.

"Abandoned by the woman I love," Em said, shaking her head. I laughed.

We set up two teams: Me, Em, and Linley, and Paige, Alivia, and Gray on the other team.

"So, what is the goal here?" Paige asked, raising her hand.

"Get the frisbee over the line of the opposite time. One of these days I'm going to get some nets so we can make it a real game," Gray said as he made the lines by dragging his heel into the sand.

Some of us were more coordinated than others, and I quickly learned that I was the least coordinated. I couldn't catch the frisbee to save my life, and my feet kept tripping in the sand. I ended up falling a lot, but I refused to let this silly game conquer me.

"You good?" Em asked, helping me up after my millionth fall.

"I'm good," I said, panting and dusting the sand off my legs.

"We're tied," Gray said. "Next point wins."

I did my absolute best to steal the frisbee, but Gray faked to one side, I fell again, and he streaked past me to flick the frisbee right between Em and Linley with a cheer. He ran around with his fists in the air as Paige jumped up and down and Alivia clapped.

"Boo! Cheating! You cheated!" Linley yelled, jumping on Gray. He caught her.

"I didn't cheat and you know it."

Linley pouted, but then he kissed her and she laughed.

"We tried," Em said, shrugging.

I went back to my towel and pulled out a book to read. That was enough exercise for one day.

My reading was interrupted by a text from my sister asking if I wanted to meet her for dinner from the little food truck that parked in downtown Castleton and had the best fried haddock sandwiches and lobster rolls I'd ever tasted..

I wrote back that I would meet her. They had showers at the beach, and I'd brought clothes to change into so I wouldn't be covered in sand.

The sun scooted across the sky and the party wound down as some people took naps, others strolled on the sand, and a few of us read.

"You ever figure out who that girl was?" Paige asked, flopping next to me.

"No, I didn't. Guess it will always be a mystery."

"Too bad," she said, fishing a soda out of the cooler. "You want one?"

"Sure."

She handed me a can and seemed thoughtful.

"You know, something tells me that you're going to run into her again somehow," she said.

"Are you psychic now?" I asked, popping the top on the soda.

"Maybe," she said with a wink.

Chapter Four

I FIGURED I should probably look like a responsible adult when I took Luna to meet her teacher, so I put on my nicest jeans and a white shirt that I'd never worn before, the tags were still on it.

"What do you think?" I asked Luna when I picked her up from daycare.

"No holes?" she asked, poking at my jeans.

"No holes," I said. She looked at me suspiciously, so that must have been a good sign.

"You ready to meet your teacher?" I asked as we drove the short distance out of Castleton to the next town over that was a bit larger and was home to the elementary school that all the local kids went to.

"I don't want to go to school," Luna said as I pulled into the parking lot of the Hartford Elementary school. WELCOME STUDENTS! A cheerful banner hung above the main entrance proclaimed.

"Why not?" I asked, turning in my seat to look at her.

She sighed as if she had the weight of the world on her shoulders. "Because."

"Because why?" I asked.

"Because it's not going to be fun."

"Who told you school isn't fun?" I asked.

"I don't know," she said, looking at her lap. Part of me wondered if she was reluctant because her mom wasn't here with her. I was going to have to do my best to make this a positive experience for her.

"Hey, look at me," I said, waiting until she did. It was such a blessing that she looked like a carbon copy of my sister, right down to the shape of her nose and the turn of her lips.

"I know this is new, and it's scary, but I promise you it's going to be fun. We'll make it fun. And I'm going to be with you the whole time, okay?"

She looked at me for a little while and then nodded.

"Okay," I said, holding my hand up for a high five. She grinned as she slapped my hand.

"Ouch, you're too strong," I said, pretending to wince.

That made her laugh.

Satisfied that I'd calmed her down enough, I got her out of the car and approached the building. Now I was the nervous one.

There were signs right at the entrance with arrows to tell us which classroom to go to. I had the paperwork in a folder Lizzie had given me.

"Okay, we're this way," I said, pointing in the direction of Miss Hardy's room.

Other adults and kids wandered through the halls, looking for the right classrooms. The air was filled with nervous energy, and the kids seemed to be feeding off each other.

Luna started bouncing along the hallway. Her energy was quite a bit different than when she'd been in the car just a few minutes ago.

We found Miss Hardy's room. It had a big construction

paper apple on the open door with her name on it and the kid's names written all around.

I took a breath before we walked in. The room was bright and organized, with a row of bins along one wall, all labeled, and a row of cubbies along the back, each with a different child's name on them.

"Let's go find your cubby, Luna," I said, taking her hand so I wouldn't lose her in the chaos of all the other kids and parents.

"Okay," she said, trotting toward the back. She could already read some words, so she found her name right away.

"That's me," she said, pointing.

"You're right, good job."

I looked around, wondering if I was supposed to be socializing with the parents.

"I'm Jackson," a little boy announced to me and Luna.

"Hi Jackson, it's nice to meet you," I said, leaning down. "I'm Sasha and this is Luna."

"Hi," Luna said, waving at Jackson.

"It's a pleasure to meet you," he said, and I had to bite back a laugh. What a polite little fellow.

"Who's your friend, Jackson?" A woman dressed in a jacket and matching skirt came over. Clearly, she'd just come from work.

"Hi, I'm Sasha. This is Luna," I said, holding my hand out to Jackson's parent.

"Nice to meet you. I'm Anna, Jackson's mom."

"Oh, I should mention that I'm actually Luna's aunt. Her mom Lizzie had to work tonight." Luna leaned against me and surveyed Jackson.

"I know how that is. I barely got out in time to get here. I work at the hospital."

"Oh, do you know Gray Baldwin? I'm friends with him and his wife, Linley."

Anna brightened up. "Yes, I know Gray. He's a great guy."

"He is," I said, relieved that I'd found someone to talk to.

"Okay, if everyone can take a seat or find a place to stand, we can get started," a voice said from the front of the room and everyone turned to look.

Oh.

Oh *shit*.

I froze, and only moved when Luna tugged at my arm. She sat at one of the little desks and I stood there behind her, trying to fight the urge to just leave the fucking room.

"Welcome everyone, I'm Miss Hardy, and I'm so excited to meet you all," said the stranger I'd kissed last weekend at the bar. She was a lot more covered up tonight. Her hair was not, in fact, dark black, but a medium blonde that she'd pulled back from her face.

I tried to swallow and failed.

Miss Hardy surveyed the room and I saw the moment she realized who I was. Her blue eyes went slightly wide for a second, and then she kept moving. A moment later, her composed smile was back in place.

"Let me start by telling you a little about myself. I'm Miss Hardy, and I've been teaching here for three years. My favorite thing in the world is chocolate, and I love going hiking on the weekends." That elicited giggles from the kids and chuckles from the parents. I just kept standing there, my palms sweating, wishing I was anywhere else.

"I'm going to pass around our agenda for the year, and answer any questions you have when I come around and speak with each child. Feel free to get up and move around if you need to."

Fuck. Shit. I was going to have to talk to her.

"She's nice," Luna said.

"Uh huh," I said.

IT TOOK Miss Hardy a while to get around to us, since we were on the opposite side of the room in the back. I tried to chat with Anna, but I couldn't stop watching Miss Hardy. Still didn't know her first name, but I bet I was going to find out. I tried to read the list that had been handed out, but the words kept blurring in front of my face.

"I hope this doesn't take too long. I have to get home and feed Jackson," Anna said in a low voice.

I looked down at Luna, but she was busy chatting with Jackson about who knew what.

How is she doing? I can't believe I'm not there.

I could feel the tension and guilt through the text message from Lizzie. I wrote back that Luna was doing fine and might have already made a friend. I told her I'd met another mom, and she should make friends with Anna. She seemed like good people.

I didn't say anything about the fact that I had recently locked lips with Luna's teacher. I was going to take that one to the grave, if I could.

By the time Miss Hardy made it to us, I was practically vibrating out of my skin with anticipation and anxiety. I had no idea how this was going to go.

"Hello, I'm Miss Hardy, what's your name?" She leaned down to get on Luna's eye level and smiled warmly. Definitely not the way she'd looked at me that night.

"I'm Luna," Luna said warily.

"I'm so glad you're going to be in my class. And who is this with you?" She looked up and our eyes met and I actually considered throwing myself through the nearest window, right through the glass. How injured would I really get anyway?

"That's Sasha. She's my aunt," Luna said.

"Your aunt," Miss Hardy said.

"My mommy couldn't come. She had to work."

Miss Hardy nodded and didn't look away from my eyes.

"I understand. I'll meet her another time. Did you have any questions for me?" That last part was directed toward me, but it took me a few seconds to realize.

"Oh, uh, no. Not right now. I'm guessing her mom might," I said, wishing my mouth wasn't so dry. I probably looked like a complete dumbass.

"Well, my email address is on there, so she can reach out to me anytime," Miss Hardy said.

I could feel her getting ready to move on when she stepped closer to me and I stopped breathing.

"My first name is Jax. Jaqueline. Just in case."

I blinked at her a few times and she smiled softly. I thought she was going to say something else, but then she was introducing herself to Jackson, and I was out from under her spell. My lungs decided to work again, and I looked around the room as if I was waking up. Right.

"Sasha, I need pizza," Luna said, tugging on my shirt.

"You 'need' pizza?" I asked, looking down at her and twirling one of her curls around my finger. The fact that she had just a little bit of red tinting her blonde hair made me happy.

"Yes. I *need* pizza," she said. She clenched her jaw in a determined way.

"What if we try a different kind of pizza?" I asked, having an idea.

"What kind of pizza?" she asked.

"You'll see. It's a surprise."

Her eyes narrowed in suspicion.

Okay, I'd have to make sure I had a backup plan.

～

STILL RATTLED, I was distracted as I made what I called Monster Pizza. First, I took a spinach tortilla, added salsa as sauce, some ground beef, cheese, and made a green purée with cilantro and fresh spinach and drew a monster face on the thing.

Luna loved it and ate the whole thing. I called it a major win. She barely fought me when I put her in the bath and washed her hair and put her to bed.

Once the house was quiet, I sat on the couch and tried to process the past few hours.

Jaqueline. Jax. That was her name. It suited her completely. Jax Hardy, Luna's teacher. She was a lot closer than I thought, and now I had to figure out what to do about it.

"HOW DID IT GO?" Lizzie asked when she got home. I'd texted her tons of updates, but she still wanted to hear everything.

"Good. No drama." No drama for my niece at least. "Oh, here is the stuff they handed out."

I gave her the folder. There had been more papers to get before we left. I was glad I wasn't the one who had to worry so much about my kid being properly educated. Sure, I did want Luna to do well in school, but I didn't have to stress over the daily minutiae.

Except for her teacher. I was probably going to obsess about her, but not in the context of my niece getting educated.

I gave Lizzie the run down, and she went in to check on Luna before coming back out and resting on the couch, pulling her feet up and wincing.

"I can't believe I missed it," she said, her voice breaking. "I'm supposed to be there for her. I'm her mom." She burst into tears and I immediately put my arms around her.

"It's okay. I know you wanted to be there. She knows you love her and you're doing everything for her." I held my sister as she cried her eyes out and I cursed the fucker who left her. I cursed the day he was born.

"I know there's nothing I can do, but it still sucks." She sniffed and I grabbed her some tissues so she could wipe her nose and face.

"There isn't any way to change your hours, or maybe get a different job?" I asked.

"There just aren't a whole lot of jobs here. And I'm stuck because of the house. I guess I could sell it, but I don't want to move and rip Luna out of everything she knows. She just enrolled in school." That was the hard part about living in a place like this. Jobs were few and far between, and you usually needed at least two of them to try and make ends meet.

"I'll ask my friends and see if there's anything out there. Linley's mom, Martha, knows like everyone in town. She'll know if someone is hiring." Plus, there was the bakery expansion. They were bound to need people for that, but it wouldn't be done for probably another year. Lizzie needed work now.

"Thank you. I love being a hostess, but it's just not enough."

"Have you thought about doing school? You could go online for a certificate or something. I bet the hospital is always hiring," I said.

"I'll think about it," she said, rubbing the space between her temples. "Right now, I'm getting a migraine."

I got her a glass of water and some pain pills.

"Thanks," she said. "Thank you for everything, seriously. I couldn't do this shit without you."

"What are sisters for?"

She hugged me again and we sat together and I put on a silly show that made Lizzie laugh.

Once she got a good job, and was able to get stable with her finances, I could think about leaving. Right now, she and Luna needed me here.

I was stuck in Castleton for the foreseeable future.

Chapter Five

"GIVE ME A BIG SMILE!" Lizzie said the following week as we stood on the porch in the cool morning air. I yawned and tried to hide it behind my hand. It was way too fucking early, but it was Luna's first day of school, and I was going to see her get on her bus, dammit.

Luna beamed as she held the little chalkboard sign Lizzie had made to celebrate her first day. She had the cutest little outfit on, and her skull-covered backpack was almost too big for her, but it was too adorable.

Luna posed for picture after picture, bouncing around with excitement. She wouldn't stop talking about seeing Jackson again, so I was thrilled she already had a little friend. I hoped that she wouldn't have any issues with the other kids. My niece wasn't a unicorn or mermaid girl. Unless it was skeletons of mermaids or unicorns. She was a spider collector, a skull drawer, a scary movie lover. I hoped the other kids would appreciate her uniqueness.

"Here it comes," Lizzie said as the big yellow school bus rounded the corner.

Luna squealed and did a little dance as she waited for the bus to stop.

"Okay, baby girl, you have an amazing day. I love you," Lizzie said, giving Luna the biggest hug. I waved as she got on the bus, did a pose for her mom to take a pic, and then the doors closed, and she was on her way. Lizzie smiled and waved until the bus was out of sight, then turned to me and had a small breakdown.

"This is ridiculous," she said, wiping her eyes. "She's fine. She's going to be fine. But I really want to get in my car and follow the bus all the way to school right now," she said, sniffing. I pulled a packet of tissues out of my jeans pocket. I'd come prepared.

"She's going to have a great day, and it will get easier. The first day was always going to be the hardest."

I brought Lizzie back inside and made her eat something. She'd made pancakes for Luna but had been too nervous to eat before Luna had left.

Since Lizzie didn't have to go to work for a few hours, we decided to hang out, even though I should have been working. It was fine, I could make up the hours later.

"I don't want anyone to see me like this," she said, so we decided to stay in and have a spa morning with face masks and one of our favorite movies. I called Sweet's Sweets bakery and ordered some cupcakes and went to pick them up.

"I can't stop thinking about how Skippy is missing this and he doesn't fucking care. How can he not care?" Lizzie said.

"Because he's a piece of shit. No, he's lower than a piece of shit. He's like a parasite on a piece of shit." If I could figure out what was lower than that, that was what he'd be.

"Fucker," Lizzie said, viciously unwrapping her third cupcake.

I pressed my lips together so I didn't remind her that she

could go after him for child support. The courts would make him pay. She said that she didn't want any of his money, but I couldn't understand where she was coming from. He owed his daughter. Hopefully, I could talk her into coming around to the idea.

"The house is so quiet," Lizzie said. "It's freaking me out."

Lizzie washed off her face mask and got dressed in her work clothes to go in for the lunch shift.

"I'm going to be so distracted it's not even worth going in," she said. "Please be sure you're here when she gets off the bus?"

"Don't worry, I will," I said. "I'm not going anywhere."

Lizzie hugged me goodbye and rushed out the door. I cleaned up a little bit and then sat down to work.

I couldn't stop thinking about the fact that my niece was being taught by the woman who had kissed me at a bar. Who was she? What was her story?

I couldn't stop myself from going online, now that I knew her full name. Unfortunately, I didn't find much in the way of social media. Just a few pages, all of them private. That made sense for her being a teacher. I wouldn't want impressionable children or their parents seeing my social media feed. I did find a few articles in local papers about different activities she'd done with her class and her winning a teaching award.

I went further back and found old newspaper articles about her academic achievements, her athletic prowess, and volunteer work. Honestly, there were pages and pages of articles singing her praises. In contrast, I looked my own name up and found a whole lot of nothing. I'd gotten through school, but I'd been solidly average. I'd played sports but hadn't been very good. I rode the bench a lot. There was nothing about me that had set me apart, and here I was, looking at the prom queen. Literally. She'd been the prom queen, and homecoming queen.

I closed the browser windows in frustration and threw

myself back into work because what I could I do? I couldn't compare to that. There was no use in even trying.

"HEY, Luna Moon, how was your day?" I asked as my niece bounced off the bus, her hair a little tangled, and a large piece of paper held in one hand.

"I made this for mommy!" she proclaimed, showing me the paper. Yet another skull. Our house was papered in them.

"Gorgeous. Did you play with Jackson?"

"Uh huh," she said. "And Ella and Ava and Isla," she said.

"Wow, that's a lot of people," I said. She chattered away and I didn't want to interrupt, but when she took a breath, I asked her if she liked her teacher.

"She is very *very* nice," Luna said.

"That's good. I'm glad she's nice." She hadn't been very nice to me, before the whole kiss thing.

"I like her," Luna said.

"It's good to like your teacher. Do you want a snack?"

"Yes!"

I made her some peanut butter crackers and carrot sticks that she munched away on happily as she told me more about her first day. I sent her mom a message that the day had gone better than we hoped, her daughter was on her way to being popular, and that she could stop worrying.

Luna finished her snack and I went through her bag to make sure there weren't any important papers in it.

"Our class has a bear, called Cookie Bear, and every week someone gets to bring him home. I didn't get picked for this week, but that's okay because I will get to do it another week." That sounded really cute.

"We'll have to do something fun when it's your week," I said.

"Can we play outside?" she asked, and even though that was the last thing I wanted to do, I went outside with her.

My sister had found a tiny trampoline at a garage sale, and so I was required to watch Luna jump and try to do "tricks" and exclaimed how impressed I was. This could last for hours. I didn't know where she got the energy, but I would like to borrow some of it.

I was ready for a nap by the time we needed to go inside and get ready for dinner. Lizzie should be home soon, and she was bringing us food from the Grille, so I didn't have to worry about cooking, which was nice.

"Baby!" Lizzie yelled as she walked in, her arms weighed down with bags.

Luna ran to hug her mom and they had their moment of sharing how Luna's day had gone. I busied myself with getting the food on plates and silverware and drinks out for everyone.

"No pizza?" Luna asked.

"Sorry, baby, no pizza. I got you chicken fingers and mac and cheese," Lizzie said. "Is that okay?"

Luna's eyes narrowed, but she picked up a chicken tender and dunked it in some ranch dressing.

"There's carrots in the mac and cheese," she whispered to me as I sat down to eat my own meal of grilled chicken, rice, and asparagus.

"Get it in where you can," I said.

We settled into our evening routine, and Lizzie took over taking care of Luna so I could get in some more work.

Check this out Hollis said, sending me a new book cover she was working on. Seriously, she was fucking talented. I didn't know how she did it. Sure, I could do some basic graphics, but I wasn't a master at creating a fantasy cover from some random stock images.

Amazing. You're killing it I said back. **It was Luna's**

first day of school and I think she might be popular? IDK. This kid is so much cooler than I am.

Hollis was very familiar with my niece and had met her over video chat many times.

Tell me about it. My little cousin is apparently famous on a new social media site I've never heard of and is making money now?

That sounded hilarious. I asked her what the social media site was because I was always looking at new places for my authors to get in touch with readers. It was a site I'd heard of once or twice, but if it was cool with the kids, then I wanted to know about it.

Can you chat now? I have something to tell you. I hadn't told Hollis about the situation with Jax, and I didn't know why. It had been a week and every time I'd tried to tell her I'd stopped myself.

I needed to talk to someone about it, though, and she was my best friend, next to my sister.

Sure, hold on.

I waited and a few moments later, the video call alert came up.

"What's up?" Hollis said. She was outside the office she rented for work, and I could hear the sounds of the streets of Boston, and I was hit with a jab of missing it so much that I couldn't speak for a second.

I walked into my room and shut the door so Lizzie and Luna couldn't hear what I was talking about.

"Okay, so remember that stranger I kissed at that bar a few weeks ago? Well, you will never guess who turned out to be Luna's teacher."

"Shut the fuck up, NO," Hollis said, her eyes going wide.

"Yes, exactly, that's the right reaction," I said. "I know that she knows who I am. I know she knows what we did. It's not like I'm going to see her all the time, you know, but still. She's like, right there." So close.

"I mean, if you aren't going to see her, then does it really matter? Do you *want* to see her?" Hollis sat the phone down and started putting her long dark hair up in a messy bun.

There was the question. Did I want to see her?

The answer: yes AND no, which is what made things so damn complicated.

"Sasha?" Hollis asked when I didn't respond.

"I'm here," I said.

"Oh, good. You were frozen there for a second."

"I don't know, Hols. I don't know!" I groaned. "I made the mistake of looking her up."

"Sasha. Why did you do that?"

"Because I'm a dumbass? I don't know. Anyway, she's been the captain/leader/winner of everything, so she's completely out of my league anyway."

"Hey, don't you say that. You are amazing, okay? You are a majestic narwhal."

I snorted.

"I'm a narwhal?" Hollis's compliments were always a little strange.

"Yes. Narwhals are majestic, just like you."

"Well, thank you," I said, laughing. "But I think you're a little biased."

"Send me a picture of her," she said. "I want to see this bitch."

"Hold on," I said. I searched online for a picture of Jax and then sent it to Hollis.

"Oh, shit. Yeah, she's hot."

"Yes, I'm aware," I said. She was even hotter without that silly wig on. Her natural hair color was like…sunlight or something.

I did not need to wax poetic about Jax's hair, thank you

very much. It was pretty. Lots of people had pretty hair.

"Hey, if I were you, I'd go for it. But that's because I have an amazing amount of unearned confidence," Hollis said. "I just assume everyone loves me."

I laughed. Hollis did assume that, but to be fair, a lot of people did. But that's because Hollis was the life of the party that everyone wanted to be near. You could never have a bad time if Hollis was around.

"Yes, but I'm not you, Hols," I said.

"And that's probably a good thing. I'm more than enough me for this world."

That made me laugh even harder. I'd been in a bad mood when I'd called her and now I wasn't. Such was the power of Hollis Carr.

"I'm not going to do anything right now. I mean, I'm not going to go out of my way to like, contact her. I don't even know what I'd say. She probably hates me anyway."

She hadn't seemed hateful at the teacher night, but she had to look nice in front of everyone. It wasn't exactly like she could tell me to fuck off in front of her students and their parents. I had no doubt she'd tell me to fuck off in private.

But then there had been that kiss…

The kiss just made everything twelve layers of complicated.

Great, now I was thinking about buttery croissants. I'd have to go get one tomorrow from Sweet's.

There was a loud pounding at my door and I knew from experience it was my sweet niece, determined to know what I was up to at all times. Even during those times when I was in the shower and trying to masturbate quietly so no one would hear me. Hollis just laughed and said she would let me go. I blew her a kiss goodbye.

I couldn't wait to have privacy again.

"What is it?" I asked, opening the door to find Luna's consternated face.

"What are you doing in there?"

"I was talking with Hollis. She had to go, but she says hello," I said.

"But I wanted to talk to her," Luna pouted.

"Next time, I promise," I said, ruffling her hair. "I have an idea. Why don't we take a picture of your painting and send it to her? I know she'd love to see it." That distracted Luna enough that she latched onto the idea and forgot that I'd dared to shut my door in her face and have a private conversation. Like a monster.

I WENT another week without thinking about Jax Hardy. Well, not thinking about her that much. Just sometimes when I was awake and also sometimes when I was asleep. She infiltrated my dreams and wouldn't leave me alone.

I kept going back to her social pages, even though I knew she was private. I also read and re-read the articles about her accomplishments like I was doing a dissertation on her. It was a sickness, really. One late night when I was trying to go to sleep after having too much caffeine to cope with a huge work deadline, I accidentally requested to follow her.

"No! No, no, no!" I scrambled to cancel the notification and then my app crashed. I got it back up and canceled the request, heart pounding in my throat.

That was close. No more social media stalking for me.

THE NEXT DAY I got an email that I'd been approved to follow maximumjax37, and I also had a message from her.

My phone slipped out of my hand as I realized that my follow request hadn't been canceled, and she'd approved me.

Okay, so that didn't mean that she knew it was me. Most of my social was for my business, with a little bit of personal stuff sprinkled in. I also had a second secret account that was just followed by a few friends that had my more salacious, silly, and non-business stuff. I rarely posted on there.

I picked up my phone and decided that before I unfollowed her, I might as well take a look at what I'd been missing.

One of the most recent set of pictures was from the night we'd met and kissed. There she was getting ready, posing as she put on the wig and made silly faces with her group of friends. In fact, it looked like Jax had a shit ton of friends. She was rarely alone in her pictures. There was one picture of her posing in her classroom next to the door with the sign with her name on it as she beamed.

I scrolled and kept scrolling, soaking up any information I could find about her. There she was in her kitchen, which was gorgeous, and huge. Okay, so she probably had money. I didn't think kindergarten teachers made bank, so maybe something from her family?

I went back and back and back, and before I knew it, I'd wasted nearly two hours with this nonsense. Then I remembered she'd written me a message. I went to my inbox and pulled it up.

Are you stalking me now?

I mean, yes? But no.

I deleted the message and went to unfollow her, but I couldn't make my finger do it. What harm would there be in following her for a few more days? She was my niece's teacher, after all. I should keep tabs on her. Make sure she was going to be a good influence on Luna. I was just being a concerned aunt.

So I closed the message and threw my phone on top of my covers.

I was a fucking mess.

Chapter Six

"WHAT'S NEW WITH YOU?" Paige asked me when I showed up at the café later.

"Oh…not much," I said, putting my bag down and taking out my laptop and earbuds.

"You sure about that?" Paige asked, closing her own laptop. "You're late and you look…flustered."

What use was there hiding this from her?

"Okay, fine. Remember the stranger I kissed?" Paige leaned forward. She was all ears.

I told her about the meet the teacher night, and then my social media fuckup from both last night and this morning.

"So, that's where I'm at," I said. "I just…I don't know why I did that, and I don't know what to do about it and I feel completely trapped, and what if I just like, made a new identity and moved to Spain?"

"Spain?" Paige asked. "Do you know any Spanish?"

"Uh, not really," I said. "But I could learn. They say that the best way to learn a language is to immerse yourself in it."

Paige laughed. "I don't think you need to get that drastic.

Just unfollow her. Everyone does that shit all the time. I mean, you're not going to see her around, right?"

"I don't think she lives in Castleton, so no." I couldn't figure out exactly where she was based on her social, but I didn't think she lived here. I definitely would have seen her before this.

"This is not a big deal. In a few months, you won't even remember her. Unless you want to…" She trailed off expectantly.

"Why does everyone keep asking me that? I don't want to see her again."

"And that's why you didn't immediately unfollow her after you accidentally followed her in the first place?" Paige said, her tone skeptical.

"I'm just keeping an eye on the woman who spends hours a week with my niece. It's called being a concerned parent, aunt, whatever. Look it up," I said.

Paige snorted. "Sure, Sasha. Whatever you need to tell yourself." She shook her head at me. "Do you want anything? I need another latte," she said.

"Yes, I need a do-over," I said.

"Small or large?" Paige asked.

"Definitely large."

"I NEED A HUGE FUCKING FAVOR," Lizzie said when I got back that evening from working at the café.

"Swear jar!" Luna yelled.

Lizzie rolled her eyes, but dutifully pulled a dollar out of her purse and put it in the mason jar that Luna had covered in Halloween stickers.

"What is it?" I asked as I pulled the potatoes au gratin from the oven. Lizzie had also made baked chicken and a nice chopped salad. Part of me wondered if the nice meal was to butter me up to ask what she was about to ask me. Lizzie always cooked more elaborately than normal when she wanted something.

"I volunteered to chaperone the class trip to the beach, and I fu-messed up and scheduled a meeting at the community college the same day. I've been thinking about what you said, and I think I'm going to look into getting at least an associate's degree. I really can't miss this meeting, because I have to get applied and my financial aid stuff sorted as soon as I can. Can you fill in? I don't want to pull out this early in the year."

So that's why she'd made the potatoes.

"Lizzie," I said with a groan. "This is a big ask."

"I know," she said. "But I'm desperate. Please?"

"When is it?" I asked.

"Next week."

What was I going to do? Say no? Make my sister look like a bad mom for canceling? Potentially hurt my niece? Not support my sister who was trying to make her life better? No, I wasn't going to do any of those things.

She knew before she asked that I would do it.

"You owe me so big for this."

Lizzie threw herself on me. "You are the best sister in the history of sisters. I owe you yet another favor." At this point, I was racking up a punch card full of favors. One more favor and I got an extra favor for free.

I wouldn't have been so reluctant to agree if Jax Hardy hadn't been involved. I mean, a beach day with a bunch of small children didn't sound like the most fun thing in the world, but it didn't sound terrible. Plus, there were bound to be other adults there, and I'd just sort of be an extra supervisor. Jax would be in charge.

Guess I was going to be seeing her sooner than I'd anticipated.

~

"LISTEN, you're going to be so busy with kids that you're not going to have time to flirt," Hollis said, when I filled her in the next day.

"I wouldn't be flirting even if I had the time," I said. "I'm not flirting with her."

"It's going to be fine. She's a professional."

"Yeah, yeah," I said. "I just can't shake the feeling that this is going to be a disaster."

"That's just your pessimism talking," Hollis said. "You need to get on my level."

"I don't think I could ever get on your level," I said.

"You should try," Hollis said. "I'm awesome."

"This has all been very helpful, thank you," I said.

"Oh, come on," Hollis said. "Do I need to send you funny shit to cheer you up?"

"Always."

I was bombarded by notifications for Hollis sending me videos, and I ended our chat to go watch them.

They did cheer me up, but a few days later when I woke up the morning of the field trip, I was once again filled with a sense of dread.

Lizzie had left the list of what Luna needed to bring, and I went over it yet another time as she ran around me with excitement. I didn't know why she was so stoked; we went to the beach all the time.

"Okay, Miss Moon, we are ready," I said, and I wondered if Jax had typed the list, or if she'd taken it from somewhere else.

"I'm going to see a whale!" Luna declared.

"You are? Well, you'll have to watch very carefully to make sure you spot one. Your mommy and me once saw a whale, but that was when we went to Florida."

"What's Florida?" Luna asked.

"It's a state," I said, trying not to laugh. "We'll look it up later."

I got her in the car, and we made our way to the school, since we'd all be getting on the bus with the kids to go to the beach. I was glad the ride wasn't more than fifteen minutes, because being trapped on a bus full of five-year-olds wasn't my idea of a good time.

I managed to get us there right on time, and Jax was loading kids on the bus, clipboard in hand. The day was unseasonably warm for September, without a cloud in the sky. The perfect beach day.

She wore tan linen pants and a light blue denim button-up. She looked too chic to be taking a bunch of kids on a beach trip. Large sunglasses hid her eyes, and when I got closer, I saw the designer logo on the earpieces. Fancy, fancy. That just lent credence to my theory that she was secretly rich. If I were secretly rich, I would simply not work and sit around in my rich person home doing rich person things.

Luna tried to run toward her friends, but I kept a hold of her hand until we got in line with the other kids getting on the bus. I was relieved to see a few other parents, including Anna. Luna tried to cut the line to go see Jackson, but I told her that we needed to wait our turn.

My heart pounded louder and louder as we approached Jax with her clipboard.

"Good morning, Luna, it's so nice to see you," Jax said, and Luna beamed up at her.

"Good morning, Miss Hardy," Luna said. I didn't know where she learned that, because it definitely wasn't from me.

"Good morning, Sasha," Jax said, her eyes flicking to mine and then back to the clipboard. I didn't think it was my imagination that she smirked just a little bit when she said my name.

"Lizzie had an emergency, so I'm the second choice," I

blurted out and then wanted to crawl under the bus.

"Don't sell yourself short," Jax said, and Luna pulled me onto the bus before I could respond.

THE BUS RIDE WAS, indeed, a nightmare, but a quick one. I glommed onto Anna, since Jackson and Luna wanted to sit together.

"I called out of work for this," Anna admitted. "Partly because I needed a day off, and partly so that the other moms won't judge me."

I hadn't known about this until Lizzie told me, but I guess this whole mom-shaming was really a thing.

"Which moms?" I asked as the bus went over a bump and all the kids squealed as they bounced in their seats.

"The ones in the front," Anna said under her breath.

I had noticed a trio of moms that hadn't said hello to me but had each given me mean-girl looks as I got on the bus with Luna.

"Details," I said.

"The one with the blonde hair is Cecily, and her daughter is London, the brunette is Sadie, and her daughter is Sabine, and then there's the one with the darker hair, Veronica, and her daughter is Capri."

Anna filled me in on the fact that all three of the moms had husbands that made bank and thought that moms who had to work were depriving their children or some shit.

"The funny thing is, they all technically work, but it's for different multi-level marketing companies. And I think Veronica has some kind of online boutique that sells shirts that say 'boss babe' on them."

I tried not to gag.

"This just keeps getting worse and worse," I said.

"Believe me, I've already had a few run ins with them when Jackson was in preschool. I tried to be friends with them, but they sure didn't want to be friends with me."

We arrived at the beach at last and Jax got up to bring everyone to attention. She'd been sitting at the front of the bus with the little trio. I wondered if being close to Jax was how they asserted their mom dominance. Proximity to power. How utterly childish.

Jax set out the ground rules and then we got all of the kids off the bus and headed in a line through the parking lot and down the wooden walkway to the soft, white sand.

"Follow me!" Jax yelled, and all the kids tripped their way across the sand as Jax led them, the parents keeping up and helping their little ones carry their stuff.

"Everyone find your spot!" Jax said, and there were a few disputes over which areas of sand were more desirable for the kids. Luna ended up with Jackson and a few of the other little girls that I'd been hearing about. One of Isla's dads was here, so I got to meet him and he was lovely.

"Remember our rules, everyone," Jax said, calling everyone to attention with a few claps. "Rule number one!"

"No throwing sand!" the kids repeated.

"Rule number two!" Jax called out, holding up another finger.

"No going in the water without permission!"

She went all the way to the fifth rule, and I was impressed, I had to say.

"Right now, it's sandcastle time, so everyone build your sandcastles. Remember, every sandcastle is beautiful and unique. If you have toys remember to…" she trailed off, waiting for the kids to fill in the blank.

"Share!" the kids yelled.

"That's right. Because sharing is…"

"Kind!"

She was really good at this.

After a few more instructions, the kids were let loose on the sand with their buckets and shovels to try and make their sand creations. I waited to see if Luna wanted me to come with her, but she was off with her black Halloween bucket and shovel.

"Guess I'm chopped liver," I said to Anna as Luna dashed down to the edge of the water to get some to make the sand wet so it would stick together.

"Yeah, same," she said with a laugh.

"They're really cute, though," I said. "Luna just loves Jackson. She won't stop talking about him."

"Same with Jackson. He just thinks she's so cool."

"She is cool," I said. "Much cooler than me."

Anna laughed.

Most of the kids did their thing, so the adults stayed back and supervised, which was how I hoped this would go.

Jax stayed with the kids, moving from group to group and supervising and offering encouragement and tips. I saw her showing Jackson and Luna how to make a drip castle, mixing the sand with a lot of water and then using your fingers to "drip" the mixture down so it made a very abstract, kind of spooky castle. Luna was all over that and I knew I was going to have to pry her away later.

"She seems like an excellent teacher. They're all just completely taken with her," Anna said. "I was hoping Jackson would get her. The other teacher, Mrs. Jones, isn't as well-liked. But you didn't hear that from me."

"Hear what?" I said, winking at her.

"Exactly."

A while later, Jax announced that all the kids had to get sunblock on again, so that was a job. There were tears, but each kid got sprayed. Luna didn't care, so I didn't have to fight with her, but a few of the other kids had some small meltdowns.

Jax spoke to each of them, and somehow, she got them back to smiling from tears in moments. I'd never seen anything like it. She was really, really good at her job.

Once the sunblock ordeal was over, she announced that it was time to look for shells and rocks. We rounded up all the munchkins and made them all hold hands as we walked slowly up and down the beach, and Jax would periodically pick something up and the kids would gather around to look at it and pass it around. Shells, interesting rocks, seaweed. Her knowledge of marine life was incredible, and she had a way of speaking to the kids that put explanations on their level, without infantilizing them too much.

Then she asked if the kids had any questions and spent a lot of time talking about whales and mermaids.

"Jackson loves mermaids," Anna said. "Like, obsessed. I got this big huge mural for his wall."

"Luna has been asking for a real skeleton for her room for every Christmas since she could talk," I said. "Her mom has done research on where we can get one, like the kind they use in classrooms to teach anatomy? We're just not sure we can fit it in her room."

My sweet, weird niece.

Our group slowly moved up and down the beach, the kids picking up shells and rocks and yelling out questions. Jax managed it all until one kid slipped and fell, requiring some comforting.

We all went back to the towels and all the kids sat down to eat.

"Do you need help, Luna Moon?" I asked as Luna trotted over with her lunchbox.

"No, I can do it," she said, sitting down next to Jackson. His mom was bringing out his food for him and setting it out. I was impressed with her little sandwiches that had been cut with a cookie cutter to make fun shapes.

I should have thought of that. The only thing I'd done was cut off the crusts of Luna's sandwich because she didn't like them.

It was surprisingly quiet while the kids ate their lunches, with the occasional whine or disagreement.

Luna dutifully ate her turkey sandwich, crackers, carrot sticks, and grapes.

"Good job, I'm impressed," I said when she showed me the empty lunchbox.

"So, I get ice cream later?" she asked.

"We'll see," I said. The snack bar had closed for the season, so it was good that we didn't have to worry about dozens of small children trying to eat ice cream. A sticky nightmare.

"How's everyone doing over here?" a voice said, and I looked up from my own sandwich to find Jax looking down at us.

Of course, I'd just taken a huge bite because I was starving, and almost choked as I tried to chew and swallow.

"Everything's great," Anna answered.

"All good," I said brilliantly, once my mouth was no longer full of food.

"Great," Jax said, looking first at Anna and then at me. "Just let me know if you need anything."

She moved on to the next group, and I found myself watching her again. Watching the way she moved, the way she emoted when she spoke with the kids. The way she smiled at them. Stunning. She was stunning.

After lunch, the kids went as a group down to the water to stick their toes in, with all the adults supervising.

"I want to swim," Luna said as I held her hand.

"I know, you do, but the water is really cold, and it's not fair to the other kids. Remember the rules?" I said and she sighed heavily.

"I guess," she said. "Can we come back to swim?"

"If it's warm enough, we'll see."

She pouted. "That means no."

"No, that means we'll see," I said, and I had a terrifying moment of realizing how much like a parent I sounded. When had that happened?

Jax waded into the water and managed to find a little hermit crab that captured the attention of the kiddos for a long time. One of the kids got the idea that the hermit crab needed a new sand home, so they all rushed off to make more castles with little pools for the hermit crab. Their enthusiasm was adorable and infectious.

Jax explained that we could make a castle for the hermit crab for a little while, but we needed to return them to their home, which was the ocean.

That didn't deter the kids that much, and the rest of the trip was spent either building castles for the hermit crab, or just digging a giant hole for whatever reason.

"She's going to sleep good tonight," I said as an exhausted and sandy Luna came to give me a hug and curl up on the towel next to me.

"Thank goodness for that," Anna said. "There is a new episode of my favorite show and some popcorn calling my name tonight."

Reading between the lines, it seemed like Anna was a solo parent, and I really wished she could meet Lizzie, because they could relate so much.

"We should have a play date," I suggested, and she loved that idea.

"Seriously, tell your sister to contact me. I'm also happy to have the kids if she needs to work and vice versa."

That was a great idea, and I knew Lizzie would appreciate having another backup plan if we needed somewhere for Luna to be.

"She is definitely going to be at the next parent thing. I don't think she'd miss it for the world."

I'd been sending Lizzie pictures all day, and she'd been sending me updates about the college and all the things she had to think about and her next steps. It was going to be a lot of work, but it would definitely pay off.

"Did you have a good day?" I asked Luna, running my fingers through her hair. She definitely needed to wash it tonight.

"Uh huh," Luna said in a sleepy voice. I didn't know if she was even going to make it to dinner without falling asleep.

It was a chore to force all the kids back on the bus. They absolutely did not want to leave.

Jax stood at the front of the bus and called everyone to attention. "If you can hear me clap once!" The kids clapped. "If you can hear me, clap two times!" The kids clapped again.

"I just wanted to thank all the parents for coming today to help out. I think we had a very successful beach day, didn't we?" The kids yelled and cheered.

The trip back was noisy and bumpy, but we all survived. The sandy and tired children were handed off to their parents, many of whom put down towels in their cars to protect the upholstery.

"Well, we made it," I said.

"That we did," Anna said, carrying a half-asleep Jackson. "So yeah, let me know about the play date. And I'll probably see you again. Let me know if you ever want to just hang out. I work all the time, but I would really enjoy some adult time."

I didn't really need more friends, but Anna was cool, and I enjoyed her company.

"Yeah, will do."

She left with Jackson and the other kids were picked up by their parents. Luna decided she wanted to wave goodbye to everyone.

"We gotta get home. See how your mom did today. And you need to wash all that sand off," I said.

"I have to say goodbye to everyone," she said, her little face determined.

"Okay," I said, even though I was ready for a nap myself.

More and more kids left and all the adults chaperoning left and then it was just me and Jax with Luna and two other kids, twin boys named River and Layke. Their dad showed up a few minutes later and loaded them into a car, and then it was the three of us.

"Thank you so much for coming today," Jax said, her eyes flicking down to Luna.

"Yeah, you're welcome," I said. Why was my heart pounding so loudly? I had no doubt that she could hear it. I mean, it wasn't like we could say anything in front of Luna, so that just left us standing there and staring at each other.

"We can go now," Luna said, tugging on my shirt.

"Okay, Luna Moon."

I met Jax's eyes again and she smirked at me. "See you around, Sasha. Or in my DMs."

That last part was a dig at me following her.

"Hey, Luna, why don't you go put your bag in the car?" I asked, hitting the unlock button. I needed some privacy for this.

Luna trotted off to the car and I had a short window.

"I didn't mean to follow you," I said, feeling myself starting to babble. "I deleted it."

Jax pulled out her phone and tapped through a few things.

"Then why are you still following me?" she asked, holding the screen in front of my face.

"Oh my god, I guess I'm not allowed to follow my niece's teacher for any reason other than I'm stalking her, I guess," I snapped and that just made her smile more.

"Seems like I might have pushed your buttons, Sasha," she

said. I wanted her to stop saying my name.

"Listen, we don't have to make this a thing between us," I said.

"What thing between us?" she asked.

I narrowed my eyes. "You know exactly what I mean."

"Mmm, I'm not sure that I do. Could you refresh my memory?" She stepped closer to me and I had to remind myself to breathe.

"You were the one who kissed me, remember?" I said.

"Sashie!" Luna called, and we both blinked. Dammit, I'd been swept up in her spell again. I had to stop letting that happen.

"Yes, Luna Moon, I'm coming," I said, not looking away from Jax.

"I have to go."

"Then go," she said. "No one's stopping you."

I rolled my eyes. Okay, it was definitely time to go.

What I wanted to do was leave her with the perfect come-back. Instead, I just sputtered a goodbye and shuffled off to my car, tripping on a pothole and nearly twisting my ankle in the process. I righted myself and kept walking. Luna bounced up and down near the car, urging me to hurry because she had to pee.

I didn't look back to see if Jax was watching.

"YOU LOOK like you had a great day," Lizzie said when we got back to the house and after Luna had used the restroom.

"I'm hungry," Luna said.

"Well, you are in luck because I stopped at a very nice pizza place and got a different kind of pizza for us to try." Luna's eyes lit up as Lizzie pulled the pizza out of the oven.

"It's spinach and artichoke," she said, putting slices on our plates. "I knew it was a risk, but I figured if there was enough cheese, she might go for it."

I thought it looked really good, so the three of us sat at the dining table while Luna gave her mom a rundown of the beach day in the way kids always told stories, with a million pauses and segues and non sequiturs. Even though she was tired from her day, Lizzie listened to every word in between bites of pizza. Luna seemed to love it, so we marked that in the win column as well.

Luna barely made it through her bath and fell asleep as her mom was combing out her hair, so Lizzie tucked her in and I got to hear about her day as we both sipped on cheap wine from a box.

"I'm going to do a little more research, but I think my best bet is being a paralegal, medical office assistant, or HR. I need to sit down and figure out which one I would be best at, that also wouldn't make me want to throw myself out a window."

We talked some more about jobs, and I filled her in about Anna wanting to have some play dates.

"Yeah, that sounds great. I'm definitely up for that. Plus, you've already vetted her, so I can feel safe taking Luna there."

A text from Hollis came through, asking for updates on how the day had gone. I'd told her that I was filling in as chaperone for the trip, and she was dying to know if I'd talked to Jax at all.

Please let me live vicariously she said.

I didn't know why she was so interested; she dated all the time.

Hold on, I told her.

"Hollis," I told Lizzie before going to my room and calling her on video chat.

"So, it wasn't that exciting," I said after she'd greeted me from the bedroom of her apartment, which was hung with lights all along the ceiling that gave it a romantic glow.

"I'll decide what's exciting, thank you. Details."

I told her pretty much everything, which didn't take long.

"I can feel the sexual tension from here," Hollis said.

"It's not so much tension as irritation. There's just something about her that just…" I trailed off, unable to find the right words.

"Sexy," Hollis said, wiggling her eyebrows.

"No, it's not sexy." Okay, it was definitely a little sexy, but that's because she was sexy. She couldn't help it.

"Whatever. I'm not going to be chaperoning anymore, so it doesn't matter." Lizzie had vowed that she would do whatever it took to be at Luna's school things from now on.

"Fine, you're no fun."

"I'm okay with that," I said. "What's up with you?"

Hollis gave me the down and dirty details of her latest conquest. She certainly knew how to charm the pants off just about anyone.

"You should teach a mastermind. Make some money," I said.

"Gross. I'm not a pickup artist," she said, making a face.

"You do pick up a lot of people, though," I said.

She grinned. "That's true."

I was grateful we'd moved on from the topic of Jax. I talked with Hollis for a little bit longer and then lay back on my bed. I wasn't ready for sleep yet, even though I was exhausted from the beach day.

I pulled up my social pages and scrolled through my feed. I almost dropped my phone on my face when I realized that one of the pictures was from the beach today. Jax had taken a shot with her toes wiggling in the sand right on the edge of the water. The caption was just a nice quote.

It was weird to think I'd been there when she'd taken that picture, just up the beach.

I really should unfollow her.

Chapter Seven

I didn't unfollow Jax, which was how I knew that she'd gone to Sweet's on Saturday morning and had a latte and a pumpkin cheesecake cinnamon roll. My mouth started watering immediately, and all I could think about was getting one for myself.

Instead, I hauled my butt out of bed, tripped over the clothes on my floor that needed to make their way to the hamper, and stumbled into the kitchen. Luna was already on the couch holding onto her Fluffy, her blanket that she'd had since she was a baby, and watching cartoons. I loved that even in the advent of streaming, some things never changed. Waking up on Saturday mornings with cartoons never went out of style.

Lizzie was in the kitchen, yawning and mixing up pancake batter. She had the rare day off, so we were all going to an apple orchard. It was still early in the season, but Luna had been begging and begging.

"Can you put the bacon in the oven and set the timer?" Lizzie asked, and I nodded. None of us were really morning people, but that was nice to have us all on the same page in the house.

I laid out the bacon strips on the baking sheet and then ducked around Lizzie to slide it in the oven as she poured out the batter to make the little silver dollar pancakes that Luna demanded.

My phone buzzed with a message from Paige.

Hey, you free today?

I wished I was.

Taking Luna to the apple orchard in Hartford, sorry. But maybe later tonight?

Luna shuffled into the kitchen, dragging Fluffy along behind her.

"I'm hungry," she said.

"Just a few more minutes, baby," Lizzie said, kissing her on the head. "Want to help me?" She pulled a special stool over so Luna could stand on it and monitor the bubbles on the tops of the pancakes and tell her mom when to flip them.

Want to come to dinner at my place? Paige asked.

Absolutely! Just let me know what time and I'll try to swing by.

"Flip!" Luna screamed and I almost swallowed my tongue.

"Okay, okay," Lizzie said. "Not so loud, baby."

Lizzie flipped the pancakes and the timer went off for the bacon and we all sat down.

"Nope, I'm doing the syrup," Lizzie said and there was a fight with Luna about whether she was old enough to be in charge of her own syrup distribution. I sipped my coffee that was drowning in lavender syrup and creamer. Linley had turned me on to lavender lattes, so I was making them at home now.

My eyes strayed to my phone and I saw that Jax had posted another picture, a selfie in her house, the sunlight perfectly kissing her cheekbones. She looked amazing and I didn't even think she'd used a filter. There were several comments about how gorgeous she was, and I looked at a few of the commenters' pages and found some of the girls that had been with her that night. Some of them were also teachers, but a few I couldn't tell what they did other that "spread good vibes" which probably meant they had inherited enough money that they didn't have to work for a living. I couldn't even mock them, because that's exactly what I would do if I was handed a pile of money to live on and didn't have to work. No jobs, just vibes.

"Sasha," Lizzie said.

"What?" I said, looking up.

"I asked if you were done." Oh.

I looked down at my empty plate.

"Yeah," I said, taking my plate to rinse it and then put it in the dishwasher.

"Let's get ready, Luna Moon," I said, taking Luna to her room to put on her clothes for the day and brush her hair and teeth.

"What do you want to wear?" I asked, pulling open her drawers. Lizzie didn't bother to fight with Luna much on her clothing choices. There were some hills that weren't worth dying on.

As usual, Luna picked out some black leggings, a black shirt with a smiley face skull on it, black socks with cats on them, and her black sparkly sneakers.

Most of her clothes were ordered online, because it was really hard to find goth clothes for a little girl.

"Very cute," I said once she'd put everything on. I brushed her hair out and braided it quickly back with a black velvet scrunchie.

"What do you think?" I asked and she turned her head side to side to check herself out in the mirror before striking a few model poses. No idea where she'd picked that up, but it was cute as hell. It was going to be all over the day she got a phone with a camera in it. She loved having her picture taken.

"You ready?" Lizzie said, sticking her head through the doorway. "Oh, Luna, you look so good. Auntie Sasha did a good job on your hair."

"Thanks," I said. It had taken a lot of practice and a few online tutorials to figure out how to do all different kinds of braids. I had to admit, it was really fun, because Luna let me try them out on her and never complained.

"Okay, now I have to get ready," I said, going to my room and yanking some clothes out of the laundry basket that I hadn't put away yet. I'd get to it tomorrow.

"Sit in the back with me," Luna begged as we got in Lizzie's car, and I caved and complied. Lizzie put on Luna's favorite playlist and away we went.

It was strange, how much my weekends had changed. Back in Boston, Hollis and I would have probably gone out for a huge brunch at one of our favorite places, and then maybe a walk around the Commons or to the aquarium or shopping. She'd always convince me to drive to some nature preserve and go on a hike and I would always tell her that I didn't do that kind of nature and then we'd compromise and go to the Arboretum, which was like, controlled nature with paved paths.

We'd get lunch and in the evening probably go out with a few other people for drinks. I'd spend the entire day gone from my apartment, arrive back late and pass out in bed.

The only place that was open past 10 p.m. on a weekend here was the bar side of the Grille, and you ran the risk of being hit on by a fisherman who was old enough to be your grandfather and who smelled like bait. Not ideal.

Now my weekends were full of Luna's activities and trying to catch up on work and laundry. True, I did have my friends to hang out with, so there was that bright spot. But everything about how I lived my life had changed. I couldn't order a burger to my apartment at 2 a.m. anymore. I couldn't order any food delivered to my house, unless I begged Linley or Charli to drop off donuts.

I also couldn't disappear when I went to the grocery store. Butch was always there wanting to chat, and then there were all the other locals who had decided to adopt me into this small, strange town. I missed being anonymous.

"Here we are," Lizzie announced as she turned into the parking lot for the apple orchard. Hartford was a little north of Castleton, and didn't border the ocean, but they did have a pond, and a small hill that I guess they counted as a mountain that had been turned into a town park with hiking trails and picnic areas.

Luna grabbed my hand and dragged me to the photo area, where there were hay bales set up, and a wooden apple with cutouts where you could stick your face through and take a funny picture. Luna demanded Lizzie's phone to take a bunch of pictures of me and Lizzie before she made me do the same for her.

"Let's go pick some apples," Lizzie said, and we paid for a bag and a long stick with a little cage on the end, which helped bring down the apples that were further up on the tree.

After a short lecture on how to pick, and which apples not to take, we headed off down the neat rows of apple trees, each one with a little sign listing the variety, some facts, and what kind of things that particular apple was good for.

"We need to find pie apples," I told Luna. The cards were a little tricky for her to read, but she did her best with some help from her mom.

Linley had also texted me a list of the best pie apples, along with her crust recipe, and some other baking tips. She just couldn't help herself.

"Honey Crisp!" Luna called out as she read the sign on one tree. Those were one of the apples on the list Linley had given me, so I pulled a few that were in range, and helped Luna use the picker to grab some from near the top of the tree.

As we walked, Luna started making up a song about pie.

Other little kids ran around, and I saw one little boy pick an apple off the ground and bite right into it before making a face and spitting it out. Luna had been informed that she was not to eat any of the apples from the ground, and so far, she was listening.

There were also plenty of adults without children, many of whom were doing more posing than actually picking any apples.

I came upon two women, one who was trying to get the perfect shot while balancing on a ladder that she was probably not supposed to be standing on.

"Let me see," she said, jumping off the ladder and walking over to the woman who'd been holding up the phone. I caught flash of beautiful gold hair, and then she turned her head, and I realized it was Jax.

I dove behind a tree so she wouldn't see me.

Here's the thing about apple trees: They aren't very wide, or tall. Not nearly wide enough to hide a whole human behind them. So, all Jax saw was me trying, and failing, to hide behind a tree.

"Miss Hardy!" Luna squealed, running over.

"Hi, Luna," Jax said. "Are you picking lots of apples today?" I'd been around her enough at this point to hear the change in the tone of her voice when she was talking to one of her students. It was subtle, but it was there.

"We're going to make pie!" Luna said, throwing her arms in the air and twirling.

"That sounds delicious," Jax said, looking up as Lizzie and I walked over. I didn't really have a choice.

Jax's friend stood beside her and was completely absorbed in her phone as Luna babbled about pie.

"Hi, I'm Lizzie Klein, Luna's mom. I'm so sorry I couldn't be there this week for the beach day," Lizzie said again, even though she'd already sent two apologetic emails.

"Jax Hardy, nice to meet you finally. Don't even worry about it. There will be lots of other times," Jax said.

"Let's do some more," Jax's friend said, not even bothering to introduce herself.

"We'll let you get back to your Saturday," Lizzie said, taking Luna's hand. "Say goodbye to Miss Hardy, you'll see her on Monday."

"Bye, Miss Hardy," Luna said, waving, and then dashing off in another direction.

I stood there for a second, unsure of what to say.

"See you later, Sasha," she said. Her voice wrapped around my name like she was caressing it with her voice. It made my skin heat up and feel too tight on my body.

"See you later," I mumbled and then almost tripped on a few apples. Why did I always have my clumsiest moments around her? It was like being around her turned off part of my brain or something.

I heard her softly laugh as I walked away, and I tried to forget the sound.

Luna kept picking more and more apples, decided that we had to bring each one home with us, and the bag got too full.

"Let's go get another one," Lizzie said, taking Luna's hand. "And we can put this one in the car."

"Do you need me to help?" I asked, and Lizzie shook her head.

"No, I've got this."

I watched as they walked back down the rows to the barn where they had a little farm stand with full bags of apples you didn't have to pick yourself, cider, honey, and other veggies.

I heard a leaf crunch behind me and whirled around to find Jax standing a few feet away.

"Hey," I said as a reflex.

"Hey," she said. I glance over her shoulder and saw Jax's friend taking more selfies.

"Do you also work as a photographer?" I asked.

"No, it just seems to happen when I'm around Casey," she said with a laugh. "She's saved my butt a few times, so the least I can do is be her hype woman."

There must be more to Casey than met the eye, because I wasn't exactly seeing what she was talking about.

Jax took another step toward me and reached right over my head to pluck an apple from the tree.

"I've been thinking," she said, inspecting the apple.

"About what?" I asked.

"I've been thinking that we should go out for a drink sometime. And not have you spill it all over my dress."

Really? We were back to that?

"Why would I go out for a drink with you if you're going to insult me while you're asking?"

She just kept turning the apple over and over in her hands. It was perfect, no blemishes or spots.

"Because I'm buying? Would you turn down a free drink?"

I'd turned down free drinks before.

I opened my mouth to say something snarky, but then her friend, Casey, called her over.

"Just think about it. Open invitation," she said, tossing the apple in the air. I watched it go up and Jax caught it one-handed. I wondered if she'd ever played softball.

"Think about it," she said, backing away before she laughed and tossed the apple toward me.

I caught it with both hands. Part of me wanted to drop it on the ground, but I didn't. I wiped the surface with the sleeve of my shirt and bit into it. Perfectly crisp.

~

LIZZIE AND LUNA came back with another bag and we filled that one as well until Luna got bored with apple picking and we went to the barn to sit down and have cider and donuts that were still warm and covered with cinnamon sugar that Luna got all over her face and fingers.

"I've got her," I said to Lizzie as she looked through her purse for wipes. I'd started carrying wipes for myself years ago, so they came in handy for my niece as well.

"Miss Hardy is so pretty," Luna said.

"She is," Lizzie said. "But you know who's prettier?"

"Who?" Luna asked.

"You!" Lizzie said, tickling Luna in her favorite spot. "And you're also kind, and smart, and strong. Right?"

"Right!" Luna said.

"I don't think she's married," Lizzie said. "Didn't see a ring."

I hadn't noticed her ring or lack thereof. I mean, kissing a stranger didn't mean she was single.

"I'm sure she's got someone," I said. I mean, how could she not?

"It doesn't really matter, but I'd like to know more about her, you know?" Lizzie said as Luna licked the remaining sugar off her plate.

"Yeah," I said. I was not going to give away what I knew about Miss Hardy.

"You ready to go, baby?" Lizzie asked Luna. She had leaves and twigs in her braid, and her cheeks were rosy from being outside. She looked like a perfect little wood sprite.

"Pie time! Pie time!" Luna chanted as we got in the car with more apples than we knew what to do with.

"I think we've made a huge mistake," Lizzie said as we unloaded the apples and set them in the kitchen.

"Did we pick this many? Or did they multiply?" I asked.

"I think they multiplied," Lizzie said with a sigh. "Looks like I'm going to be looking for lots of apple recipes."

Lizzie set me to the task of washing and peeling the apples while Luna "supervised" and she worked on the crust.

"I can't remember the last time I made pie crust," Lizzie said. "Maybe because it's so much work."

She rolled out the chilled crust between two pieces of plastic wrap and then put it in the fridge to chill before laying it in the pie pan.

I followed Linley's directions for preparing the apples, and Lizzie cut up strips of dough for the lattice top. Luna hadn't gotten bored of watching us yet, and Lizzie had given her a little piece of dough to play with so she didn't stick her fingers in everything.

"Okay, wish the pie good luck," Lizzie said, holding the pie out to Luna to bless before she shoved it in the oven and set the timer.

"Be good, pie!" Luna called, waving to it as Lizzie shut the oven door.

"Okay, now we wait. And clean."

Flour and apple peels littered the kitchen.

"I've got this," I said, starting to gather the apple peels that I'd tried to keep in the bowl, but had failed.

Luna got a burst of energy and started dancing around the living room.

"I don't know where she gets it from," Lizzie said, yawning and going through the pictures she'd taken on her phone. She put a few of them together and posted on her social media. I got a notification that I'd been tagged.

"I'll ask Linley for more apple recipes," I said. "You good on your own for dinner?"

"Yeah, yeah. I've got some spaghetti and sauce and meatballs in the freezer. Mom of the year!"

She frowned and I gave her a hug.

"You are literally doing your fucking best," I said, whispering so Luna didn't hear me swearing. "You literally just made your daughter pie from scratch. You're allowed to take the easy road on dinner."

As for me, I decided to take a few of the apples with me to Paige and Esme's.

"Just picked today," I said, handing her the bag.

"Wow, thank you! I'm going to have to make some apple butter or something."

I had to be inspected by Esme's husky, Stormy, and Paige's orange cat, Potato, before I could walk all the way into the little house. You couldn't beat the little furry welcoming committee. I would love to have a pet, but it wasn't in the cards right now.

"Drink?" Esme asked as I walked into the kitchen. That was where all the action was.

"Yes, please," I said. Esme handed me a glass that looked and smelled a lot like cider.

"Apple Pie Old Fashioned," she said, and my eyes lit up.

"I love an Old Fashioned, how did you know?" I asked.

Esme wiggled her fingers. "Magic."

"You are magical," Paige said, kissing her on the cheek and wrapping some of Esme's long dark hair around her wrist.

"Who else is coming?" I asked, taking a sip of my drink and relishing the sweet and smoky flavor. Perfection.

"We think everyone?" Paige said. "It's going to be a full house. We might run out of chairs."

Fortunately, the weather was nice, so we went out the back of the cottage where Paige and Esme had a little grassy yard that sloped down to a rocky border with the ocean. Or was it a bay? A cove? I wasn't sure. The smell of saltwater was sharp, and seagulls wheeled through the sky, calling out to one another.

"It might get a little chilly, so we have extra sweatshirts and blankets," Paige said. She and Esme really were the best hostesses.

I helped them bring the food and utensils and plates out to the picnic tables outside. Since their friend group had expanded, they'd had to buy a second table to seat all of us.

Linley and Gray arrived with two cakes, followed by Natalie and Em with two massive casseroles in aluminum trays, then Charli and Alivia joined us.

It was a full house. Stormy couldn't decide who to be excited about, so she just ran around, checking on everyone before Esme threw her a bone for her to chew on in a corner of the yard. Potato watched us from the window, angry that he couldn't be part of the fun.

I loaded up my plate with casseroles and salad and Esme topped off my drink. It was such a nice change from earlier at the apple orchard.

I still hadn't gotten the taste of that apple Jax had thrown at me out of my mouth.

"How's everything going with the house?" Paige asked Em and Natalie and they both rolled their eyes simultaneously. They'd gotten a place in a new development, and it was almost finished, but they kept getting caught with little delays that were preventing them from moving in.

"At least another month," Em said. "Please kill me."

"No, no killing," Natalie said, hugging her close. "It'll be fine. There are always little setbacks like this."

I wouldn't know. I'd never owned a house, but I knew that Lizzie was always calling someone to fix something in her place.

"I just want to be in. I can't take this waiting," Em said, shaking her head. "But we are planning a housewarming, whenever that will be. Probably in twenty years."

"It will all work out," Paige said.

"I just want a dishwasher," Em wailed dramatically, and everyone laughed.

"Hey, imagine living in a hotel room. Alivia didn't even have a stove," Charli said, smiling at Alivia.

"To be fair, I had an entire professional kitchen downstairs and pretty much never cooked for myself," Alivia said. They were such an interesting pair. Charli was all pink hair and flouncy skirts and vibrancy, whereas Alivia had short dark hair undercut on both sides, and nearly always dressed in a suit since she managed The Honeysuckle Inn that her parents owned. I had the feeling that Alivia and Luna would get along in the fashion department.

They hadn't moved in together, but at least Alivia had gotten out of the inn, and was living nearby in a little rented cottage that was just cozy enough for two. Charli was still technically living with Natalie, even though Nat was staying most of her time with Em until they got the keys to their house.

"I wouldn't mind living in an inn if I could get room service delivered and my room cleaned," I said. "That would be the real benefit."

"It wasn't like that for me," Alivia said with a laugh. "I ended up cleaning not only my room, but everyone else's."

That made us all laugh.

"I think we're good where we are," Linley said. "I have great neighbors." She was referring to Charli and Natalie, who lived on the floor above them in an apartment building within walking distance of downtown Castleton. This whole group of friends was so interconnected in so many ways.

And then there was me, just sort of... here.

"I'm just waiting until the day when I can pee alone and not have someone bang on the door and demand to talk to me," I said. Luna didn't understand the meaning of privacy.

"How long are you planning on staying?" Charli asked. She'd also come to Castleton temporarily, but under much different circumstances. Her ex had kicked her out of her apartment, and she'd come to stay with Linley, her cousin, and work at Sweet's. Pretty perfect arrangement. Then she'd fallen in love with Alivia and had moved in with Nat and had officially joined the Castleton Crew. I'd started calling them that in my head.

"I don't know," I said. "Luna is in school now, but Lizzie is thinking about starting college classes, and maybe getting a different job with better hours, so I'm not going to bail on her until everything is stable." I really shouldn't tell these people so many details of my life, but they just seemed to spill out. It was a real problem for me.

"You're such a good sister," Charli said, patting my arm.

"Thanks," I said. I really liked Charli. She was so sweet and fun and bubbly.

"It's fine for now," I said. "But I am not doing a full winter here. No thank you." I shuddered, thinking about how many horror stories my sister had told me about Castleton winters. Hard pass, no way.

"Oh, it's not that bad," Paige said.

"Then why do I have to hear about it whenever your mom calls you to shovel her walkway?" Esme said, poking her in the arm.

"Listen, this year I am hiring someone. I will pay them and she will have no say. I'm not doing that anymore." Paige and her mom had an interesting relationship where Paige sometimes acted more like the parent than the other way around. They were still close, but Paige had had to draw some boundaries to protect herself.

"I should think about doing that for Lizzie. She doesn't have time for that shit." I'd also tried to get her to hire a cleaning person, but she absolutely balked at that too. I was almost at the point that I was going to start randomly transferring money into her account. What was she going to do? I mean, I guess she could send it back, but I hoped she would just give in and keep it.

The conversation turned from Castleton winters to favorite vacation destinations to the latest shows everyone was watching.

"Lizzie and I are absolutely hooked on the one where the guy is like, a murderer, but he's obsessed with making a girl fall in love with him. We've stayed up way too late with it."

"Oh, we want to start that one," Linley said. "But I was waiting for the next season to come out in a few weeks so we don't have to wait."

"Is this one going to make me mad?" Gray asked. He was an extremely level guy, but shows with medical inaccuracies drove him up a wall.

"I can't help it," he said when we all looked at him. For the only guy in our group, he was really comfortable with his role.

"You can just cover your eyes," Linley said, putting her arm around him. He sighed heavily.

I filled my belly with delicious and cheesy casserole and topped that off with a piece of chocolate butterscotch cake and then a piece of toasted coconut cake because I couldn't say no when Linley offered me a piece.

The air got too cold to stay outside, so we moved inside to the living room, and there definitely wasn't enough seating for everyone, so some of us squished on the couch, the wing-back chair that Paige had found at a yard sale, and then Esme went to the basement and brought out some beach chairs and a few extra folding chairs. We made it work. I ended up being shoved up against Paige's puzzle table, which had a half-done puzzle on it. According to the box, it was over a thousand pieces. Paige had quite the puzzle habit, but Esme was a book collector, so it all evened out. The cottage was small, but cozy, and had plenty of little tchotchkes around. From what Paige told me, there had been even more before Esme had moved in, and I couldn't even imagine what that had been like.

Stormy came over and put her face in my lap, probably hoping I might have some treats hidden in my pockets.

"Sorry, girl," I said, petting her head. She gave me a disapproving look and moved on to Charli.

Paige broke out the hot chocolate and Baileys and handed out mugs topped with homemade whipped cream.

I covered myself with a blanket that Esme handed me and let the chatter ebb and flow around me. Usually I talked a lot, but tonight I wanted to take a backseat. Like I did at the bar.

I hadn't been to a bar since that night with the incident with Jax.

I was itching to go out again, and she had asked me to let her buy me a drink.

I mean, would it be so bad? Maybe I could swing a free meal out of it. I'd find the most expensive place I could think of and order the most expensive thing, eat fast, and then be out of there.

Sure, I'd have to deal with her smirk and her comments, but I'd been through worse. There was no way she could top my worst date—when the girl I'd talked to online demanded that I pick her up from her house and then go to an extremely sketchy steakhouse where she proceeded to order enough food for five people, only eat some of it, get the rest to go, and then claim she forgot her wallet when the bill came. Oh, and don't forget the part where I took her home, and when I walked in, her wife and her mom were in the kitchen baking a cake together.

She hadn't told me she had a wife, and non-monogamy wasn't for me. And then her mom made me eat a piece of cake while I died inside.

There was no second date.

Maybe. Maybe I would let Jax buy me a drink. But I

couldn't tell anyone that's what I was doing. Well, except for Hollis. I'd have to tell at least one person in case I went missing.

"Oh my god, you have to read it," Natalie said, bringing me out of my head and back to the present moment.

"I don't know," Paige said. "It sounds more like an Esme book."

"We should read it together," Esme said. Paige was practically sitting on her lap as they shared a piece of cake with two forks.

"Okay, but if there are too many scary parts, I'm out," Paige said.

"What book is it?" I asked.

"The latest Jack Hill book," Natalie said.

"Oh, I just ordered a copy of that," Alivia said. She also had a love for more spooky type books.

"Nice. Maybe we should do a buddy read of it," Natalie said. "I mean, there are enough of us that it would be fun."

I'd read a few other Jack Hill books. It was hard not to, they were everywhere. The horror writer was one of the best-selling authors in the world, and he also happened to be from Maine. People were always telling stories about spotting him in the wild or seeing him on a plane or something.

"I'd be up for reading it together," I said.

"Me too," Paige said.

"I don't want to be left out," Em said.

"Me neither," Charli said.

"I can read it or listen to it on my breaks," Gray said.

We agreed on a start date for everyone to get through the first five chapters, and then we'd all get together and talk about it. I was kind of excited. This was one of the only kind of small-town activities that I wanted to participate in.

"Oh, I love this," Charli said, clapping her hands. "It's going to be so fun."

We finished our cocoa and then the couples started filtering out.

"We're so old," Paige said. "We need to go out and stay out late to remind ourselves how young we are."

"Next weekend," Esme said as I helped them clean up and bring the dishes to the kitchen.

"I might be busy," I said.

"Doing what?" Paige asked.

Shit. I shouldn't have said anything. My mouth was always getting me into trouble.

"Oh, I don't know. I think Luna has something," I lied.

"Okay. Well, it's not set in stone. You could always meet us late or something."

"Yeah, sounds good."

I left Esme and Paige kissing in the kitchen while they poured themselves more boozy cocoa.

Lizzie was dozing on the couch and Luna was fast asleep in her pajamas with glow in the dark bats on them when I checked on her.

"Hey," I said, nudging Lizzie's shoulder.

"Hey," she said, blinking her eyes open. "I wasn't asleep."

"You were, but it's okay. Luna's fine."

Lizzie groaned.

"Do you want some pie?" I was still pretty full from the food at Paige and Esme's, but I wasn't going to turn down pie, especially since I'd helped make it.

"Yeah, you want some? I'll get it."

Lizzie yawned and I went to cut us two slices and throw them in the microwave for a few seconds to warm up before topping both of them with a hefty dollop of vanilla ice cream.

"Bless you," Lizzie said as I handed the plate over.

"No problem," I said, taking a bite of the pie.

"Oh my god, this is perfect." It was. Just the right amount of sweetness and tart from the apples, and zing from the spices. The crust was just the right combo of buttery and crumbly.

"No soggy bottom," I said, my mouth full.

"No soggy bottom," Lizzie agreed, taking a huge bite.

We both devoured our slices of pie and Lizzie seemed like she wanted to talk about something.

"What's up?" I asked, to get the conversation moving.

"I did something bad," Lizzie said, her cheeks getting red.

"Oh god, what?" I asked.

"I looked up Skippy's social media," she said, holding up a pillow to hide her face.

"What the hell is wrong with you?" I asked, almost yelling before I remembered that there was a sleeping child just down the hallway.

"I don't know," she moaned. "I just... I don't know. Maybe I enjoy pain?"

"There are ways to enjoy pain without looking up your ex. Just get some nipple clamps like a normal person."

Lizzie stared at me. "Can you not talk about nipple clamps while my child is sleeping?"

"Lizzie. I know he's Luna's father. I know you loved him. But you've got to just...cut him out. It's done. He's gone." I couldn't understand why she couldn't just move on. He certainly had.

"You don't get it," she muttered.

There it was. She was always throwing it in my face that I'd never been in a really serious relationship. Sure, I'd dated, but I'd never lived with anyone, and I'd never even been close to engagement or marriage. Plus, I was her little sister, and she liked to hold the fact that she was three years older over my head.

"Do you really want to do this right now?" I asked.

"It's just not that easy. You don't just turn the love switch off, especially when you have a child together."

I kept my mouth shut so I didn't snap back at her, because fighting with Lizzie was pointless. I had to live with her, and we had to get along in front of Luna.

When we'd been growing up, our parents had been constantly fighting and I didn't want my niece to live like that.

"What did you see on his social media?" I asked, changing tactics.

"Oh, just him being blissfully happy with a girl who looks like she was ripped out of a sexy billboard. They're always going out dancing or walking the strip or going on fabulous vacations."

"And where the hell is he getting the money for that?" I asked. Skippy hadn't exactly been rolling in cash when he'd lived in Castleton. He'd hopped around from job to job, never really landing on anything he could stick with for more than six months.

"Her," Lizzie said. "She's got money."

That explained a lot. Skippy really had it made. I wondered if they'd had a prenup. Seeing as how they got hitched in Vegas by an Elvis impersonator, I was guessing probably not. So even if he bailed on her, he could ride the alimony pony all the way to the bank.

Maybe Skippy was brighter than I gave him credit for.

"You can't tell me that his daughter isn't in the back of his mind. Maybe not much right now, but there will be a day when he has to look himself in the mirror and reckon with what he's done. And he's going to suffer."

"He should suffer," Lizzie said. Then she shook her head and groaned. "I don't want to talk about him anymore."

"You really should block him. Do you need me to do it for you?"

In a show of trust, Lizzie handed me her unlocked phone and I went to each of her social pages and blocked Skippy's profiles. He sure did look like he was having a good time, but karma would come for him. Hopefully soon.

"What's going on with you? I feel like all we do is talk about my bullshit life and Luna. I've been a bad sister lately," Lizzie said when I handed the phone back to her.

"Not much. Work. Work, work, work, Luna, work, sometimes hanging out with friends, work, Luna." And sometimes running into Luna's teacher that I'd kissed, but I didn't say that.

"You're not thinking about dating anyone?" Lizzie asked.

"Not really. I've got too much other shit going on," I said. Plus, there wasn't anyone I wanted to date.

"Well, you shouldn't let me or Luna stop you from having a good time if you want. I don't want you to have any regrets about coming here."

"Lizzie. I don't have any regrets," I said, reaching out and taking both her hands.

She and I hadn't talked about my exit plan, because I didn't want to put a deadline on her getting her shit together.

"I'm here for you and I'm here for Luna. I'd do anything for both of you."

"I know," Lizzie said, sniffling. "You really are the best sister."

We hugged and I kept my mouth shut about wanting to get the fuck out of Castleton.

Chapter Eight

I HAD a message on my social media the next morning. From Jax.

I'm just putting this out there: I'll be at this address on Saturday evening at 6 p.m. If you decide to meet me, you can. If you don't decide to meet me, I'll have a drink by myself and flirt with a waitress. Your choice.

My mouth dropped open. The audacity! Who did that? I copied the address and put it in my GPS. The restaurant was about thirty minutes outside of Castleton and located in a swanky little seaside town that had been settled mostly by rich people with second homes, because they were the only ones who could afford it. Every single business in town catered to them, so there were a lot of expensive pottery shops, an organic juice bar, a hot yoga studio, and restaurants with expensive steaks, including the one that Jax had invited me to. I looked at the menu prices and almost choked. Oh, I was definitely going to get my money's worth. If she wanted to pay an arm and a leg to get some time with me, so be it.

I didn't respond to her message. She wasn't going to know if I was going to meet her until I walked in the door. I wanted to give her some suspense. It was only fair.

Now I had to figure out what the fuck I was going to wear.

THE REST of my Sunday was spent trying to amuse my niece, and also trying to get a bunch of promo set up for one of my authors. I had all the graphics and copy, it was just getting everything scheduled right, and making sure they coordinated with the paid promo. I didn't love spreadsheets, but they were necessary so I didn't fuck anything up.

Another one of my authors sent me her new book that I needed to pull teasers from and start promo on as well. Next week I had a video chat with a potential new author, which was always nerve wracking. I could do things via email, but I always liked to see people so I could figure out if our styles would work well together. I wasn't for everyone, and that was okay. Better to find that out sooner rather than later. I'd learned a lot in this business, and I'd made a lot of mistakes in my early days. I was much better at figuring out who I wanted to take on as a client now, and who had the most realistic expectations for what I could do for them. No matter how much money someone paid me, I couldn't make one magic graphic that would rocket their book to the top of the bestseller list.

I ate pie for brunch and had zero regrets about it.

Lizzie had to work a few hours in the afternoon, so it was just me and Luna, so I pretty much let her get away with whatever, since it was Sunday and she had school tomorrow.

"Can you watch me jump?" she asked, pouting in that way that made me immediately give in.

"Okay." I did bring my phone with me, and put on some silly music, and hoped that she would wear herself out and not be jumping for two hours.

"Can we go to the beach?" she asked after about ten minutes of jumping and "tricks."

"It's too cold to go in the water, so we can go and play in the sand and pick up shells," I said.

Luna thought about that.

"Okay," she said. I was much happier going to the beach than watching her on the mini trampoline, so I got a bag together with essentials, grabbed a few towels, and we were off. Luna sang made-up songs as I drove.

The beach had officially closed for the season, so the snack bar wasn't open, and the parking lot was pretty empty. Most people were here to walk their dogs or get in their daily run. I knew Alivia came and ran her frequently, so I hoped I'd bump into her.

Luna found the perfect spot to spread out our stuff and immediately started working on a sandcastle down near the water where the sand was still wet. She seemed lost in her own world, so I took that time to open a book on my phone. I needed to start reading the Jack Hill book so I could talk about it with my friends. Romcoms were much more my speed, but I was willing to take a risk.

I'd only read a few pages when someone called my name and I looked up.

"Hey, Alivia," I said. She was panting and had on a base-ball cap, a sweatshirt, and black yoga pants.

"Hey, just saw you and thought I would say hi," she said, checking her fitness watch.

"Is Charli here?" I asked, and Alivia laughed.

"She's more of a hiking girl. I just came down for a short run. She's at the library right now." I needed to bring Luna to the library more. I knew they had activities for kids, and it would be nice for her to have some social time with other kids outside of school.

"Luna begged me to come here, and I'm bad at saying no, so here we are," I said. "I'm actually reading the Jack Hill book."

"I really need to start. Every time I try to read, Charli distracts me in some way."

"Sexy," I said, and that made her laugh again.

"I'm not complaining." She checked her watch again. "Okay, my heart rate is dropping, so I'm going to get back at it. Nice to see you."

I waved goodbye and she was off. I'd never seen someone who was so graceful when they were running. She wasn't my type, but I had to give Charli props for landing her.

I went back to the book, but it was pretty slow going to get into the first chapter.

Luna came over, asking about snacks, so we had a little snack party on the towel before she dragged me over to show me her castle.

"That's a really good moat," I said. She'd gone all out, with added wings and pools and shell decoration on the turrets.

"You could be an architect someday," I said.

"What's a artech?" she asked.

"An architect," I said, enunciating. "It's a person who designs houses."

Luna thought about that. "I could do that. When I have free time not being a witch."

I bit back a laugh. "Okay, Luna Moon."

I WENT a little overboard for dinner and mixed up some pizza dough and helped Luna top hers with lots of veggies and cheese and pepperoni. She was so stoked to have her own individual pizza that I was going to start buying frozen dough so we could do this more often. It was easier to get her to eat a variety when she made it herself.

"Maybe next summer we can grow some tomatoes and make our own sauce," I said before realizing that I probably wasn't going to be living with her next summer. We'd have to make do with store-bought for now.

Luna ate her whole pizza and didn't fight me on taking a bath. I made sure her school bag was packed and brushed out her hair before settling her in with Fluffy on the couch with a movie.

Lizzie came home just as I was going to check on Luna, who had fallen asleep on the couch. I carried her to bed, and tucked her in.

"Thanks," Lizzie said.

"We went to the beach for a little bit, and she's decided she wants to be a full-time witch and a part-time architect."

"Sounds like a plan," Lizzie said with a snort. "Oh, that kid. She is something else."

"That she is."

THE REST of my week was somewhat uneventful, and I didn't tell anyone I was meeting with Jax for a drink until Thursday night during my talk with Hollis.

"I need you to help me pick out an outfit," I said. I didn't have a whole lot of clothes suitable for a fancy restaurant, so my options were slim.

"Okay, what kind of occasion are we talking about here?" Hollis had much better fashion sense than I did.

"Uh, drinks? At a fancy restaurant."

Her eyes went wide.

"And who might you be having these drinks with?" Hollis asked.

"Uh, Jax. She invited me and I decided to go because she's buying."

"Oh really?" Hollis said. "You're just going for the free drinks and food?"

"Yes," I said, not meeting her eyes.

"You're such a liar," she said, shaking her head. "You're totally into her. There's no shame in that, Sasha. Go get it."

I laughed.

"It's just a drink. And maybe a disgustingly expensive steak," I said, opening my closet and cringing at how much shit was shoved in there. I was greeted by a little avalanche of crap.

"Girl, you need to hire an organizer. Or an exorcist for that closet."

"Yeah, shut up," I said, flipping through the hangers and pulling out what might pass for a nice outfit.

"Okay, what do you think?" I laid out the options on my bed and then held them up for her to see.

"Nope," Hollis said as I held up the first dress. "Nope," she said to the second.

"Definitely not," she said to the third.

"Okay, well, I only have one more, so you'd better not hate this one." I held up a dress that I'd actually bought when I was with Hollis at an outlet store just outside the city. I hadn't had any reason to buy it, but it had called to me anyway.

It was a dark green velvet with long sleeves and a plunging neckline, and it fell all the way to the floor. It looked like something an actress might have worn to a movie premier in the golden age of Hollywood.

"Oh, definitely that one. It's going to look incredible with your hair."

"Okay, that's good." I set the dress down on a chair and put the others back in my closet.

"You're going to be a smoke show. She's not going to be able to resist," Hollis said.

"I don't know about that. I'm just hoping I don't spill anything on myself, or fall off the chair, or trip."

"Speaking of that," Hollis said, pointing at me. "What shoes are you wearing with it?"

I would love to wear heels, but every single time I'd tried to wear heels, I'd ended up with some kind of injury. Once I'd even fallen down some steps and fractured my ankle and ended up in a boot for weeks. Never again.

"I've got black flats," I said, showing her some flats with pointed toes. "They're going to be hidden under the dress anyway," I said. "Part of me wants to wear sneakers, but I don't want her to make fun of me."

Hollis asked about my hair and gave me some tips.

"If you get laid because of this, you have to call me after," Hollis said.

"I'm not sleeping with her, Hols," I said, rolling my eyes.

"You say that now," Hollis said in a singsong voice.

"I can promise you I am not sleeping with Jax. You can take my word on it," I said.

"Okay. I'm going to hold you to that," Hollis said.

"I have some self-control, unlike some people," I said, giving her a look.

"Hey, I have self-control."

"Really? Because I've never seen it."

She glared at me.

"Now you're just being rude," she said, but she was laughing.

SATURDAY ARRIVED and I had to tell my sister that I was going out that night.

"Oh, where are you going?" she asked as she wiped Luna's face free of ketchup. Luna's new thing was dipping her grilled cheese sandwiches in ketchup.

I told her the name of the restaurant and her eyebrows went up.

"Isn't that a really swanky place? Why are you going there?"

I took a breath. "I have a date. Sort of. I'm meeting someone."

Lizzie's eyes went wide. "Who?"

"Just…someone," I said, pretending to be casual. "It's just a one-time thing."

"Wait, hold on. Is this a set up?"

"Uh," I said and then Lizzie grabbed my shoulders.

"Oh my god, I'm so excited you're going on a date! Have you picked out your outfit yet?"

I showed her what I was going to wear, and she insisted on helping me with my hair. I sat on one of the kitchen stools while she curled my hair and then pinned it back over one ear with some bobby pins that had little crystals on them.

"Let me make you glam," Lizzie said, and I had no choice but to let her, as Luna bounced around and offered to help by handing her mom brushes.

I wasn't against makeup at all. I wore a little bit most days when I left the house, but glam had never been my forte.

"Now I'm going to need every single detail so I can pretend it was me. I can't remember the last time I went on a date," Lizzie said with a sigh as she applied mascara to my lashes and then curled them.

I had to go to my room to get the full-length view in the mirror on the back of my door, but once I saw myself, I had to admit that I looked pretty fucking great. The velvet dress really loved my body and made me feel sexy as hell. Then there was also the fact that I wasn't wearing anything under it. I hadn't wanted to risk any lines showing.

"Isn't Auntie pretty?" Lizzie asked, picking Luna up.

"So pretty," Luna said.

"Thanks, Lizzie," I said. "I really appreciate your help." I slid into my flats and grabbed my favorite brown leather jacket. It didn't exactly go with the dress, but it was my go-to jacket.

"She isn't picking you up?" Lizzie asked as I grabbed my keys.

"No, I'm meeting her there," I said, grabbing my bag and putting it over my shoulder.

"I guess that's safer," Lizzie said. "But you call me if you need anything. You remember our code." Lizzie and I had a code word that we'd say if we were somewhere and needed to bail. All one of us had to do was ask the other one if we needed to pick up some ice cream on the way home. The other one would come to wherever the location was and pick the other one up, or, say that there was some kind of emergency that the other had to get home for.

"I'll be fine," I said. I'd given both Lizzie and Hollis the address of the restaurant. Plus, there was the fact that I was going to be with my niece's teacher, so I was pretty assured of my own safety.

"Have a good time," Lizzie called.

"I wanna go on a date," Luna whined as I shut the door.

I GOT MORE and more nervous as I drove to the restaurant. It was a bitch to find parking, so I finally had to go put my car in a lot that was a short walk to the restaurant. I made sure to walk carefully and hope the wind didn't mess up my hair too badly.

When I got to the door, there was a man in a crisp suit standing behind a podium.

"Reservation?" he asked.

"Oh, uh, I'm actually meeting someone." Hopefully she was already here. It wasn't like I had her number to call and ask.

"Name?" The man asked.

"Jax Hardy?" I said.

"Hardy, party of two," he said, scanning the book in front of him before grabbing a menu.

"Follow me."

I inhaled once through my nose and followed him toward the back of the restaurant.

JAX SAT at a table in the back that was right next to a cozy fire-place and had a view of the ocean via a window next to the table. It was also relatively private and cozy.

Jax looked over her shoulder when she heard the footsteps of both me and the host, and I couldn't read her expression as she stood up.

"Hello, Sasha," she said. I took in her outfit. I'd been a little worried that I would be overdressed, but my fears were unfounded.

Jax wore a silver sequined dress with short sleeves and a cutout back. Not to mention a pair of the highest heels I'd ever seen that no doubt had red bottoms.

Her hair was pulled back in a loose updo, and diamonds twinkled in her ears.

Knockout. She was a complete knockout.

"Wow," I couldn't stop myself from saying.

She laughed and did a little twirl.

"You look incredible," she said, her eyes bright.

"I didn't know if I was going to come," I said, and then realized the double entendre.

Jax laughed softly. "Let's just start with dinner and drinks."

She moved to stand behind my chair and it took a second to realize that she was pulling it out for me to sit down. I mean, I guess.

I sat down and then she resumed her seat and picked up her menu.

"Did you find the place okay?"

"Not that hard with GPS," I said, then realized how bitchy that sounded. "Sorry. This place is really nice." They were going to kick me out for not being fancy enough, even in my pretty dress.

"It's one of my favorite spots," Jax said. Oh, so she'd been here before. I kept getting more and more vibes that she didn't have to worry about money. Curious.

I looked at the menu and even though I'd looked up the menu online, seeing the prices in person was still shocking.

"What would you recommend?" I asked. I wondered if duck was good. I'd never had it before.

"The roasted duck is fantastic," she said. "But so is the beef tenderloin. And I never come here without getting the cheese plate as an appetizer." The beef tenderloin was the most expensive, so that's what I was getting.

"A cheese plate sounds good," I said, moving on to the drinks menu.

"Do you mind if I order drinks?"

"Sure," I said, shifting in my chair. The wine list alone was making my head spin. I was so completely out of my element.

Soft piano music played through the restaurant, and I realized that they had an actual player in a tux sitting at a shiny baby grand.

"Do you think he takes requests?" I asked, and she laughed.

"For enough money he does," she said.

"Interesting," I said, thinking of all the songs I could request, but then I'd definitely get kicked out.

"I'm really glad you decided to show up," Jax said as a waiter in a crisp suit arrived to take our orders.

"Yes, we'll have a bottle of the 2002 Bollinger, and the cheese plate to start," Jax said easily.

"Excellent choice," the waiter said, nodding his head to Jax.

"I'm not sure if I'm happy I showed up yet," I blurted out. "I'm still deciding."

Jax smiled, as if this didn't bother her at all.

"How is Miss Luna?" Jax asked.

"Feisty as ever," I said.

"Good," Jax said. "She's a fun kid."

"She is," I said, at a loss for what to talk about with her.

The waiter arrived with an ice bucket and a bottle of champagne, pouring a glass for each of us and then leaving the bottle.

"Should we toast?" Jax asked, raising her glass. I raised mine with trembling fingers, praying I wouldn't spill any on the tablecloth.

"What should we toast to?" I felt put on the spot.

"Let's toast to new experiences," Jax said, and I was fine with that. I tapped my glass to hers and did spill a little.

"Shit," I said, and then looked around. You didn't say a word like that in a place like this.

"Sasha, it's okay. You can relax."

I sipped nervously from my champagne and it was very good. I hoped it was expensive.

Jax sipped carefully and put her glass down.

"Why the hell did you want to ask me out?" I blurted out.

Jax leaned back in her chair and studied me.

"Why not?"

"Because you were pretty unhappy with me that night we met. You never got in touch with me about the dry-cleaning bill, by the way," I said. Not that I wanted to pay it.

"I'm sorry I was a bitch that night. I had other things going on," she said, waving her hand.

"What kind of things?" I asked, even though I didn't care.

"Life," she said with a tight smile.

"That's very specific," I said.

She didn't answer, just picked up her champagne and took a long sip.

Our cheese plate arrived, and we ordered our entrées. I wondered if it was okay to eat the bread with my hands, or if I was supposed to use a special fork or something, so I waited to see what Jax would do. She grabbed a piece of bread and spread some of the softer cheese on it. Looked like Brie. I loved Brie, especially when Paige baked some inside of Philo dough with some jam on top. Perfection.

I copied Jax, and bit into the bread, which wasn't as good as the bread at Sweet's, but it was a close second.

"So, Luna has told me what you do for work, but it was hard to understand her," Jax said.

"I'm basically a virtual assistant for a number of authors." I watched her face to gauge her reaction. I got a lot of blank stares when I explained my job sometimes. You'd think in this tech age that people would realize that jobs can be remote, including being an assistant, but I guess not.

"That's really interesting, how did you get into that?" She tried one of the other cheeses, eating her bread daintily. I hoped I didn't have Brie on my face.

"I've been an admin in an office before, and I made a friend who does freelance book cover design, and I wanted to have more freedom with my life, so she hooked me up with some of her authors," I said. "What made you get into teaching?" I was guessing her life was much more interesting than mine.

I gulped some champagne and then went for more cheese.

"I could give you the cliché answer that I wanted to help the next generation, but that's not the whole reason. I wanted to…" she inhaled, thinking as she swirled the liquid in her champagne glass. "I wanted to do something normal."

I was confused. "What do you mean by normal?"

"I had the opportunity to...to not work. To be the kind of person who doesn't need a job. And it would have been too easy to be that person, but I didn't want to. I wanted to be normal." She shrugged one shoulder.

"So, your parents are rich," I said.

Jax laughed. "More or less."

That explained so much.

"You could have been one of those people who just like, goes to the country club and plays golf and eats luncheon with people from Connecticut," I said and that made her throw her head back and laugh loudly. It was a delightful sound.

"Is that what your perception of rich people?"

"Maybe," I said.

"It's not that far off," she said.

"You play tennis, don't you?" I asked.

"I've had a few lessons," she admitted.

Our entrées arrived, and the steak smelled amazing and had a serving of polenta and some kind of special sauce on the side. Jax had gotten the roasted duck, and I definitely wanted to try it.

The knife slid into my steak as if it was going through butter and my first bite was pure heaven and melted in my mouth.

"Oh my god," I said, my mouth full. Oops.

"Good?" Jax asked, poised in the act of cutting her duck.

"Yes," I said after I swallowed. "Best steak I've ever had."

"That's what I want to hear," she said, cutting a bite of duck. "Do you want to try this?"

"Yeah," I said, and she held her fork over the table, one hand under the bite so it didn't spill.

I leaned forward and bit the meat from her fork, and there was something extremely sexy about that action, and I didn't know why. The champagne made me feel warm and dizzy.

"That's good too," I said. Not as good as my steak, though.

"Do you want some of mine?" I asked. It was only fair to offer.

Jax beamed. "Uh huh."

I fed her a bite of my steak and then we just sort of pushed our plates to the center of the table and started sharing.

There were other people in the restaurant, but we were safe and tucked away in our little corner. I could still hear the music from the piano, which was being played by extremely skilled fingers. The fire flickered beside me, and I started to relax a little more.

Jax poured me more champagne and asked me about my life, but all I wanted to know was more about her.

Against my will, I was completely intrigued. Who were her parents? Were they famous? Was my lack of celebrity knowledge biting me in the ass right now?

To be fair, no one else who had been around her had said anything, and I'd been around a bunch of parents at the beach when she'd been there and hadn't heard a word.

Instead of outright asking, I decided to pick up clues and see if I could solve the mystery on my own.

"So, what do you do when you're not working or hanging out with your niece and spilling a drink on me at a bar?" she asked. The plates were empty and I was well on my way to tipsy. I was going to have to wait a while before I was good to drive.

"I don't spill that often," I said, and she raised one eyebrow. "Okay, I spill a lot. It's part of my charm?"

She smiled at me, and it wasn't a patronizing smile.

"I don't know, I feel like I just work a lot. Oh, I'm sort of doing a book club with my friends. It's not really a book club, because we didn't want to put that much pressure on it, but we're reading the first five chapters of the latest Jack Hill book." At the mention of the author, her face fell for a moment.

"Something wrong?" I asked. Was she against reading? She couldn't be. She was a teacher.

"No, I just remembered that I didn't finish part of my lesson prep for Monday," she said smoothly. The waiter interrupted further questions by asking us if we wanted dessert.

"The chocolate mousse," Jax said, without even looking. "And a slice of the chocolate cake. Anything for you?" She looked at me.

"Oh, uh, that sounds good," I said, handing the menu back.

"Better make it two chocolate mousses," Jax said, and the waiter nodded.

"You really like chocolate?" I asked.

"Mmm, I do," she said. "It releases endorphins in your brain similar to those of an orgasm." I almost slid off my chair as she casually mentioned orgasms in this restaurant. I did a quick glance around, but no one was paying attention to us.

"Is that right?" I asked. "What other kinds of trivia do you know?"

"Oh, all kinds," she said, leaning forward. The glow of the fire flickered on her face and I was struck by just how incredibly beautiful she was.

I felt something on my leg, hiking my dress up.

"Are you trying to seduce me?" I asked, my voice a little breathless.

"Is it working?"

"Yes," I said. Oops. I really couldn't keep my mouth shut in front of her.

"Good," she said, and our desserts arrived. The waiter set a crystal bowl of silky chocolate mousse that was whipped lighter than a cloud in front of me.

I almost moaned again when I had a spoonful.

"Try the cake," Jax said, holding her fork out with a bite on it. The cake was thick and rich.

"I'm going to have a chocogasm," I said, and that made Jax giggle. I liked making her laugh.

"I like the way your mind works," she said.

I almost licked the rest of the mousse from the bowl, but I did have some decorum.

"That was perfect," I said, sitting back and basking in the warmth of the fire.

"I'm so glad you enjoyed it." The waiter came back and asked if we needed anything else, and then set the bill on the table.

"Oh, do you mind splitting it?" Jax asked, and I almost had a small heart attack. I had money, but not fancy steak and champagne money. Everything I had extra was socked away in an account to get me back to the city.

Jax saw the panic on my face and then her face broke into a smile.

"I'm fucking with you. I said I would pay." She slid a black card out of her wallet, and I didn't know much about credit cards, but I had the feeling there was an astronomical limit on the one she tucked into the bill and set upright on the table.

"Don't do that," I said, annoyed. "How much was that champagne?"

"Do you really want to know?"

"Yes."

"About six hundred dollars," she said, as if it was nothing.

"Six hundred dollars?!" My voice squeaked into a new octave.

Jax just looked at me.

"You're just on a whole other level, Jax Hardy," I said, shaking my head. I knew I should be mad at her for spending so much on fermented fizzy grape juice, but the champagne had been good. And I had come here with the intention of making her buy me an expensive meal.

The waiter nabbed the bill and then brought Jax her card

back. She signed the receipt with an elegant hand and then it was time to go. I realized I didn't want to get in my crappy car and go back to my sister's house and my messy room that I still hadn't cleaned.

"You okay?" Jax asked.

"I don't know," I said honestly. "I… I don't want to go home just yet."

"We could go back to my place…and have some tea." Our eyes met and I knew she wasn't talking about tea.

I'd been on enough dates to know a sexy invite when I got one.

I shouldn't go. I definitely shouldn't go.

"Okay," I said instead.

Chapter Nine

To GIVE myself a little more security, I did take my own car, and Jax gave me her address, so I followed the robot in my phone to her place in Hartford.

"You've got to be fucking kidding me," I said when I pulled into the driveway.

The house was a yellow Victorian with a turret and wrap-around porch. Sure, it wasn't on the water, but it was still very impressive. I parked behind her car and got out. The lights were on inside and I walked up the steps of the porch slowly. I could still back out if I wanted to.

Jax opened the door for me. She'd already taken her shoes off.

"Come in," she said, and I slid my shoes off and set my purse on the table next to the door. There was a chandelier above my head that I chose to ignore.

"Come with me to the kitchen," she said. The entryway opened to the entire downstairs, with the living room, dining area, and kitchen all flowing into each other with a staircase on the left that led to a landing on the second floor. I really wanted to go up in the turret, but I didn't want to ask.

What the fuck was I doing here? I should have just gone home.

Jax filled a copper kettle and put it on the stove.

"What kind of tea would you like?" she asked, keeping up with the ruse that I was here for tea and not for sex. Hollis was going to laugh when she found out.

She pulled a little tray out of the walk-in pantry and set it in front of me. I selected a packet of tea and she pulled one out for herself as we waited for the water to boil.

I had never been in a situation like this, and I really, really wished Hollis was here to give me tips.

Maybe I read too much into things and she did just want to have tea?

"This house is really nice," I said.

"Thank you. It's been a labor of love. I had to completely remodel it when I bought it, and I wanted it to be just right."

The kettle whistled and she poured water into both of our mugs.

"Lemon? Honey?" she asked.

"Yes, to both."

Okay, we were having tea, not sex. I completely misread things.

Jax fixed my tea and handed it to me.

"Want to sit in the den?" she asked.

Of course there was a den. Not something so ordinary as a living room. I gritted my teeth together and followed her into the den.

Jax sighed as she sat on the couch.

"You okay over there?" she asked.

"Yes. I'm fine," I said, my voice a little sharper than intended.

"You don't have to be here if you don't want to be," she said, setting her cup down on a silver coaster.

"I'm fine," I said, and then set my tea down too. "It's just…you ask me out and then we end up at this fancy fucking restaurant and you're buying bottles of wine that are like, the price of my student loan debt and then there's this house and I'm just…" I couldn't finish. I stood up. "I don't know why I came here. I should go."

"Wait," she said, standing up and taking my arm to stop me. "Why are you so angry at me?"

"I don't know!" I yelled, not caring if I was being loud. "There's just something about you that's so… so…"

"So what?" She bit out the words and before I knew what I was doing, I was shoving her up against the wall of the den and kissing the shit out of her. She gasped a little, but then her hands were in my hair, pulling out the pins and mangling the curls that my sister had curled so carefully.

I wasn't gentle, and she didn't seem to care. I kissed her hard, hard enough to bruise her lips and have our teeth and tongues crashing into each other. It was a ferocious kiss, and I didn't want it ever to end.

I ripped at her dress, trying to get at more of her skin.

She paused the kiss just long enough to fumble with the zipper under her arm. I may have torn a few seams getting the sleeves down her arms.

"Ruining another dress," she said breathlessly.

"Who gives a fuck," I said, sliding the top of the dress to her waist. "Why is it so fucking tight?"

"Hold on," she said, pulling the dress and shimmying it over her hips and down to the floor in a shiny puddle.

"There," she said, and I realized I wasn't the only one who hadn't been wearing anything under their dress. The only thing that covered any part of her were two little stickers on her nipples that were shaped like flowers. Everywhere else was…bare.

I looked her up and down, taking her in.

"Oh shit, I forgot about these," she said, peeling the little stickers off and tossing them aside.

"Can't have the world knowing you have nipples," I said.

"Shut up and take your dress off," she said, and I wanted to say something snarky in reply, but I pulled my arms out of my sleeves and shoved my dress onto the floor. It was a lot easier for me to get out of mine.

"There, are you happy now?"

Jax grinned. "Very."

Her fingers clasped mine and she moved until I was the one up against the wall. She pressed my hands above my head and pressed her body to mine and I think I blacked out for a second at all the contact of her naked body with my naked body. Our curves and valleys fitting in and around each other. She was just a little bit taller than me, and she used it to her advantage to dominate my mouth. Now I was at her mercy, and I wasn't complaining. She attacked my tongue with hers and pressed her body into mine so hard that I think I was going to leave a permanent mark on her wall.

I ground my hips against hers, begging her silently for more. I hadn't fucked anyone in a while and I had a lot of pent-up lust boiling in my blood that Jax had somehow ignited. There was only one solution, and she was the person to help me with it.

She licked my neck and sucked just a little bit and then nibbled her way down to my collarbone. I couldn't stop talking, begging, asking her for more. Did I care that she was probably leaving marks all over my body? Nope. Did I care that I was probably going to have a lot of regrets about this tomorrow? Nope. Right now, all I cared about was Jax Hardy fucking me so hard that I didn't remember my own name.

"You're so impatient," she said, sliding her hand between my legs to brush my center just barely. I almost screamed in frustration. I was so close and so wet already it wouldn't require much. She still had two of my hands held in one of hers above my head and they were starting to ache, so I pushed against her hand and she let me go.

"I'm not an acrobat," I snapped when she looked up at me.

"Didn't say you were," she said, and then got on her knees and my legs almost gave out.

This beautiful girl was on her fucking knees in front of me and I couldn't even remember how we'd gotten to this point.

"I'm going to fuck you with my tongue and you'd better come and make it worth my while," she said, before she ran one hand up and down my leg then setting it on her shoulder.

I wobbled just a little bit as she licked the inside of my thigh.

"Results not guaranteed," I said, but it was a lie. I was so close already.

"I'm not wasting my time unless you come," she said, leaning closer and then kissing just below my belly button. "You need to come for me."

"I don't need to do anything," I lied. I never needed to come so badly in my life.

"Shut up," she said, just before she kissed her way downward, pausing right above my clit. For a terrifying moment, I wondered if I'd recently groomed down there, but then remembered that I'd trimmed everything up in the shower yesterday. As if I'd been preparing for this.

Jax proceeded to kiss all the way around my clit and entrance, and I knew she was doing it on purpose. I would have called her a bitch, if I was capable of speech.

I was just about ready to scream in frustration when she licked my center and grazed my clit with the barest touch that it almost made me jerk in surprise.

Jax kissed my clit slowly, and then fluttered her tongue at my entrance and I didn't know how I was still standing. With every subtle lick, she brought me closer and closer, and I just started making incoherent noises at this point.

"Make as much noise as you want," Jax said. Her voice was irritatingly calm, and it was only more arousing. Just when I thought she couldn't torture me anymore, she sucked on my clit, and then thrust her tongue inside me, sucked my clit, and thrust, going back and forth and landing me toward an orgasm so powerful that it gripped my entire body, shot me into space, and scattered me among the stars.

I was lost completely, and the pulses seemed to go on forever.

When they slowed at last, I found myself on the floor. Didn't remember how that had happened, but it would have been a miracle if I'd remained standing through all that. Jax sat in front of me, her face wet, and her lips set in a satisfied smile. As my eyes went back into focus, she deliberately licked her lips.

"Very good," she said, patting me on the foot. As if I'd earned a gold star for an orgasm.

"Fuck you," I panted.

She laughed. "You can, if you want. But I suggest we go upstairs. My bed is much more comfortable."

I was up for that, as soon as I could actually move. It took all of my effort to push myself up on trembling legs. My skin was so sensitive that I cringed at the coldness of the floor and feel of the wall against my hands as I pushed myself up.

"Let's go," I said with more confidence than I felt.

"Hold on, don't forget the tea," she said, picking up both mugs.

I just stared at her.

"I'll just warm them up," she said, taking both mugs to the kitchen. I guess Jax didn't have any issues with modesty. I mean, if I looked like her, I'd probably walk around naked too. I tried not to compare our bodies because this wasn't the time to get all insecure. Instead, I slid my dress back on and went to the foyer and retrieved my phone. I had to be at least a little responsible. I sent Lizzie a message that I was staying the night with my setup date and I was safe, and I'd see her tomorrow. She sent back a flurry of responses asking for details, but I just repeated that I'd tell her all about it tomorrow, then put my phone on silent.

"You ready?" Jax said, standing at the foot of the stairs, completely nude, and holding two steaming mugs of tea.

"Did you get cold?" she asked, looking at my dress.

"No, I just..." I guess I wasn't as comfortable prancing around her house nude as she was.

I slid my dress off again and left it under the chandelier and followed Jax up the stairs.

She took me down a short hallway to the left and back into a massive master bedroom. She was right; her bed was definitely going to be more comfortable than fucking on the floor or up against a wall.

I watched her move around, watching as the lights she turned on lit up her skin. She really was perfect. Jax handed me my tea and then went to light some candles and...oh, a fireplace. Of course. She used a remote to start it, so it must be gas.

I sipped my tea and watched as she pulled some decorative pillows off the bed and piled them on a couch at the end of the bed. Every move she made was methodical, and I didn't know what to make of her.

Jax hummed softly to herself as she opened a few drawers in her nightstand and pulled out a few items.

"Oh," I couldn't help myself from saying.

"I like to be prepared. I don't normally keep lube in my den," she said by way of explanation. Not only did she have one type of lube, she had several.

"Do you have any allergies?" she asked, and I just blinked at her.

"Uh, no," I said when I realized she was serious.

"Oh, good," she said, selecting a bottle and setting it next to a box of tissues on the stand.

I finished my tea and looked around for a place to set the mug and settled on the mantel of the fireplace.

Jax seemed to be done with her sex preparations, and I wasn't sure what I was supposed to be doing.

"Hey," Jax said, and I stopped myself from looking around the room. "Come here." She crooked her finger at me and I went, as if she'd pulled me toward her.

"We can take this slower, if you want," she said.

I didn't want to take things slow. If I took things slow, I might start thinking about what a bad idea this was and end up leaving before I got to see how she looked when she came. I was determined to see that.

Instead of answering her, I just kissed her again, pulling her bottom lip between my teeth, and using that as my answer.

I walked her backward until her legs hit the bed, and she made a little startled sound. I was tired of her hair being up, so I turned her around to kiss her upper back as I removed the pins from her hair and tossed them on the floor. Her hair fell down in soft waves, and I couldn't resist running my hands through them as I kissed the very top of her spine. She arched back into me and I ran my hands down her back and over her stomach. Wrapping my hand in her hair, I used it to pull her head to the side so I had better access to her neck. Judging by the sounds she made, this had been a good idea.

"Now who's being demanding?" she asked, almost completely breathless. Good. I was going to pay her back for what she'd done to me, and then some.

"Get on the bed," I said with more confidence than I felt. When it came to my past sexual experiences, I'd kind of just gone with the flow, as long as the flow wasn't toward, like, shoving fruit inside me and then eating it erotically. That was just a recipe for a yeast infection, if you ask me.

I talked a big game, but when it came to sex, most of my thoughts became mush, and I couldn't have come up with any sort of plan if I wanted to. But tonight, with Jax? My head was clear. My goal was simple: make her come so hard she would never fucking forget me. Ruin her, just a little.

Jax obeyed me, and I could see her waiting for me to make my next move.

She lay on top of the covers against the pillows, and then she sat up as if she'd forgotten something.

"Hold that thought!" she said, rolling off the bed and then getting down on the floor to pull something out from under the bed.

I hoped it wasn't, like, a giant dildo, because I didn't think we were ready to add any kind of toys until we'd figured each other out a little bit first. All kinds of possibilities ran through my head, each one more shocking than the last.

Jax popped up and I breathed a sigh of relief.

"Just so we don't have to change the comforter," she said as she laid out several towels on top of the bed.

Sex towels. The woman had sex towels. I thought I was the prepared one, but she had me beat.

"Good thinking," I said, and I wasn't being completely sarcastic.

"I like being prepared," she said, and I understood her more in that moment than I ever had before.

"Now," she said, getting in her previous position, "where were we?"

"Touch yourself," I said. The easiest way for me to figure out how to touch her was to watch how she touched herself. Plus, it was hot as fuck.

"How do you want me to touch myself?" she asked before licking her palm and fingers.

"Show me how you get yourself off," I said.

Her eyes narrowed as she dragged her hand between her breasts and then pinched one of her own nipples. Like I said, hot.

"Oh, so you can make me do all the work while you watch?" she asked, but her eyelids flickered closed and her back arched into her hands as she pinched her other nipple and rolled it between her fingers. I took note of the technique.

She licked her hand again and slid it down her stomach before she met my eyes and deliberately spread her legs wider so I could see.

"Pay attention," she said, and I leaned closer. "Come up here so you can see."

I fumbled my way onto the bed, nearly sliding off the sex towel before I situated myself in front of her, almost right between her legs.

One of Jax's hands went back to her nipples and the other stroked just outside her entrance, up, and over, just avoiding touching her clit. The motion was similar to what she'd done with her tongue on me earlier, and I got wetter just remembering it. Watching Jax touch herself gave me ideas, so I copied her and licked my fingers, even though I didn't need to.

"Don't you dare touch yourself right now. You're supposed to be paying attention," she said. I guess I wasn't in charge after all.

"Get over here," she said, and motioned for me to get behind her. I scrambled on the sex towels and to adjust the pillows, but I got myself situated behind her, my legs around her, and her back resting against me.

"Give me your hand," she said, and I did. She put her fingers on top of mine, and then ran my hand up and down her stomach.

She was using me, and I didn't mind. Not even a little bit. Her skin was so warm, and I was getting sensory overload from having her up against me. There was absolutely no way for me to seek my own relief, and that was extremely annoying, but there wasn't a whole lot I could do about it.

Jax continued to use my hand to circle around, and I was completely at her mercy. Again.

"Are you paying attention?" she asked, her breath hitching in her throat.

"Yes," I said. She dragged my fingers through her wetness, and I gasped.

"Fuck," she hissed through her teeth.

Our hands made another circle, and then she curled my fingers so I just penetrated her. The angle wasn't ideal, but it didn't seem to matter to her. She let me find her clit at last, and we circled the little pleasure nub before teasing her entrance again. I wanted to fuck her properly, but she wasn't letting me.

Extremely frustrating.

"Grab the lube," she said, and I fumbled for one of the bottles, not even looking at what it said.

Jax moved so she was beside me, laying down. I sat up and squirted some lube on my fingers. The scent of cherries filled the air.

"What the?" I looked at the bottle and I'd picked the cherry-flavored lube. Oh well, it worked as well as the other shit, I assumed.

Of course, I had to give it a little taste. I did get a cherry vibe, but the overwhelming taste was chemicals.

"You okay over there?" Jax asked, looking up at me with a question in her eyes.

"Yeah, sorry. I got distracted by the lube."

Jax giggled in the cutest way, it made my heart do a little squeeze in my chest. Hey, if you couldn't giggle during coitus, what was the point of the whole thing?

Jax's giggle turned into a gasp as I slicked my now-lubed hand over her, and she threw her head back. I had particularly long fingers and good wrist dexterity, if I did say so myself.

"Now it's your turn to fucking come," I said, circling her clit and then sliding inside her with two fingers. I loved the feel of her inner muscles trying to milk my fingers and listening to her sounds as she gasped and gave me encouragement and told me when I hit the right rhythm that would push her over the edge. I watched her face, and when her legs started to violently shake, I started an all-out assault and fucked the shit out of her with my fingers, making sure to hit her clit with the heel of my hand.

She started coming apart in my hands and I felt it with my fingers and watched her arch her back and her entire body shake and spasm.

She was completely under my control and that was so fucking hot, I nearly came myself. I rode the wave with her, continuing my work with my fingers until the little clenches of her body slowed.

"You're such a bitch," she said, looking at me with glassy eyes.

"So are you," I said, and then licked the rest of the cherry lube off my fingers as she watched.

Chapter Ten

THE MOMENTS just after sex were the worst. You thought about all the things you'd done, all the faces and sounds you made, and all your insecurities came roaring back. Plus, you remembered all those things you forgot to do, and all the shit you had to do the next day. It was a rude awakening.

Jax turned on her side and looked up at me.

"What are you thinking about?" she asked.

"If I pulled the chicken out of the freezer to defrost," I said. "I can't remember."

That startled another laugh out of Jax.

"At least you're honest."

"Sorry, I should have told you I was thinking sexy things. Defrosting chicken isn't sexy," I said. I wanted to go back to a few moments before when I'd been fucking her with my fingers.

"I'd prefer honesty over bullshit. Always," she said.

"Me too," I agreed.

"Do you want some more tea?" she asked. This change from fucking to tea was really giving me whiplash.

"I guess?"

"Was there something else you wanted?"

"I mean, I'd really like to get off again, but I can handle that on my own," I said, studying her bottles of lube. I wondered if she had one of those that increased sensation or heated up. I'd never tried them, but I'd always been curious.

Jax had both. I wondered what would happen if I mixed the sensitizing lube with the lube that heated up. Would my clit fall off? I didn't know if I was willing to risk it.

Jax jumped on the bed and the lube bottles all tumbled to the floor.

"No one is getting you off but me," she said, pushing my shoulders back on the bed and straddling my hips.

"That works," I said, completely taken aback and completely aroused by this turn of events.

Jax did get me off. Four more times.

"SHOWER?" she asked when I could barely keep my eyes open or move any of my limbs.

"If you can get me there," I said. My bones had turned into wet noodles.

"Come on," she said with a laugh as she dragged me to her absolutely massive bathroom.

"Holy shit," I said. It was like a spa in there. Huge tub with jets, a walk-in shower with multiple showerheads, and double sinks. There was also a damn sitting area, right in the middle of the room. Who had a sitting area in their bathroom? Jax Hardy.

"This house really sold me on the size of the master bath-room," Jax said, opening the shower door and turning the main showerhead on.

"Yeah, I can see why," I said.

"Come on," she said, getting into the shower. I stepped in

behind her and shut the door. There was a bench and enough room to fit at least four more people.

"You could have an orgy in here," I said as Jax turned on one of the other showerheads, so we were both standing under the hot water.

"I've never done that, but I'll keep it in mind," she said, tilting her head back and letting the water run down her back. The pressure of the showerhead was amazing. It felt like I was getting a damn massage.

"Okay, I would buy the house just for this shower," I said, closing my eyes and surrendering to the sensation.

"I know," Jax said, and I opened my eyes and watched as she let the water run all over her body. I had already come so many times tonight but watching her bathe herself was just getting me riled up again.

"You're watching me," she said.

"Obviously," I said.

"Like what you see?" she asked.

"What gave it away?" I asked. "Come on, you know you're fucking hot, Jax, don't patronize me."

She just smiled and grabbed a bar of what I thought was soap, but which turned out to be shampoo, and started scrubbing it through her hair.

"Want some?" she asked.

"Sure," I said, and turned around so she could apply it for me.

"Your hair is so gorgeous," she said. "I couldn't stop staring at the way it looked in the light of the bar that night. You were just...glowing there. Like a copper beacon."

I'd had a lot of compliments on my hair before, including some weird ones, but that was one of the nicest.

"I couldn't stop looking at you, either," I said.

"Yeah, I noticed," she said, putting her fingers in my hair and massaging my scalp.

"Oh, that feels good," I said, leaning into her touch.

"I wanted you then," she said.

"Is that why you yelled at me, or why you kissed me?" I asked. Her fingers stopped moving for a moment as she thought about it.

"Both," she said. I turned to rinse my hair out, and Jax grabbed a bottle of some conditioning goo that smelled minty and was probably really expensive.

There were all kinds of jars and bottles in her shower, including a chocolate body scrub that I really wanted to try, but let Jax soap me up and slide her hand between my legs and get me off one more time instead.

Once we were squeaky clean, Jax wrapped me in the biggest, softest towel I'd ever touched, and was probably hand-made by angels, and then commanded me to go back and get in bed while she made me something in the kitchen downstairs.

I waited for her footsteps to fade down the stairs before I secured my towel and went ahead to explore while she was occupied. I found two more bedrooms on the second floor, including one that had the curved walls of the turret. It was smaller than the master, which was a huge shame. One of the bedrooms looked like a guest room, and the other was an office. That one had the turret.

I snuck up to the third floor and found just two rooms: what looked like a gym, and a library.

A huge fucking library. Floor to ceiling bookshelves, a mahogany desk, yet another fireplace, and books as far as the eye could see. I knew I'd spent a lot of time exploring, so I didn't get to see everything, but I did scan some of the shelves and Jax had quite the literature collection, both old and new.

I scampered back down the stairs and got myself situated on the bed as if I'd been there the whole time.

Jax came up the stairs a few moments later with a full tray

with more tea, and what looked like a professionally arranged charcuterie tray.

"Before you ask, no, I did not make this. I order them and they come shrink wrapped. I just took off the wrapping and set it on the tray."

She put the bounty between us on the bed and then handed me a robe. She put one on as well, and we sat together on her bed and munched from a variety of cheeses, nuts, crackers, and dried fruit. I'd eaten so well tonight.

"I didn't know you could order charcuterie," I said.

"I found this place online and it's so great for parties. I never know what to bring, but you can't go wrong with something like this."

Maybe I'd bring one the next time I had dinner with all my friends. Like an appetizer.

"You don't have to go home," Jax said out of the blue. "In case you were worried I was going to kick you out. I'm not."

I hadn't been worried about that. I'd still been sort of floating in a sex haze.

"Oh, good," I said. "I told my sister I was staying out all night. She thinks one of my friends set us up. I just… I couldn't tell her I was going to see you."

Jax put a piece of cheese carefully on a cracker and then added a little folded piece of prosciutto.

"Yeah, I get that. I mean, you don't have to lie to her, but I'm not going to stop you from telling her the truth. I know it makes things a little complicated."

Yeah, understatement.

"Would you like, get into trouble? At work?"

Jax shook her head. "No. I can date and fuck as I please. I just keep things discreet so I don't have to share my personal life with all the parents. You'd be shocked at what they're willing to ask you about at parent-teacher night," she said. Actually, I wouldn't be. People in small towns got comfortable asking all kinds of completely inappropriate questions. It was a lot to adjust to.

"I just think… we should keep this between us," I said. I wasn't going to lie to anyone, but I was going to tell them that this was my personal business and they didn't need to know who I was fucking. Because right now, that was pretty much all we'd done. I mean, the date was a one-time thing. I wasn't planning on repeating it. The fucking on the other hand…

"So, does that mean you'd like to see me again?" she asked.

"Maybe," I said. "I'll think about it."

Her face fell and then I poked her.

"I'm kidding. Yes, I would like to see you again. As long as we can keep things casual. I'm not… Castleton isn't the place I'm going to be staying. I'm only here until my sister gets her shit together. I'm saving up enough money for an apartment in Boston again."

"Okay," she said. "So, we'll just have fun while you're here. I can do that."

"So can I," I said. "It doesn't have to be anything serious. We're adults."

"We are," she said.

"Good. Then it's settled."

I almost wanted to reach out and shake her hand, as if we were sealing a transaction or something.

We finished the tray and exhaustion fully came over me.

"You can borrow some of my clothes," Jax said, going to her massive walk-in closet and bringing out a matching pair of shorts and tank top with little blue flowers on them.

"You can have some underwear, if you don't mind wearing mine."

"No, I'm good." I usually slept without underwear.

"Great," she said, slipping out of her robe and then getting into bed. After a second, she sat up. "If you want to sleep in one of the guest rooms, you can."

"No, this is fine." I took off the robe and put on the pajamas. I hadn't checked the tag, but if they weren't organic cotton, I would eat one of her decorative pillows.

I got under her covers and almost moaned at the sheets. I'd never felt anything like them. Everything Jax owned was the best of the best. No wonder she put down sex towels.

Jax turned on her side and faced me. All the lights were still on, and I wondered if I was supposed to turn them off.

Then Jax said "turn off the lights," and a robotic voice said "okay. Turning off the lights." And then the room went dark, with the exception of the fireplace.

"Of course you have a house robot," I said.

"It's not exactly a robot," Jax said. "I just don't like getting out of bed to turn the lights off if I'm already cozy."

It was hitting me how utterly different our lives were. There would be time to think about that later. For now, I was going to bask in the expensive bed with the expensive sheets and the hot, naked woman beside me.

THE NEXT THING I KNEW, I was holding something warm that made little contented noises. As my consciousness returned, I realized I was holding a naked Jax and I was still in her bed. The night came rushing back, and I opened my eyes to confirm that my arms were full of Jax. Naked Jax, who was looking at me.

"Good morning," she said. Our faces were close together, and I really wanted to kiss her.

"Good morning," I said. Her hair was all disheveled and her cheek had a mark from the pillow on it. This was the most devastatingly beautiful she'd ever been, and I stopped breathing for a second.

"Something wrong?" she asked.

"No," I said, my voice catching. "Nothing at all."

The royal treatment continued as we ventured downstairs and I sat in the breakfast nook, nursing a latte as Jax whipped up a frittata. I got bored by myself, so I brought my cup into the kitchen and sat on one of the counters. It was granite, and cold, so I yelped a little bit.

Jax asked the house robot to put on some music, and apparently, she had a breakfast playlist.

"I like to have good vibes in the morning," she said.

All of the tunes were upbeat, and I knew nearly all of them, from the classics, to the newer stuff.

"I always do a big breakfast on the weekend," she said. "Since during the week it's not really feasible."

"Yeah, I don't know how you go and teach to a bunch of kids in the morning. I'm lucky that no one in my family is really a morning person, so we all suffer together." Luna was always so cute and grumpy when she woke up.

"It's not easy," she said. "But I don't mind getting up early. There are a few perks of being a teacher, including having the time off."

"What do you do during the summer?" I asked as she babysat the frittata.

"Travel, mostly," she said.

"Where to?" I asked.

"Here, there, and everywhere," she said. Okay, she was back to being vague again. Fine. I put that avoidance away in my mind for later pondering.

"If I could go anywhere, I'd go to Tuscany," I said. "My mom loves that movie, and she used to play it all the time, so I think it affected me. Or I'd want to see the North Pole and the aurora borealis. Or both," I said.

"I've never seen the aurora borealis. Maybe that will have to be my next trip." She could no-doubt afford it.

"This is almost done," she said as a little tension fell on the room. We should probably stop talking about money.

I hopped off the counter as Jax plated our beautiful breakfast.

"Let's sit here," she said, motioning to the breakfast nook.

"This is excellent, thank you," I said as I tasted the frittata. It was full of veggies and cheese.

"Thanks," she said. The sun filtered in through the curtains and lit up her golden hair. She looked absolutely incredible in the morning, and it wasn't fair at all. I hadn't checked myself in the mirror yet on purpose. I didn't want to know how puffy my eyes were, or how much of a nest my hair was.

Jax pulled one of her feet up on the chair and I could sense she wanted to say something.

"Do I have something on my face?" I asked, picking up the napkin and wiping, just to be sure.

"No. I'm just thinking that I'm really glad you came back with me last night," she said, sipping her coffee.

I was still hungry, but I wasn't going to ask for seconds. I'd just eat when I got home, which should be soon. I didn't want to overstay and ruin the mood. Things always looked different in the daylight.

"I'm glad too," I said, putting my fork down. "Thank you for everything." I got up from the table.

"Oh, are you leaving?"

"Yes? I need to get home and do some work." Not a complete lie, but also not the complete truth. I always had work to do, but I tried to have as normal weekends as possible.

"Oh, right. Of course," she said, standing and taking the plates to the sink.

"Do you need something to get home in?" she asked. Right. I'd come here in a full-length green velvet dress. Not exactly Sunday morning attire.

"I don't believe in the walk of shame," I said.

"Are you sure?" she asked.

"Yeah," I said, going to where I'd left the dress on the floor. It was a little crinkled from sitting there in a pile all night. I took it with me upstairs and changed out of the sleepwear she'd given me. I hadn't brought anything else with me but my phone, and I retrieved that from the entryway table.

Jax still had her robe on and wiped her hand on a dish towel and came to the foyer to say goodbye to me under the chandelier.

"So, stay in touch," she said. "And send me a message to let me know that you got home okay."

"Okay," I said, even though it was like a ten-minute drive. "I guess I'll talk to you later?" How were you supposed to end these things?

"Absolutely," she said, leaning forward to give me a kiss. It was short and...awkward? How could a kiss between us be awkward when we'd just spent the whole night fucking?

"Take it easy," I said as I opened the door and then wanted to fling myself down the stairs. Take it easy? Was I eighty years old?

"Bye, Sasha," Jax said, and I heard the smile in her voice as I walked down the steps, being careful to hold up the gown so I didn't trip.

I stood for a second at the door of my car and looked back at where she leaned in the doorway. She fluttered her fingers in a little wave and I waved back before getting in the driver's seat and backing out to the road.

LIZZIE GREETED my return with a round of applause and a knowing smile.

"Yay, auntie!" Luna said, also clapping, but she had no idea why.

"Thank you, thank you," I said, doing a little clumsy curtsy with my dress.

"You certainly look like you had a good time," Lizzie said, handing me a cup of coffee. I'd slept amazingly well at Jax's, but I didn't turn down free caffeine.

"I'll get the full details later," Lizzie said, looking pointedly at Luna, who did not need to hear the details of my sexcapades. "But tell me just a little bit?"

"Well, we went to an extremely fancy dinner. I had the best steak and chocolate mousse of my entire life." Talking about the restaurant seemed to enthrall Lizzie, so I told her plenty of non-Jax details.

"I know you don't want to tell me who she is, but is she hot?" Lizzie asked.

"Yes," I said. "Very. And she has a gorgeous house with a library and everything." There was so much to tell that didn't involve Jax. Luna got bored and went back to the living room to watch cartoons and sing to herself with Fluffy.

"Are you going to see her again?" Lizzie asked.

"I think so? We left it kind of weird. I told her to 'take it easy.'" It still sounded bad.

Lizzie cackled. "You nerd."

"I'm just not very good at this," I said. "I need tips."

Lizzie sighed. "I miss dating."

"Seriously? Dating is terrible." So much anxiety and wondering if they liked you as much as you liked them, and if you were being too much or not enough and hoping you didn't get your entire heart broken.

"No, it's fun. You get all pretty and it's new and exciting and there's that possibility of something." She shrugged one shoulder. "I don't know, that's how I always felt."

"You should start dating again." Now that she wasn't obsessed with Skippy, she could actually find a decent guy.

"Sasha. There aren't a whole lot of guys who are going to sign up to date someone with a kid," she said.

"You're not giving yourself enough credit. There are plenty of people that aren't scared by that," I said, but she didn't look convinced.

"Have you even tried dating here?" I asked.

"I mean, no, but I've been busy," she said.

"That sounds like an excuse. I mean, if you're not ready to date, you're not, but if you're stopping yourself just because you don't think anyone will want you, that's a whole different thing."

Lizzie sighed again and looked at Luna, who was dancing in the living room and wearing Fluffy as a cape.

"I just want something better for her. She deserves someone who wants to be her father," she said. "Guys like that don't just fall out of trees."

I made a note to start asking some of my friends if they knew of any eligible guys that might be on the same page as my sister. There had to be a nice guy in the Castleton town limits, or nearby. We just hadn't met him yet.

"You're going to find him. Or he'll find you. It's going to happen." I rubbed her shoulder and she gave me a sad look.

"I really need to take a shower," I said. "And get out of this dress."

"Go on, you little sex maniac." She whispered the last part so Luna didn't hear.

I'D COMPLETELY FORGOTTEN to let Jax know that I got home okay, and I ended up getting a message from her on social media with her phone number.

I thought about looking at Luna's emergency

contact list, but that seemed like it would cross a line, so here we are.

I went ahead and just sent her a message.

Got home fine. Thanks for the date. This is Sasha, btw.

Definitely not the smoothest text I'd ever sent, but I didn't know what else to say.

I had a good time too. We should definitely do that again.

Oh, I definitely wanted to have a night like that with her again. Sooner rather than later, preferably.

I have my non-book club book club next Friday night, but I'm free on Saturday night.

That would give me something to look forward to on the weekend, besides non-book club book club. I still had two chapters left to read, and I wasn't going to slack, even though we'd planned this as a no-pressure situation.

Saturday night it is. Do you want me to make reservations? She sent back. I wanted her to make reservations as long as she was footing the bill.

Sure I answered. I had to admit, it was kind of nice letting someone else do the planning and just tell me when to show and where. All I had to do was look good and eat food. Ideal situation.

Just let me know what kind of thing to wear I added, because I didn't have a whole lot of fancy clothes. I might have to borrow something from one of my friends. Lizzie and I weren't the same size, so we couldn't share.

Wear something that you feel comfortable in. No black tie required.

That wasn't helpful. I needed to know the vibe. Getting lobster rolls from a truck was a different vibe from the place we'd gone this weekend.

Think cocktail attire she said, and then I went to google "cocktail attire." I hoped that pants were still considered cock-tail attire. I liked a dress every now and then, but pants could be glamorous too.

Got it I sent back to her.

I took my shower and put on a tie-dye sweat set that Lizzie had gotten me last Christmas.

"Wanna make some hot chocolate?" I asked Luna and her eyes lit up. I felt just a twinge of guilt for being gone last night.

I got out the crockpot and Luna helped me pour in the milk and the chocolate chips, the condensed milk, the heavy cream, and just a little bit of spices for the hot chocolate. Luna kept stealing chips and popping them in her mouth, thinking that I couldn't see her.

"I'm going to run to the store and get a few things," Lizzie said, coming into the kitchen to check the fridge and finish her shopping list.

"You be good," she said, and Luna fed her a chocolate chip before she grabbed her keys and left.

"Did you miss me last night, Luna Moon?" I asked.

"Yes," she said, as she clumsily stirred the mixture in the crockpot, almost slopping it all over the counter.

"But I came back today, and now we get to spend the rest of our Sunday together," I said.

"Okay," Luna said, thinking for a moment.

"Are you going on a date tomorrow?" she asked.

"Nope, but I'm going on one next week." For a little kid, a week was an eternity. "Is that okay?"

"Are dates fun?" she asked. I wondered if, in her mind, dates seemed like boring adult things.

"Yes, dates can be very fun. Sometimes they're not fun, but if you don't have fun, you just don't go on another date with that person." I hoped I was explaining this right. I didn't want to give her date anxiety for the future.

"Was your date fun?"

"Yes, very fun."

She nodded. "Can I come on your date?"

"Sorry, Luna Moon. Maybe sometime you can come, but right now my date and I are still getting to know each other," I said.

Luna sighed. "Okay. But will you bring me back a cookie next time?"

I laughed. "Yeah, I'll bring you back a cookie."

LATER THAT NIGHT I gave Hollis the details of my date, after I'd given some to my sister.

"I'm so proud," Hollis said, pretending to wipe a tear from her eye.

"Shut up."

"My baby's all grown up and fucking on the first date!"

"Don't say that so loud," I said, getting up and making sure my door was closed.

"You're still glowing. I love this for you," she said. It was nice to have my sister and my best friend so supportive of me hooking up with Jax.

"You don't even understand, Hols, her house is enormous. It just kept going. And there was this massive library upstairs."

"Yes, but was the sex good?" she asked and I groaned.

"Yes, the sex was amazing, but think about the library," I said.

"I mean, you can fuck in a library, I guess."

She was getting on my last nerve.

"Is sex the only thing you can think about?" I asked.

"I mean, it's one of the only things I think about, yes."

I rolled my eyes. "There's more to life than sex."

"Is that what you told her last night?" she asked.

"No. It was… So, the sex was great, but she has this laugh, and she made me this amazing breakfast and everything."

Hollis's eyes narrowed.

"You sound like you're falling for her," she said.

"No! I'm absolutely not falling for her. It was just nice to be spoiled, I guess. It's not every day that happens." I honestly couldn't remember the last time I'd gone on a date and hadn't split the bill or had to look at the menu prices before making a reservation. And I didn't have to worry about going back to someone's apartment and worrying about waking up their roommates, or if it was going to be a mess, or if there would be a bed with a frame for me to sleep on. Jax had everything, and I was definitely going to see that library next time.

"Just be careful," Hollis said.

"I am. We're just hooking up. That's it."

"Okay, if you say so," Hollis said in a tone that told me she did not buy it.

Chapter Eleven

"So, I went on a date last weekend," I told Paige on Tuesday when we met for our little work session at the Castleton Cafe. I had a latte in my hand and my laptop open, and a bunch of spreadsheets to work on and paid advertising to fiddle with. It was going to be a good day.

"Ohhh, tell me," Paige said, practically slamming her laptop shut. "Work can wait."

I gave Paige similar details to what I'd told Lizzie. Not all the details, but enough. And I left the fact that it was Jax out of it completely.

"Wow, take advantage of that," Paige said when I talked about the restaurant. "Let her spoil you."

"I plan to," I said.

"Now that makes me want to take Esme out for a fancy dinner. I feel like we spend too many nights at the Grille or eating at home. We need to change things up. Plus, then I get to see her in her special leather pants." Paige looked off into the distance as if she was picturing it.

"Sounds hot," I said, and Paige just made a noise of agreement.

"Sorry," she said, coming back a few moments later. She immediately got out her phone and typed out a message. "We are doing that this weekend, for sure."

I was happy to inspire my friends to spice up their lives.

"I don't know where we're going this weekend, but she said I should wear cocktail attire, and I don't think I have anything that works for that. I'm not sure what to do." There weren't any really big clothing stores in Castleton. Just a few little boutiques, and they were mostly for Maine-themed t-shirts and sweatshirts.

Paige stood up.

"Come on," she said.

"What are you doing?" I asked.

"We're going shopping," she said, shoving her laptop in her bag.

"But what about work?" I asked.

"Work can wait," she said, pulling out her keys. "I'll drive."

Normally I would have been the one to suggest a spontaneous outing, but this time it was Paige.

I shoved my work bag in the backseat and hopped in her car. She was grinning from ear to ear.

"Listen, I need to write copy for this science-y website about like, soil, and my other job is to transcribe a podcast about changes in real estate law. I need to gear myself up for that." She made a face and backed out of the parking space.

"Sounds riveting," I said.

"Oh, it won't be, but they're paying me really well to do it, so here we are." Paige turned out of the parking lot and onto Main Street, heading south.

The nearest place to buy any kind of trendy clothes was twenty minutes away, so Paige put on a fun playlist and we chatted about how much we hated Mondays.

"We're not leaving until we find you something," she said as we pulled into the huge lot for the closest strip of discount stores, including one that had prom dresses and other formal wear.

"If we can't find something there, then there's that other place a few minutes away that's a little more fancy that might have something."

We tried the formal shop first, and it was hard to not find a dress that wasn't made for a teen going to prom, or a mom or aunt for a wedding.

"I don't think this is the place," I said as we poked through the racks.

"Yeah, definitely not what you need. Let's go somewhere else." We also hit a few of the casual discount stores, but I didn't see anything.

Paige drove us over to the other side of town, where the ritzier people shopped.

"This seems more like it," Paige said as we got out of the car in front of a boutique that had leather purses and mannequins posing in what looked like vintage dresses in the window.

"Let's go," I said.

"What do you have that counts as cocktail attire?" Paige asked the salesperson the minute we walked in. "She's got a date." Paige pointed at me and I waved, then felt like a dork.

The salesperson looked me up and down and then went to a few racks near the back.

"What do you think of this?" she asked, presenting me with a black dress that had a halter top, and what looked like a leather skirt that would fall about to my knees.

"Oh, I kind of love that," I said. "It would make me feel like a badass."

"Go try it on," Paige said, shoving me toward the dressing room.

I fumbled a little bit getting into the dress, but once I had the halter done, I turned and checked out the back, then twirled to see the action of the skirt.

"Come out, come out," Paige chanted.

I pushed back the curtain and struck a little pose.

"What do you think?"

"You look hot. Seriously hot," Paige said, clapping. "You have to get that."

I checked the price tag and cringed a little, but it wasn't as bad as I thought it would be. I went back into the dressing room and took off the dress, getting back in my regular clothes.

"You nailed it, thank you," I told the salesperson.

"It's a gift," she said with a smile as she wrapped the dress in tissue paper and then rang me up.

"Come back anytime you need a dress," she said, and I made a note that the name on her tag said Amber.

"Thank you so much, Amber. You're a life saver."

Dress squired, Paige and I had no choice but to go back to the café and get on with our work.

"That was fun. I wish we could do things like that every day instead of working," Paige said with a sigh as we pulled into the large Castleton parking lot behind the main row of shops. It directly bordered the ocean, so in addition to the shoppers, there were several boats parked near the dock, and in the water. The food truck that had the best lobster rolls in the world was still serving eager customers, locals and tourists alike.

Great, now I was craving a lobster roll. Since I'd just spent a lot of money on the dress, I couldn't really splurge like that for the next week. I had to keep control of my spending so I could save enough money to get an apartment.

Paige and I set ourselves back up at the café, and I was somewhat soothed by a latte and the dress sitting in a bag at my feet.

"Oh, Esme and I are going this week to that restaurant you went to on your date. We'll probably get like, a few pieces of free bread and water, but she had a look at their drink menu and got excited." As a bartender, Esme had an appreciation of a fine cocktail, and she didn't get a whole lot of chances to make them with expensive ingredients.

"Sit in the back near the fireplace, if you can. It's really nice back there. Oh, and I hear the piano player takes requests if you tip him," I said with a laugh.

"Oh, that could be fun," Paige said.

I downed the rest of my coffee and went back to my inbox before settling into the rest of my to-do list. I loved my job, but it definitely wasn't as fun as finding the perfect dress.

THE REST of my week was spent finishing the chapters for Non Book Club, taking care of Luna, and trying to get ahead on work. Leaving things until the last minute gave me hives, so I was happiest when I was on top of things at work. Somehow that tendency didn't cross over to staying caught up on laundry, or car maintenance.

The dress hung on the back of my door, and I would stare at it every now and then when I was in my room. Hollis had given her stamp of approval and said it was definitely sexy. Since I'd already worn the flats with my other dress, and this dress had a different vibe, I was breaking out my black fall boots to wear with it.

I didn't hear much from Jax, but I figured it was just because she was busy with teaching. I didn't want to be too aggressive with contacting her, so I settled for constantly scrolling through her social media and staring at different pictures of her. Totally healthy.

Lizzie was distracted with figuring out what career path she wanted to take. She'd fallen into a research hole, looking up various careers and salary ranges and figuring out how much student debt she was comfortable with having.

"I can't fuck this up," she said one night as she clicked away on her laptop while I'd been on my phone looking at Jax's social pages.

"If I fuck this up, then I am not only going to ruin my life, but my daughter's life." She moaned and I reached over to close the laptop.

"That's enough for one night," I said. "Why don't you see if you can find some people to talk to that are in the fields you're considering? See if you could set up a meeting, or even ask questions via email. That might help you narrow things down."

She looked at me and I saw the dark circles under her eyes. Lizzie had been consumed with this decision, and I needed to be a more present sister. She needed me.

"That's a good idea. I just keep thinking I'm going to make the wrong choice." She rubbed her eyes.

"Okay, I'm making us some tea, and we're going to watch something silly," I said, getting up to brew some lavender tea.

"Thanks," she said, setting her laptop on the coffee table.

I made the tea and found some biscotti from Sweet's that I had in the pantry.

"Here we go," I said, bringing everything over.

"Thanks, Sasha. I know I'm being dramatic, but being responsible for someone else is fucking terrifying. I have no idea why so many people sign up to be parents." She munched her biscotti and then dunked it in her tea.

"You're doing the best you can, Lizzie. And look at what you've already done. You have this house, and you're paying for it on your own. You're taking charge of your life and going back to school to make things better. Not every parent would do that," I said.

"You're right. I know you're right. Okay, I'm going to see if

I can talk to some people, because I need to just make a decision, and start doing something. This indecision is what's killing me."

She talked some more about her job research, and I listened to her. She'd really gone all-in with this decision, and she was being mature and sensible about it.

I was really proud, but I didn't want to say that. Luna had an amazing mom.

$\sim$

FRIDAY AFTERNOON I went with Paige back to her house to help get ready for Non Book Club. Linley was bringing a tray of goodies from Sweet's, and Esme was in charge of drinks, as usual. I'd thought about getting a charcuterie tray from somewhere but ended up just getting a bunch of things from the grocery store and figured I could assemble it at Paige's as my contribution.

"Look, we have more chairs," Paige said as I walked into the living room.

"Oh, this is so cozy," I said. She'd re-arranged the couch and pushed it back, so she could place the chairs in a circle so we were all facing each other, with a table in the middle for drinks and food and so forth.

"I mean, I'm going to have to move the couch back again, but it's fine," Paige said. Esme was on her way back from stopping at the bar to grab a few things.

"This looks great," I said.

"Thanks. I can't wait until we can do things at Em and Natalie's house because they're going to have a lot more room. Alivia said we could use her house too, but I think that's even smaller than Em's cabin." It was a problem. None of us had very large homes to accommodate entertaining. Too bad we couldn't use Jax's house. There was enough room to have three times as many people with room to spare. Hell, we could have it in the library. How nice would that be?

Paige fussed around making sure everything was perfect while I set out to arrange everything on the wooden tray she gave me. I looked up some pictures to help give me some ideas, but I ended up just going freestyle with it.

"How does this look?" I asked Paige.

"Very nice! So fancy." I took a few pictures of the tray and posted them on my social.

I got a message from Jax not five minutes later.

Did you arrange this yourself? It looks great

I thanked her and couldn't stop smiling at her approval.

"Oh, who are you talking to?" Paige asked, getting cups down from the cabinets for everyone.

"No one," I said, putting the phone down.

Esme walked in the door a second later and completely distracted Paige from asking anything further.

"Okay, we are ready," Esme said, plunking several bottles of alcohol down on the counter.

"We've got boozy drinks and non-boozy drinks. Drinks for all," she said with a laugh.

"Anything I can do to help?" I asked, but Esme waved me off. "I've got this."

There wasn't much for me to do, so I went to play with the animals and wait for everyone to arrive. Alivia was next, along with Charli, followed by Linley and Gray, and then Em and Natalie. Yet again, I was the only one not with a partner, and I had to swallow my jealousy. That was easier to do when Esme put a drink in my hand, an Old Fashioned, my favorite.

There was a little bit of chaos as everyone got themselves settled in the living room and filled their plates.

"So, since this isn't an actual book club, we can just sort of...do what we want," Paige announced.

"Who had nightmares?" Charli blurted out. Several hands went up.

"Seriously, this book is so creepy!" Em said.

That kicked off a lively discussion about the book, what parts we liked, what parts we didn't, and what we thought was going to happen next. I found myself laughing more than I thought I would and putting in my own two cents as someone in the publishing industry.

"None of my authors write horror, but it would be really fun to make graphics and stuff for this," I said.

"You should reach out to him," Linley said. "See if he needs someone."

I shook my head. "Jack Hill has teams of publicity people who have actual degrees that cater to his every whim. When you're bringing in that much money, you can pretty much do what you want."

We somehow got into a discussion of the publishing industry and the horror genre as a whole. Esme was the one who'd read the most and recommended some books to those of us who wanted to read more. She had a blog where she gave out personalized recommendations every month, so she was really good at finding books people would like.

"I'm guessing there won't be a lot of kissing in this book?" Charlie asked, flipping quickly through her copy.

"Uh, no," Esme said. "There might be some, but not what you're looking for in the romance department. Jack isn't exactly known for that."

What a shame. He could learn something from my romance authors.

"So, we'll do the next five chapters for next time?" Paige said.

"I could do a presentation about Jack Hill's other books and his writing history," Esme suggested.

"Oh, I love that idea!" Paige clapped her hands happily. I

thought it was a cool idea too. I'd love to know more about what drove him to write these kinds of books.

"I can look up some of his publishing stats, if anyone is interested," I said.

"We like data," Paige said, beaming.

"And I'll make themed desserts next time," Linley said. "I was a little rushed for tonight due to the construction at the new kitchen." She rolled her eyes.

"How's it going?" Paige asked.

"Oh, we're getting there, but just about every piece of equipment we need is on backorder, so my dad has been calling around to see if we can buy off someone's old equipment for a better price, and so we can get it quicker. Mom is wrangling everything else, so I'm trying to keep everything together at the bakery. I'm going to be so relieved when we are finally done and can hire more staff."

It sounded exhausting, but at least they were on their way. As Lizzie had said, the hardest part was just before you'd made the decision.

"Hey, Gray, I have a question for you. Are you friendly with anyone in hospital admin? My sister is thinking about getting a degree or certification, but she wants to do some research beforehand," I asked him.

"Yeah, absolutely. Let me reach out and I'll email you some names. I know a couple people who wouldn't mind sharing their expertise at all."

It wasn't an overstatement to say that everyone loved Gray, and for good reason. I wish he was single, because I'd set him up with Lizzie. She needed to be cared for the way Gray cared for Linley.

Any of my friend's relationships were the blueprint of how to respect and love each other. It was hard to believe that I'd ever have something like that myself. At least I had something going on. I wasn't about ready to call whatever I was doing with Jax a relationship, but it was *something* at least.

Non Book Club slowly broke up, with everyone saying they needed to get home for one reason or another. My charcuterie board had been demolished, so I only had to wash the wooden tray and put it in the dish drainer.

"Thanks so much for coming," Paige said, giving me a hug.

"Yeah, sure. It was really fun. I'll see you on Monday?"

"Ugh, don't remind me of that word," Paige said, covering her ears.

"Sorry!" I said, grabbing my bag and pulling out my keys. "Bye Esme, bye Potato, bye Stormy!" I called. Esme said goodbye from the living room where she was attempting to shove the couch back into position, and Stormy barked. Potato remained silent but hopped up on the windowsill as I walked down the steps and got into my car.

I WALKED into a completely different house when I got back from Non Book Club.

"Hello?" I asked as I stared into the living room, which was filled with blankets draped over chairs and the couch.

"Come in the fort!" Luna's little voice yelled. I got down on my knees and pulled aside one of the blankets.

"Wow, this is amazing," I said. Not only had they made a blanket fort, but the floor was covered in more blankets and pillows, making a soft nest. One blanket had been draped over the TV, so you could only watch it while in the fort.

"We have snacks," Lizzie said, handing me a bowl of popcorn.

"Nice," I said, settling in with my back against the couch.

They'd even gone the extra mile and strung twinkle lights up.

"This is the best fort I've ever been in," I said.

"Well, we had a lot of practice," Lizzie said. When she and I were younger, we'd made forts all the time in the basement. There was an art to it, and you had to have the right supplies.

Luna came over to snuggle in my lap and I kissed the top of her head.

"I'm going to sleep in the fort," she said.

"Just for tonight," Lizzie said. "Forts aren't special if we have them all the time, right?"

"Right," Luna said in a sad voice.

"Let's enjoy it while we have it," I said, putting the bowl of popcorn in Luna's lap so she could have access to it.

"What are we watching?" I asked.

They'd just started a movie, so they went back and played it from the beginning for me so I didn't miss anything.

"How was book club?" Lizzie asked as the studio logo filled the screen.

"It wasn't book club, and it was good. You could come next time." I'd invited her at least three times, but she declined.

"I need to make my own friends," she said. "You have your own thing going on."

That was true. Since Lizzie had moved here, she hadn't gotten out much. Mostly because she was so busy with Luna, but I also thought she used that as an excuse.

"You should set up a play date with Anna. Then you could have a mom friend."

"You're right, I'll do that," she said.

"Shhh," Luna said, putting her little finger to her lips.

"Sorry," Lizzie and I said at the same time.

LUNA FELL ASLEEP HALFWAY through the movie, but Lizzie and I kept watching and eating the snacks. It was a fun cartoon movie we'd seen before, but it was a good comfort movie, and watching it in the fort made it so much cozier.

I slid Luna onto the pillows beside me and tucked her in as the credits rolled.

I kissed her forehead and her mom did the same.

She unplugged the twinkle lights and we both crawled out of the fort reluctantly.

"If only my problems could be solved by watching a movie in a blanket fort," Lizzie said as we cleared up what was left of the snacks.

"Life would be so much easier," I agreed.

"So, you know I'm going on another date tomorrow. Don't know if I'll be back, but I'll let you know when I figure out where we're going to dinner."

"You could at least give me her address, so I know where you're going to stay," she said.

"Why? I'll have my phone on me the whole time, so if there's an emergency, you can get in touch with me," I said.

"But what if there's an emergency with you?" she pointed out.

I had anxiety about giving out Jax's address. What if Lizzie looked it up and somehow connected it to Jax? I was so not ready to have that conversation.

"I'll be fine. I'm not going to be that far away." Lizzie glared at me, and I thought she was going to try and tickle the answer out of me, but she didn't.

"Okay, okay. You're an adult and you can take care of yourself. I'm not your mom, so I'm not going to nag you. But I'm still curious," she said.

"It's really not that interesting," I said.

"I think it is. I spend my day seating people at tables and trying to keep a five-year-old alive. Going on dates and having sex is way more exciting."

The sex and the dates were exciting, I couldn't lie about that.

"You'll just have to find your own," I said.

Lizzie sighed. "That's the problem."

～

I DECIDED to go for a different look for this date and used the dress as inspiration. I pulled my hair back into a high ponytail that I'd probably need to take down within an hour, but for now looked really cute. I paired it with my black boots, and small silver hoop earrings.

This time I broke out the eyeliner and did a little fancy wing that took me way too long to get even, but I was happy with the results once I was done.

"Verdict?" I asked Lizzie as I came into the living room and twirled.

"Hot," Lizzie said.

"Black dress!" Luna yelled, jumping up and down. "I want!"

"It's too big for you right now, Luna Moon. You can have it when you're bigger," I said.

"Promise?" she asked with wide eyes.

"Promise."

"Okay, auntie has to go on her date," Lizzie said, putting her hands on Luna's shoulders.

"You look really hot," she mouthed at me.

"Thanks," I said, grabbing my gray coat and purse. I had a black leather jacket that I'd worn to the last date, but it seemed like overkill with the leather of the skirt on the dress. Since the coat was more of a wrap, it covered the dress just enough that when I took it off, the reveal would be more dramatic. I wanted to stun her speechless.

Chapter Twelve

YET AGAIN, I was meeting Jax at the restaurant. It wasn't as far from Castleton, which was nice. I hadn't known where I was going until she texted me about an hour before I had to leave. This time we were meeting at a less-fancy place, but it was still nice. The menu was a lot more affordable and familiar too. I couldn't lie, I was a little relieved. I was able to find a spot in the small lot next to the restaurant, and I looked around for Jax's car. Since it was a fancy model, it was easy to spot among the other vehicles and several trucks also in the lot. If there was one thing that Maine did not have a shortage of, it was pickup trucks.

I walked over to her car, but she must already be inside. I sent her a message that I was here, and she told me to meet her just inside.

I kept my coat on so I could do the dress reveal when we sat down.

Jax also had a coat on, and tonight, she wore wide-leg black pants. Her coat was a warm wine color.

"Hi," I said, smiling at her as she turned.

"Hi," Jax said. "She's here," she told the host.

"Follow me," he said, grabbing two menus. He wore a polo shirt with the logo of the restaurant on it. Very different from our last date.

He took us all the way through the restaurant and to a back deck.

"Oh, wow," I said. The restaurant was inside a brick building that used to house an old mill and sat right next to a roaring river. The view from the deck was spectacular.

I took off my coat and made sure to twirl just a little as I did.

"Wow, yourself," Jax said, pausing in the middle of taking off her own coat. I stopped remembering how to form words when she revealed a completely see-through white shirt with a black bustier underneath.

Help.

The host seated us at a table right next to a heater, so even though the air was chilly, we'd stay warm. Good thing, because her top was more air than fabric, and my dress was almost completely backless.

"Enjoy," he said, and then left us.

"This is seriously cool," I said, looking up at the sky that was aflame with the setting sun.

"I thought you might like this," Jax said.

I couldn't take my eyes off her. A giant sparkly ring caught my eye as she picked up her menu.

"That's beautiful," I said, pointing at it.

"Oh, thank you. It's a family heirloom." She looked at the ring fondly. I wish my family had heirlooms. The only things I'd gotten from my family were some cursed and ugly paintings, and weirdly shaped toes.

"It really is gorgeous," I said again. I didn't care about the menu. I just wanted to look at her.

A waitress came over to fill our water and take our drink order.

"I need some more time," I admitted.

"No problem," the waitress said.

I scanned the menu quickly and saw they had a special Old Fashioned, so I decided to order that.

"I haven't eaten here in a while, and they have some new appetizers. Want to get the sampler?" Jax asked.

"Sounds great," I said. Honestly, I cared much less about the food than thinking about peeling that top off her later.

What was happening to me? I was thinking about ditching food in favor of sex.

"You okay?" Jax asked.

"Yup," I said, and held up the menu to block most of her body so I could actually look at it. They had a great selection of burgers, so I picked one of those when the waitress came back to take our drink orders. Jax ordered the baked lobster mac and cheese with a side garden salad. I was definitely going to be taking a few bites of that.

I was happy once my drink arrived. It was delicious and I had to remind myself not to drink it too fast.

Jax had ordered a dirty martini. That seemed like such a grown-up drink. I'd never had one because I was afraid I wouldn't like it.

"I thought about you this week," Jax said.

"Yeah?"

"I think you've rubbed off on your niece a little bit," she said with a laugh. "She looked at me one day, and I swear, it was the exact same expression I've seen on you."

I didn't know why that made me feel so good, but it did.

"Yeah, well, I'm not her mom, but I do my best to set a good example. It's not easy."

"No, it's not," Jax said, sipping her drink. "You don't know how many euphemisms I've had to come up with so I don't curse when one of my kids has a tantrum and throws a toy that hits me."

I leaned in.

"Like what?"

"Sugar is a popular one. I've also used names of cereals too. Coconuts works too."

I laughed. "I remember once when I was in high school I said 'schist' during a geology lesson and my teacher thought I said 'shit' and I almost got into trouble, but everyone at my table stood up for me."

"Schist is a good one. But a little too close to the real word, so you might slip and say it instead."

"I say 'holy cow' a lot around Luna. It's very old school."

"You could always change it up with an 'oh my heavens!'"

I laughed. "I will definitely add that to my repertoire."

The appetizer platter came, and it was almost a meal in itself.

"I don't like mozzarella sticks," Jax admitted.

I just stared at her.

"How can you not like fried cheese?" I asked. I'd never heard of such a thing.

"I'm sorry! I've tried. I just don't. They're all yours."

I scooped them all onto my plate, along with the little bowl of marinara.

"This night is already going in my favor," I said, dipping one of the deep-fried bites into the sauce and then into my mouth, nearly burning my tongue.

Jax selected a pretzel bite and dipped it in some honey mustard sauce. I was surprised to see her eating with her fingers and not a fork. She seemed too classy for finger food, yet here she was.

We split the spinach and artichoke dip and the honey buffalo wings. I was about to lick my fingers clean but wiped them on my napkin instead. I didn't want Jax to think I was an uncultured heathen.

This restaurant had music too, but it was jazzier, and piped through hidden speakers. Made the whole night feel very New Orleans.

My burger arrived and it was messy and drippy and got sauce all over my face, but it was so tasty, I didn't care.

"How bad do I look right now?" I asked halfway through eating as I set it down to reach for some of the Parmesan truffle fries.

Jax just laughed. "Come here," she said, and I got up and got down next to her chair so she could wipe my face. What I didn't expect was for her to take my chin, turn my head, and lick the sauce from my cheek.

I froze, hit by a shot of lust so intense that my legs almost gave out.

"I just wanted a taste," she said before she used her napkin to take care of the rest of my face.

I somehow managed to get myself back in my chair, but I couldn't speak for a few seconds. Jax just gave me a wicked grin, because she knew exactly what she'd just done to me. I carefully glanced around, but no one was staring at us, so I didn't think any of the other diners had seen it.

"If you wanted to taste my burger, all you had to do was ask," I said, picking up a fry.

"Where's the fun in that?" she said. "I like my way better."

So did I.

JAX DID GET a few bites of my burger, and I had some of her meal as well. When the waitress came back to ask about dessert, Jax's eyes lit up. We both perused the dessert menu, and Jax asked what I was thinking.

"Well, I'm thinking you probably want the triple chocolate chip cookie skillet," I said.

"And what do you want?" she asked.

I almost opened my mouth and said "you," but I stopped myself at the last minute.

"I think that sounds amazing," I said.

"Perfect," she said, and when the waitress came back, she ordered the cookie skillet.

It came a little while later, and it was one of the biggest cookies I'd ever seen.

"There's no way we can finish this," I said, picking up my spoon. The cookie was topped with a massive scoop of ice cream that was quickly melting over it.

"I like that challenge," Jax said. "We'll bring it back with us and eat it in bed later if we don't finish."

That idea definitely had its appeal.

Jax and I stuffed our faces with the cookie that had not only milk chocolate chips and white chocolate chips, but dark chocolate chips.

"Have a chocogasm?" Jax asked.

"Definitely," I said.

"You can never have too much chocolate in my book," Jax said.

WE DIDN'T FINISH the cookie but took the rest to bring back with us, and I made sure to get a smaller one for Luna. Once again, I used the GPS on my phone to navigate to Jax's house.

Was it me, or had the house grown in size since I'd been here last week? It somehow looked bigger than I remembered.

I shook my head and grabbed the overnight bag I'd brought this time from the passenger seat. As much as I enjoyed wearing her clothes, I liked having my own toothbrush and a change of clothes for tomorrow.

Jax had already shed the white top when I opened the door,

so I was greeted by Jax only in her bustier which was…quite something.

My bag slid off my shoulder and fell to the floor.

"Hey," Jax said.

"Uh huh," I replied, which didn't even make any sense.

Jax laughed. "Should we go right upstairs, or would you like tea first?"

Yes, I absolutely wanted to go upstairs, but there was something I liked about this little tea ritual beforehand. I guess she'd already planned for tea, because I heard the kettle in the kitchen before I could answer.

"Tea, please," I said.

I hung up my jacket and put my bag on the entry table.

Soft music piped through the house, controlled by her house robot. I listened to the piano music and realized it was a cover of a song from a very popular cartoon movie. One of Luna's favorites.

"Guess you can't get away from the kid's stuff," I said, pointing upward to indicate the music.

"Yeah, it's kind of an occupational hazard," Jax said, stirring honey and lemon into my tea.

We took our mugs to the den and sat down together.

Jax kicked her shoes off and tucked her feet up under her.

There was something sensual about sitting here and looking at her, knowing what we would be doing later, and denying myself from touching her.

Waiting, and anticipating that first kiss.

"What are you thinking about?" Jax asked.

"Kissing you," I said automatically.

"You can, you know."

"I know."

"So why don't you?" she challenged.

"Don't tell me what to do," I snapped back. "If you want to kiss me so bad, then you go for it."

Jax carefully set her tea down and stood up. She put both hands on the arms of the chair and leaned down to look into my eyes.

"I thought we were having a nice cup of tea? But, if you've changed your mind, I can roll with that," she said, reaching back and taking hold of my ponytail.

Tea sloshed onto the skirt of my dress.

"Shit," I said, and Jax used her other hand to take the cup from me and set it down safely. Could tea ruin a skirt?

"Are you ready to go upstairs?" Jax asked.

"Yes," I said, and she pulled just a little bit to get me to stand.

"Let's go," she said, taking my hand and tugging me toward the stairs.

I WALKED UP to Jax's bedroom in a daze. How was it that I turned inside out when I was with her?

Jax closed the door to her room behind me.

"Turn around," she said. I did, showing her my back.

She ran her fingers down my spine before taking hold of the zipper and pulling it all the way down and pushing my hair out of the way so she could undo the halter part at my neck.

The dress fell right off me and onto the floor.

"Can I just hang it up so it doesn't get creased?" I asked, as if I needed her permission.

"Sure," she said, going to her closet and then bringing me back a hanger. I hung the dress on the back of the door. I'd have to deal with the tea damage later.

I faced Jax, completely naked.

"Fuck," she said, looking at me with her head tilted to one side. "What am I going to do with you?"

"Whatever you want," I blurted out.

Jax laughed. "Let's start with a kiss, shall we?" she asked.

A kiss was a very good place to start.

Our lips met and I pressed my full body against her, wishing that she was naked too.

"Take your clothes off," I said in between kisses when I took a pause to breathe.

"Okay," she said, and then she started unlacing the front of the bustier and I watched, transfixed.

"How do you breathe in that thing?" I asked.

"Carefully," she said as she slid her shoulders out of the straps and then pulled the rest of the top over her head. Her pants went next, but this time she wore something under them. It was a little scrap of black lace, but still. Something told me Jax Hardy had an extensive lingerie collection that I hadn't seen yet.

"Happy now?" she asked.

"Very," I said, reaching for her breasts and pinching both her nipples, making her jump.

"Not yet," she said.

"Not yet what?" I asked.

"I get my way first," she said.

"Doesn't that mean you get off first?" I asked.

"No. It means I get my way with you," she said, sliding her hand down and cupping me.

Okay, we were getting right down to business.

"Go sit on the bed," she said, and I did. Of course, I did.

"Lay back," she said, putting one hand on my chest to push me back so my legs were still on the ground, but I was looking up at the ceiling. It was very ornate. I didn't know what kind of architectural feature it was called, but it had a nice effect, with raised squares, almost like frames.

"You'll have to spread your legs wider for me," Jax said.

I did as told, and I heard a sound of satisfaction from her. I sat up, so I could see what she was doing.

Jax got on her knees and looked up at me, running her hands up and down my thighs.

"I've been thinking about making you come since the moment you left last week. Haven't been able to get it out of my mind."

Uh, same.

"Let's make all that anticipation worth it." She kissed the inside of each thigh and then ran little kisses up toward where I needed her, stopping just short.

I watched her hair shimmer in the light and lifted one hand to her head.

"You can try to direct me all you want, but I'm not letting you come quickly. I'm not that kind of girl."

"What kind of girl are you?" I asked and she looked up at me.

"I'm the girl who's going to make you come harder than you ever have in your life."

And she did.

I GOT to use the tub. Jax turned on the tap and let me select which bubble bar I wanted to use. She had a whole drawer of them, and a special knife to shave off pieces to drop into the water.

I picked one that was dark blue and kind of glittery and smelled like jasmine and a bunch of other lovely things.

While the tub filled, Jax went down to the kitchen to unwrap another charcuterie board and pour us both a glass of wine.

"How much did this bottle cost?" I asked when she came back upstairs with the whole snack situation.

"Do you really want to know?" she asked, handing me a glass.

"Probably not," I said. The wine was red and rich, and slightly warm. "This is nice," I said, taking another sip.

"I'm glad you like it," she said.

I almost moaned when I slid into the frothy water. Jax even had special bath pillows for our necks, and her house robot piped whatever music we wanted into the room. Jax even had a special tray that sat on the edges of the bath, so we could have the food and wine between us.

Jax faced me with a smile on her flushed face.

"This is the most relaxed I've been in probably ten years," I said. The orgasms had unhinged my joints, and the bath was soothing every single muscle. Plus, I got to stare at an incredibly gorgeous woman. And there was cheese. What more could you ask for?

"I might want to marry this tub," I said.

"Just wait," she said, and then she turned on the jets.

"Oh yeah, I'm definitely marrying this tub."

"Then should I leave you two alone?" she pretended that she was going to get up.

"No, don't go anywhere," I said reaching out and grabbing her arm. "Get back in this tub."

"Okay," she said with a pretend sigh. "If you insist."

The water sloshed as she got back in.

"So, when do I get the grand tour of the rest of the house?" I asked.

"I don't know, haven't you already seen it?" she said, deliberately making eye contact as she drank her wine.

"What do you mean?" I asked, even though I was a terrible liar.

"You're not as sneaky as you think you are. In fact, you're not sneaky at all. You'd make a terrible burglar."

"That's an extremely insulting thing to say."

"Oh no, are you mad?"

She sat up and then moved the tray so it wasn't between us.

Jax dove toward me like some kind of mermaid.

"Don't be mad," she said, and then kissed me.

I pulled her until she was on top of me, straddling my thighs.

"I'm not mad," I said. "But I wouldn't have had to go on my own if you would have just taken me to see the library in the first place."

Her face was just an inch from mine. I could see the little flecks of green in her blue eyes and practically count her eyelashes.

"Do you want to see the library right now?" she asked, slowly grinding her hips against me.

"I mean, not right now, at this second," I said. "I'm a little too distracted to be looking at books." I reached between us and stroked her, causing her to tremble.

"Make me come and I'll show you the library," she said, her eyes opening.

"Challenge accepted," I said.

I DID MAKE HER COME, and so we hopped out of the bath, and I wrapped myself in one of her thick robes and a pair of fuzzy slippers that were so soft, it was like walking on clouds. If I wasn't careful, I was going to get used to this luxury, and it would be a rude awakening when I had to go back to my normal life with coupons and apps to give me special sales so I could afford to get a new pair of jeans.

I followed Jax up the stairs to the library. She told the robot to turn on all the lights and the room was bathed in a warm glow.

"Browse if you like," Jax said, going to the little nook in the turret to sit down on the bench. She watched me walk around and look at the books.

"You have a very interesting collection," I said. "You've got these leather-bound ones, and then you've got all these paperbacks, too," I said. There didn't seem to be any kind of organization that I could see.

"Are they arranged any particular way?" I asked, running my fingers along a few of the spines. There was no dust on anything, so someone must clean in here frequently. I wondered if it was Jax, or if she hired people to clean the house.

"I mean, they're arranged in my mind. I know where everything is, but it doesn't really make sense to anyone else. I do keep series together," she said, getting up and leading me over to a section of shelving. "See?"

I saw a popular fantasy series all arranged. She had both paperbacks and hardcovers. Something I hadn't noticed before were several shelves of children's books.

"Wow, you have a lot," I said.

"Yeah, I like to keep backup copies, and I also like to see what's new so I can get them for my classroom." Jax absolutely bought books for her classroom with the money out of her own pocket, I was sure.

I found one of Luna's favorite books and pulled it out, making note of where it was so I could put it back.

"I've read this one to Luna hundreds of times," I said. "I could tell you what's on each page of this." I flipped through the book and then put it back.

"Yeah, that is a guaranteed winner with the kids. I've read it to every class too," she said.

I sat down on the thick rug that sat under the desk and covered a huge swath of the dark hardwood floor.

"This really is a special room," I said. "I can imagine just sitting in here during a rainy afternoon and reading with the fireplace on," I said.

Jax sat down next to me.

"Do you have any really rare books?" I asked.

"Give me just a second," Jax said, getting up.

She walked over to some shelves on the other side of the room, selected one title and carefully brought it over.

"This is my favorite of my rare books," she said.

I was shocked when she set the book into my lap. Was I allowed to be touching this?

"Wow," I said, reading the title. Pride and Prejudice by Jane Austen.

"It's a rare illustrated edition," Jax said. "Not the most expensive of my collection, but it's probably my favorite." She opened the green leather cover and showed me some of the bright illustrations.

The book had a little bit of damage, but it was over a hundred years old, so it was bound to.

"Wow," I said again.

"I'd love to get a first edition, but those go for thousands upon thousands," she said. "Someday."

She gingerly took the book back from me and returned it to the shelf.

"You really should join Non Book Club," I said. "We could even have it here. This would be the best place," I said.

"But wouldn't that mean admitting to everyone what we're doing?" she asked.

"Oh, right." I'd forgotten about that part. If I told everyone, then I was opening myself up for not only scrutiny, but criticism, and I did not need that.

"Never mind," I said, but I really did like the image of all my friends here in this lovely library, all eating and drinking and chatting. They'd like Jax, I was sure of it.

"So," she said, standing up. "Should we go get in bed?"

"Yeah," I said, getting to my feet.

Chapter Thirteen

IT WAS another perfect sleep in a perfect bed with this perfect girl. Then I got to get up and have fresh fruit, croissants, poached eggs, and coffee in the sun-drenched breakfast nook.

I felt so spoiled.

"You don't have to leave yet, you know," Jax said. "We could do something today." I mean, I didn't have to get home right away. I had a change of clothes. It was a beautiful fall Sunday. Lizzie was off work and had planned to take Luna to the movies. Not a big deal if I missed that.

"Okay, what did you have in mind?"

"The foliage is just starting to get pretty, so I thought we could go on a little hike."

My smile froze on my face.

"A hike?" I asked, because I had to confirm.

"Are you not a fan of hiking?" she asked, sipping her coffee with the cup in both hands.

"Oh, um, I'm just not very experienced," I said. I wasn't experienced because I hated hiking. Going to the apple orchard was one thing. Venturing into the woods to walk up a mountain or whatever was something completely different.

What about bears? What if I tripped and broke my ankle? What if I fell off a cliff? There were so many dangers; it didn't seem worth it.

"Don't worry, I know a perfect little trail that's very beginner friendly. The view is worth it, I promise. And when we get down, I'll buy you lunch."

I mean, how could I say no?

"Will there be melted cheese?" I asked.

"As much melted cheese as you want," she said, getting up and kissing me on the forehead.

This could be a disaster, but at least there was cheese to look forward to.

IN A FREAK COINCIDENCE, Jax and I turned out to have the same size feet, so she lent me a pair of her extra hiking boots. I guess my boots from last night weren't good enough.

Jax also supplied me with an extra backpack, and loaded me up with snacks, and a bottle of water.

"I've got a first aid kit in my car, do you want me to grab it?" I asked.

"No, I've got one," she said, pulling a little red zippered bag out of her backpack with a white cross on it.

"Well, aren't you just prepared?"

"Another occupational hazard," she said. "Kids are always hurting themselves, so I keep first aid kits literally everywhere."

Once Jax checked our packs, making sure we had enough water and sunscreen and bug spray, we got in her car with the leather seats and all the tech bells and whistles. I didn't even want to think how much it cost.

Jax drove us north of both Hartford and Castleton, toward the center of the state. Farms and trees flashed by me, and I got a little twitchy being this far inland. I got nervous when I was too far from the ocean for some reason. That was why I loved the city of Boston. You got city and ocean, with beaches just a short drive away.

"You doing okay over there?" Jax asked as we pulled into a tiny parking lot that was tucked on the side of the road. A huge wooden board announced the name of the trail and had a little plastic container of maps. I was definitely grabbing one of those, even though I'd read a paper map exactly never.

Several other people got out of their cars with walking sticks and dogs on leashes and packs that looked like they were for serious hikers.

"Are you sure I'm going to be okay?" I asked. You couldn't even see the mountain from this vantage point. It was like walking into fog, or something. Not knowing what the hell you were going to find.

"You're going to be fine. We just stick to the trail, take breaks, and we can always come down if you want. Going down is a lot easier than going up."

"I like going down," I said to her, raising and lowering my eyebrows.

Jax rolled her eyes, but she was laughing.

"Come on, that was good," I said as we got out of the car. I made sure my hiking boots were tied so I wouldn't trip on my laces and adjusted the straps on my pack.

A family with two small children headed into the woods, the kids skipping along, their cartoon-covered backpacks bouncing on their backs.

Okay, if a small child could handle this hike, then I could. I liked walking. It was the woods I didn't like.

"Ready?" Jax asked, sliding on her designer sunglasses.

"Yup," I said, putting on my aviators that were scratched to hell, but were my favorite pair.

I let Lizzie know that I was going on a hike for the day and to let Luna know I would (hopefully) be back for dinner.

Have you been kidnapped? I thought I just read that you're going on a hike.

I shook my head and typed a message back to her.

Yes, I'm fine. It's just incredible what I will do for a hot girl.

Lizzie sent back a laughing emoji. **That sounds about right for you. Have fun. Don't get, like, eaten by a bear or something.**

"Come on," Jax said, waiting for me. She looked so sexy in her hiking gear. The boots were definitely doing it for me.

"Okay," I said, putting my phone in my backpack. "Let's go."

FOR THE FIRST FEW MINUTES, I could still hear the noises from the road, which was comforting. It was when I couldn't hear cars anymore that I started getting nervous.

"You doing okay?" Jax asked. I knew I was slowing her pace.

"Yeah, I'm good," I said, looking around. I couldn't shake the feeling that something was going to jump out at me any moment.

"Why are you twitching?" she asked, walking closer to me, stepping right over a root that probably would have tripped me.

"I'm not twitching," I said and then there was a loud sound to my right.

"What was that?" I dove for Jax, grabbing onto her to shove her in front of me.

"A woodpecker," Jax said in a dry voice, looking down at me as I crouched behind her.

I heard the sound again, almost like a knocking. I'd definitely heard that sound before.

160

"Didn't you grow up in Maine? Haven't you ever heard a woodpecker before?" she asked.

"Yes," I snapped, standing up. "I'm fine. Let's go." I stepped away from her, embarrassed and annoyed by what she'd just seen. Jumping behind her at the sound of a woodpecker wasn't sexy. It wouldn't make her want to drag me off the trail and fuck me senseless.

This had been a very bad idea.

I NEEDED a break a little while later, and we stopped to rest right near a little stream that crossed the trail.

I sat on a rock and willed my body to stop sweating so much. I chugged my water and pulled some of the snacks from the pack.

Jax was pretty quiet and hadn't said much since my little outburst.

"I'm sorry," I said. "About earlier."

"It's okay. I just wish you'd told me hiking wasn't your thing. I wouldn't have dragged you along."

"You didn't drag me along," I said. "I'm an adult who agreed to come with you. I can make my own decisions." Now I was getting heated again. I just didn't like being treated like I didn't know my own mind.

Jax looked at me for a long moment.

"Okay," she said. "I'm going to ask you one more time if you want to turn around, and if you say keep going, we'll keep going and I won't ask you again. Do you want to keep going?"

Not really.

"Yes," I said. Now I was determined. Something about this damn hike had lit a fire in me, and I was going to finish this thing, even if I had to crawl to the top. I was doing this shit.

Jax nodded and we finished our snacks in silence.

When we started walking again, I tried to be a better sport by asking Jax to point out the various plants that we saw.

"Look," she said, pointing at a little crop of flowers with a dark brown center and yellow petals that almost looked like a daisy, but with the wrong colors.

"Black-eyed Susans."

She picked one and pulled the stem off, then tucked it behind my ear.

I felt myself blushing from my cheeks to my ears.

"Very cute," she said.

Jax told me other things, like not to drink the water and what poison ivy looked like. She was smart. Obviously, I'd known that, but the depth of her knowledge about so many subjects was almost terrifying. I felt woefully inadequate in comparison. I mean, what the hell did I know?

"Do you take your students hiking?" I asked.

"There's a little nature trail we take them to, but they're too young for anything like this. I mean, not as a big group. Can you imagine?" No, I couldn't. All of them at the beach had been enough, and that was when they were all in one place.

"I feel like you'd also have fewer parent volunteers," I said.

"Definitely," she said, laughing.

I wanted to ask if we were close to the top because we had been walking for a thousand years. Somehow, my pack felt heavier than when I started.

Jax and I passed a few people on the trail, and Jax told me a little bit about trail etiquette.

"What happens if I need to pee?" I asked. That was an inevitability that I wasn't looking forward to facing.

"Haven't you ever been to a concert and had to use a shady bathroom? It's a little like that."

Oh. Got it. I was going to wait as long as possible before doing that.

We stopped and had another break, and I finally asked how much longer we'd be hiking.

"Probably another twenty minutes or so?" Jax pulled the map out and consulted it. We'd passed little trail signs, but I hadn't been paying attention. Oops. I was a really bad hiker.

We had almost made it to the top when I said I had to pee, so Jax told me where to go, and handed me a little bit of TP so I didn't have to drip dry. Somehow, I managed to get the job done, but my dignity was a little bruised as I returned and Jax squirted some hand sanitizer in my palm.

"Feel better?" she asked.

"Yeah," I said. Hopefully we could get to a public bathroom before I had to go again. "Let's do this."

We finally, *finally* made it to the top of the mountain, and I had to admit, the view was pretty great. I didn't get too close to the edge, but I took a few pictures of the view to show Luna. The little town below us looked like it was made for ants, and the cars were minuscule. Some of the leaves were just starting to turn yellow on their way to orange and then brown before they all fell to the ground.

"It would have been nice to be up here during the height of the foliage season, but this is still pretty good," Jax said, standing with her hands on her hips and surveying the land as if she owned it.

She looked incredibly hot, and not half as sweaty as I was. I'd had to put my hair up in a bun so my sweaty pony would stop slapping my neck as I walked.

"Let's celebrate," Jax said, pulling some items from her pack. They included little collapsible champagne glasses and a tiny bottle of bubbly.

"I didn't see you pack this," I said.

"Sorry if it's not very cold," she said. "I did pack it with an ice pack, but I could only do so much." The champagne was chilled, surprisingly, when Jax handed me a glass.

"We shouldn't have too much, but I thought we could have a little treat. Congrats on making it to the top, Sasha."

I tapped my glass with hers and sipped. Jax also had some more snacks, and a little blanket to lay everything on. I hadn't known there would be special treats at the top. There was even a little box of chocolate truffles.

"It wasn't so bad," I said.

"Mmm, tell me how your legs feel tomorrow," Jax said, and I narrowed my eyes.

A hawk made slow circles in the sky, and I took video of it for Luna.

"You don't have to be a hiker. The important part is that you tried," Jax said.

"You don't have to placate me. I'm not one of your students," I said.

"I know," she said, her face falling. Shit.

"I'm sorry. This is all just very out of my comfort zone," I said, waving my hand around. "I'm not a woodsy person."

"Yeah, I kind of picked up on that," she said, and I smacked her in the arm.

"Hey, I have other skills, okay? We can't all be…like…some woods woman." I had been trying to think of some famous hiker but couldn't come up with anyone.

"I'm only outdoorsy because my parents took me hiking when I was a kid. My dad traveled a lot, so when he wasn't working, he loved just hiking in the woods with the quiet." This was one of the first times she'd ever talked about her parents. Honestly, I didn't know if they were still alive, or where they lived, or anything else. Since she'd never mentioned a sibling, I'd assumed she was an only child.

"Was he an airline pilot?" I asked.

"No, just did a lot of traveling," she said, sipping her champagne and looking out at the sky. I guess that was all the information I was going to get.

To be fair to Jax, I didn't really talk about my parents either. Maybe she didn't have a good relationship with them anymore. That, I could understand.

Several other hikers made their way to the peak and Jax and I watched as they took pictures and got way too close to the edge.

"I prefer the less dangerous view," I said as we packed up the remnants of our peak picnic.

"Me too," Jax said. "Things can go wrong even on the simplest hike, so it's best to be overly cautious."

My legs were stiff from sitting, so it took a few steps for my joints to start working again as we took one last look at the view.

"Selfie?" I asked Jax. "Just for us."

She nodded, and we smushed together as I held my arm out and smiled.

I knew I wasn't going to post the picture anywhere, but I wanted to have it to remember this day. Remember this day with her.

~

JAX WAS RIGHT; the trip down was a lot faster. I had to keep focusing so my feet didn't get ahead of my brain and send me tumbling down the trail. I ended up having to pee again, and it was just as unpleasant as the first time, but then Jax went and I had to be vigilant by myself. It was a huge relief when she came around the corner and smiled at me.

"No bears?" she joked.

"No, but I did make eye contact with a squirrel that seemed suspicious," I said.

"Come here," she said, motioning to me. I stepped toward her and she led me around the large rock she'd used to shield herself from anyone that might be passing by.

"What is it?" I asked, going from interested to terrified in about half a second.

"Calm down," she said, pushing me up against the rock.

"Jax, what are you doing?" I asked, and then she reached for the button on my jeans.

"Do you want anyone walking by to hear you?" she asked, sliding her hand down my jeans to cup me.

"Oh, shit," I said, my hand slapping at the rock, grabbing to hold onto something.

"Shhh," Jax said, stepping closer and leaning against me. "You've got to be quieter."

That was easier said than done as she stroked me with her fingers. My eyes shuttered closed as she dipped one finger, and then another, inside me, cupping her hand so the heel of it pressed against my clit.

I whimpered and she used her other hand to cover my mouth. That just made me moan.

"You really don't know how to be quiet, do you?" she said in my ear as she fucked me slowly with her hand. Distantly, I heard voices, but Jax didn't stop.

Several people were coming up or down the trail and they were being really loud about it, but I was so lost in what Jax was doing that I couldn't be too worried about it. We were out of sight, at least, so the chances of them seeing us were slim. As long as I could be quiet.

"Does it make you excited? To think we could be caught?" Jax whispered, picking up the pace.

Yeah, it definitely did. There was an edge of the forbidden that added another dimension, and I could feel myself getting ready. I clutched her as I came, and she muffled my noises with her hand. I slumped against her, panting as she withdrew her fingers.

"What was that for?" I asked when I could speak.

"You've been pretty tense today. I thought you could relax a little." She smiled at me and then gave me a quick kiss.

My legs were less agile as I followed her from behind the rock and back to the trail.

∾

I WAS MORE relaxed for the rest of the hike back to the car, but I was thrilled when I saw the glint of Jax's car through the trees. I almost wanted to hug it.

"You hungry?" Jax asked as we threw our gear in the back and I sat down in the passenger seat. Sitting had never felt so good in my life. I was hungry, and then I was ready for a nap. The hike and orgasm combo had made me drowsy.

"Definitely," I said. The snacks had been fine to sustain me during the hike, but now I needed a full meal.

Jax drove us to a small diner that didn't look like much on the outside, but Jax told me it had amazing reviews, and she'd eaten here before.

"You'll like it, trust me."

I was a little surprised she had picked this little hole in the wall, but I followed her as a waitress seated us at a little table. The entire place was decorated with vintage Coke memorabilia and had a fifties feel. I liked it immediately.

The menu was massive, and I couldn't decide what I wanted to order.

"What's good?" I asked.

"All of their burgers, definitely, and the fried chicken sandwich will change your life." Since I'd just gotten a burger the night before, I decided to go with the fried chicken. It came on a butter-grilled bun and dripping with a honey sauce that I couldn't stop licking off my fingers. Jax got the cheeseburger salad, which also looked amazing.

"I'm sorry if I'm being rude, but I'm so hungry," I said, taking massive bites of my sandwich.

"It's okay," Jax said with a laugh. She had much better manners than I did, and I wondered if she'd learned them from her parents. Probably.

"Did you do cotillion?" I asked.

"What?"

"Did you do cotillion? With the white gloves and the coming out and everything?" I only knew about it from movies and TV shows.

"Uh, no? Why would you ask that?" she said, pouring a little more dressing on her salad.

"I guess because you have such nice table manners, and because, you know…" I trailed off.

"Because my parents have money," she supplied.

"I mean, yeah."

Jax shook her head. "No, my parents weren't like that. They didn't always have money. My dad came into it after they'd already been married, so their lives didn't change all that much." I found that hard to believe, but I kept my mouth shut.

I wasn't going to ruin this by asking too many questions.

"That must have been quite a change," I said. Maybe he'd won the lottery? That would explain why she was so cagey. Lottery winners had people coming out of the woodwork to beg them for money all the time.

"It was, but I don't remember it. I was born after," she said.

"Do you have any siblings?" I asked.

"Nope, only child." She grinned. "So, you could say I'm a little spoiled, but I own it."

Huh. I'd never heard anyone own something like that.

"Good for you," I said.

"Really?" she asked. "A lot of people would think that's a negative."

"I mean, I haven't seen you be much of a bitch. I mean, except for the night we met. You were kind of a bitch then."

I half expected her to throw her salad in my face.

"I was kind of bitch, wasn't I?" she said.

"Yeah, you were."

We smiled at each other across the table.

I DOZED off during the ride back to Jax's house to get my car, and I wasn't looking forward to the short drive back to Castleton.

"Thanks for pushing me out of my comfort zone today," I said.

"You're welcome. Maybe sometime we can do something out of mine. Keep things even."

Now I'd have to come up with something.

"You're going to let me plan one of our dates?" I asked.

"Why not?" she said.

"You might regret agreeing to this," I said, leaning against my car.

Jax laughed. "We'll see."

She kissed me goodbye in the driveway, and then went back into the house. She waved from the open doorway as I got in the car.

I didn't want to leave.

"OH MY GOD, where have you been?" Lizzie asked as I dragged myself into the house.

"Hiking, I told you," I said, throwing my purse down and then completely collapsing on the couch where Luna was snuggled up with Fluffy.

"Give me snugs," I said to Luna, holding my arms out. She crawled into my lap and I kissed the top of her head.

"I missed you, Luna Moon," I said.

"You were supposed to come with us," Luna said, and I could tell she was upset I'd missed our movie date.

"I'm sorry, sweetie. I'll make it up to you next weekend. We'll do something just us," I said. I didn't know when I was going to fit that in with the date with Jax, but I'd make it work. I could do both.

Luna thought it over. "Okay."

"How was your hike?" Lizzie asked, leaning over the back of the couch.

"Exhausting," I said. I wasn't going to tell her about the orgasm part. "I don't know how people do that all the time. For fun!"

"I know," Lizzie said, shaking her head. "Remember when I decided to do cross country in high school?" We both burst out laughing.

"If I remember correctly, you were doing it to impress a boy."

"Correct," Lizzie said. "Never again!"

I slid my shoes off and put my feet up on the coffee table.

"I'm making goulash for dinner, is that okay?" Lizzie asked from the kitchen.

"Yeah, that's fine."

Goulash was a dish we used to make when we were younger. Basically, you took whatever pasta you had in the pantry, whatever meat you had in the freezer, and whatever sauce you had in the fridge, and put it all together. Usually that meant elbow macaroni with pizza sauce and ground beef. Add some cheese on top and a veggie on the side, and you were done.

Something told me Jax had never eaten goulash. I really did wonder what her childhood had been like. She claimed her parents didn't act like rich people, but I'd really like to know. Had she cut coupons from boxes of cereal ever in her life? Had she been able to choose whatever college she wanted and not have to worry about loans? I wasn't resentful, just curious.

"How was the movie?" I asked Luna, and she spent the next twenty minutes telling me each and every detail, and I pretended to hang on every word. It was actually really cute. We all ate our bowls of goulash on the couch, and Lizzie had to cut Luna off from completely drowning hers in cheese.

"She's probably at least sixty percent cheese at this point," I said.

"I know, that's what I'm trying to avoid," Lizzie said, going to put the cheese away so Luna couldn't sneak any more.

Luna wasn't happy and started having a little meltdown that didn't have anything to do with cheese.

I shared a look with Lizzie as she tried to comfort the crying Luna.

"Let's go have a nice bath, okay?" Lizzie said, but Luna just sniffled.

Luna perked up a little in the tub and was falling asleep by the time Lizzie started detangling her hair. We both tucked the passed-out Luna in bed.

"She'll be fine tomorrow. She's just having a hard time dealing with disappointment," Lizzie said as we cleaned up the living room.

"I know how she feels. I can barely deal with it, and I'm fully grown."

Lizzie laughed as we finished and then sat on the couch.

"So, how was your date?" she asked. "I'm dying to know who your mystery woman is. It's not someone embarrassing from high school, is it?"

"No, definitely not. We're just sort of…figuring things out."

"She's not married, is she?" Lizzie asked, and I just gave her a look.

"I'm not a cheater."

"Well, you wouldn't be the one cheating," she pointed out.

"No, but I'd be helping a cheater. She's definitely not married."

Lizzie yawned. "I'd still like to know who she is."

At this point, I didn't think I'd ever tell Lizzie about Jax. I mean, why would I? We weren't going to be getting serious, ever, and it would just cause drama over nothing.

"We'll see," I said, and then changed the subject.

Chapter Fourteen

"CRAP, I forgot that was coming up," Paige said as we stood outside the Castleton Cafe. She pointed to a bright orange poster announcing the dates of the Fall Festival that Castleton was celebrating for the second year. It had been an addition to the Summer Daze sale last year to get more people to visit Castleton and patronize the businesses one last time before winter set in and everyone went into hibernation mode until Christmas.

"You going?" I asked.

"Esme is helping the Grille with their cider and beer booth, so I've been roped in to help. I know Sweet's is doing something too," she said as we walked in and got in line to get out first shots of caffeine.

"It's definitely going to be bigger than last year. They didn't plan it super well, and not a lot of places participated, but Martha is on the planning committee this year and she's whipping everyone into shape."

I'd met Linley's formidable mother a few times and I could imagine that she wouldn't put up with a half-assed festival.

"Sounds fun," I said.

"Hey, Blue, can you surprise me today?" Paige asked.

"You got it," Blue said, tapping the screen of the register.

"And I'll get one of those little egg things," Paige said. The café had recently partnered with a local farm and had added egg sandwiches and these little egg muffins to the menu.

Paige paid and then I ordered a mocha latte with an extra shot of espresso and an egg muffin as well.

"You make my job too easy," Blue said with a grin as he handed the order receipts to Tabitha, the owner of the café, to heat up the egg bites before they went to make our coffee drinks.

I shoved a few bucks in the tip jar before I went to sit with Paige at our favorite table.

"Before we get started, I have to know how your date was," Paige said, right before Blue called out her name to come pick up her order. She grabbed mine as well and set the plates and cups down on the table.

"It was good. We went to this place on the water, and the food was amazing."

Paige waved her hand. "I don't care about the food. Well, I don't care that much. Get to the good stuff."

I rolled my eyes. She was shameless.

"I'm not giving you every detail, you perv," I said.

"I don't need every detail. Just, like, a few."

"Well, we went back to her place and we were supposed to have tea, but that kind of led to us going upstairs." Paige ate her egg muffin and leaned in to catch every word.

"And we did…stuff. And then we took a bath together."

"Ohhh, sexy." It was. I told Paige all about Jax's tub and the charcuterie and so forth.

"It sounds so romantic, Sasha," Paige said.

"It was. It really was. I can't let myself get too attached."

"Why not?" She wiped her fingers and started drinking her mystery drink from Blue. Paige let them experiment on her, making all kinds of wacky latte combinations that she drank and rated. I think they liked to get a chance to be creative. They also did cool latte art with the frothed milk.

"Because I'm not sticking around. It's pointless to start something serious if I'm going to be moving. Just setting me up to get hurt. No thanks. I'll have fun while it lasts and then move on." I shrugged one shoulder.

"You know, deciding you are trying to keep feelings out of it, and actually doing that, are two different things," Paige said. "Trust me, I should know."

"What do you mean?" Was she talking about Esme?

"Let's just say that my intentions with Esme were to hit-it and quit-it and obviously, that didn't work out." She held up her left hand, where her engagement ring sparkled.

"I mean, that's you. We're completely different people."

Paige just sighed and shook her head. "Okay. If you say so."

"I do," I said. "Not everyone hands their heart over to a hot bartender."

"Ouch, that was rude," Paige said, but she was smiling. "To be fair, have you seen her?"

"Okay, you do have a point there," I said.

We both laughed and decided it was time to actually get to work.

"OKAY, I'VE DECIDED," Lizzie announced at dinner later in the week.

"What have you decided?" I asked.

"I've decided that I'm going to get my degree in healthcare management." She beamed, and I could tell she had been bursting to tell me.

"Really? That's awesome."

"I know, I can't believe I finally decided. But I talked with Gray's friend at the hospital, and she told me what kinds of jobs I could get, and it just sounds perfect. Now I just have to apply and do my financial aid and cross my fingers," she said, her words coming out in a rush.

"Did you hear that, Luna Moon? Mommy is going back to school," I said.

"You're going to school with me? I don't know if Miss Hardy would let you," Luna said, and Lizzie and I laughed.

"No, sweetie, I'm going to college. It's like a school for grownups."

"Do you get a lot of crayons?" Luna asked.

"I don't know, but I'm going to find out," Lizzie said, giving me a wink.

Lizzie told me more about her program, and what classes she was going to have to take, and that it was definitely going to mean me watching Luna more than I did now. It was absolutely going to cut into my time with Jax, but what was I going to do? I'd make it work. I'd literally come here with the purpose of helping my sister, and nothing was going to come before that, not even mind-blowing sex with the hottest woman I'd ever seen.

"I WISH I could see you more than once a week," Jax said on Saturday night as we lay in bed after another intense sexsion. She'd asked me if I wanted to plan this date, but I'd declined, since I was exhausted. Next time. During this particular date, I learned that she had a complete arsenal of sex toys under her bed, all pristine and waiting to be used. I'd never seen a more complete collection.

Jax Hardy was thorough in anything she did.

"Yeah, I know," I said before I could think better of it.

"But I know you're busy and I'm busy, so this is what we have."

Her fingers walked up and down my back, tracing lazy circles as I lay on my stomach, propped up on her expensive pillows.

"My sister is starting school soon, so I'm going to have to watch Luna more, so it might not be every weekend," I said.

"I understand," she said, but I could tell she wasn't happy about it. "Then we have to make the most off the time we have," she said, and she shifted until she was on top of me. "Right now, I'm going to make the most of my time by worshipping your spectacular ass."

I moaned into the pillow and she laughed.

This woman was going to be the death of me.

"YOU DON'T HAVE to cook me breakfast every time," I said the next morning when I went downstairs to find her in the kitchen with music playing as she stood at the stove and swayed from side to side, her blonde hair hastily pulled back.

"I like cooking," she said, taking whatever was in the pan and putting it on a plate.

"Hash browns topped with hollandaise and microgreens and a poached egg," she announced as she pushed a plate toward me.

"Wow," I said. I was honestly impressed. "One of these days you're going to have to show me how you poach an egg. I love them, but I have no idea how to make them."

"Sure. I'll show you anytime," Jax said, handing me a fork.

I should offer to cook, but if she enjoyed it, then why would I take that away from her? I should probably feel guilty for her paying for everything and cooking and always staying at her house, but if she had the resources, then why make a big deal out of it?

"Can you stay for a little bit?" Jax asked as I cut into the egg that oozed all over the potatoes.

"Yeah, but not like last weekend. I have to take Luna to the movies this weekend to make up for not going with her last time." My niece really could get away with anything.

"You're sweet. Okay, that's fine. Casey has been begging to have lunch, but I've been ditching her to hang with you, so I'll let her know I'm free."

I munched on a perfectly crispy potato. "How long have you been friends with her?" I knew so little about her social life, but it was clear she had lots of friends, judging by all the pictures on her social pages and in frames around the house.

"A few years? We actually met at the bar and started hanging out."

"What does she do for work?" I asked, even though I thought I knew the answer.

"She does social media." And there it was. "To be honest, she doesn't need to really work. She just does social media for fun."

I was trying really hard not to say anything.

"She seems...interesting," I finally said. Jax met my eyes.

"You know, you're not that good at hiding your thoughts. I can feel your judgment from here."

"I'm sorry. It's just...all I have to go on is that day in the orchard," I said.

"She's not always like that," Jax said. "She's actually really generous. And she's gotten me out of a jam more than once." If she said so. Who was I to judge?

"People get the wrong idea about my friend Hollis too. She's just really confident and doesn't put up with bullshit, so people just think she's a complete bitch. Which she is, sometimes, but only for a good cause." I smiled, thinking about how

Hollis would always stand up for someone who was being hurt, no matter who that person was.

"Sounds like she and I would get along."

I thought about that for a few seconds. "Yeah, I think you would."

We finished breakfast, and I fiddled around getting my stuff together. I needed to leave, but I didn't want to.

"Do you maybe want to do something next week?" I asked.

"Next week I have fall break. I'm going to be doing some workshops, but I do have some spare time." Worked for me.

"Let me take you out," I said.

"What did you have in mind?" Jax asked.

"This time, it's my surprise," I said, and watched her eye twitch. If there was one thing I knew for sure about Jax Hardy, it was that she loved being in control. She loved being the one orchestrating everything. It was probably why she made such a good teacher.

"You're not allergic to snakes, are you?" I asked, just to wind her up.

Her eyes narrowed. "What would we be doing where I might encounter snakes?"

"I don't know," I said, throwing my bag over my shoulder. "You'll find out when we get there."

I laughed as I walked out the door, enjoying her frustration.

I WAS tired when I got home, but I sucked it up and had some coffee and took my niece to the movies where we snuck in candy and covered our bucket of popcorn with so much fake butter sauce that I needed to wipe her down before we went home.

We found Lizzie doing school applications at the dining table. I felt her stress as soon as we walked in.

"Hey, Luna Moon, why don't we go outside?" I asked. Lizzie shot me a grateful look. I kept Luna outside for a while until Lizzie finished and said she should start dinner.

"I've got this," I said, pulling some frozen chicken strips out of the freezer. I ended up making a kind of dinner charcuterie, with cut up veggies and ranch and the chicken strips and crackers and cheese.

"It's snacks for dinner," I told Luna.

"Yay!" she said, so I called that a win.

"I can't believe I'm going back to school. What if I end up failing?" Lizzie said. I could tell she was tired and stressed about this school thing.

"In that case, we just start making videos of Luna and post them online and turn her into a child influencer and then ride on her coattails," I said. Lizzie rolled her eyes.

I TOLD Lizzie about my date and said that I was going to plan the next one, and I needed ideas. I was absolutely kidding about the snake thing. I didn't even know where you'd find snakes in Maine.

"You could always bring her here," Lizzie said pointedly.

"That's a no," I said.

"Yeah, I get it. Can't really get in the romantic mood with a five-year-old running around and singing." The idea of having Jax in my room with my little bed made me cringe. She definitely didn't want to see any of that. She'd never fuck me again.

"You know what? I got a coupon for a free night at The Honeysuckle Inn from Alivia when they gave me that silly little welcome basket," I said. What could be more romantic than a charming inn that was right on the ocean?

"Oh, that is perfect. I'm a little jealous," Lizzie said.

"You need a spa day. We should find a babysitter and go and get massages some time," I said. I'd had so many plans to do stuff like that with Lizzie when I first moved in, but then we got busy and those things got put aside for activities with Luna.

"Ohhh, that sounds like heaven," Lizzie said. "Can you make sure my masseuse is a really hot guy?"

I laughed. "I'll see what I can do, but I am not paying for a happy ending."

Lizzie smacked me. "I don't mean it like that! I just want a little bit of fantasy."

She yawned and closed her eyes and I knew she was probably going to fall asleep on the couch.

"You're gonna find the right guy," I said, but she was already asleep.

I ENDED up texting Alivia to ask if I could cash in my coupon for the following weekend. She responded back right away that they had an opening, and she would let me have one of the best rooms. I told her that wasn't necessary, but she wouldn't take no for an answer.

All I had to do was make sure that no one saw me with Jax at the same time.

Don't worry. I can sneak you in the side door Alivia said when I asked if we could keep things secret. She didn't ask why, and I was relieved.

It was a risk, having Jax in town, but if I snuck her in and out and we didn't leave the room, who was going to know? Besides, the majority of the people staying at the inn weren't even from here.

We'd get room service and fuck all night. What could be better?

THE REST OF THE WEEK, I couldn't concentrate.

"You're twitching," Paige informed me on Thursday as I attempted to work on newsletter content for one of my authors.

"Sorry," I said. I needed to get my act together, but I was really excited about my date, and I couldn't hide it. Jax had been pestering me the whole week via text to tell her what we were doing and annoying her with random suggestions hadn't gotten old yet.

"Big date this weekend?" Paige asked, as if she knew.

"Maybe," I said.

"Ohhh, what are you doing?" I couldn't tell her, because my friends would absolutely show up at the inn and try and figure out who my mystery woman was.

"Just hanging out," I said. Not a lie, so I didn't feel bad about it. I didn't need to give Paige every single detail.

"You getting serious yet?" Paige asked, nibbling on her scone.

"Definitely not," I said. "We're keeping things casual."

"Uh huh," Paige said in a tone that called that into question.

"Can we not?" I asked.

"Okay, okay, I'll keep my comments to myself," she said, holding her hands up in surrender.

"I appreciate that," I said.

"You gonna be ready for Non Book Club?" she asked.

"I still have one more chapter. I've gotten behind this week." My reading time had really been suffering lately and I wished I had more of it in my life. Once I moved back to the city, I'd have to schedule myself some reading dates at some of my favorite little bookstores.

"Esme and I already finished, but don't worry, we'll keep it spoiler free," she said. That made me picture the two of them sitting on the couch together and reading, which then led me to picture doing the same thing with Jax in her library. It would be so cozy.

"What are you thinking about?" Paige asked. "You got all dreamy there."

"Nothing," I said, looking back at my computer.

"Uh huh," Paige said with a smirk.

I WAS late for Non Book Club, and I ended up dropping the charcuterie in the driveway, so everything that was so carefully arranged ended up all over the place.

"I'm sorry," I said, setting the muddy container on the counter as everyone chilled in the living room.

"It's fine, it's an abstract charcuterie," Paige said, rubbing my shoulder.

She shoved me toward the living room as she dealt with the mess of a tray I'd brought.

"Hey," I said to Alivia as I took one of the chairs next to the couch.

"Hey," she said, giving me a wink.

"I know too, but I won't say anything," Charli whispered, leaning over. "I can keep a secret."

"Yes, you can," Alivia said, and their eyes met. They smiled at one another and shared a soft kiss and I felt like I was intruding.

"Thanks," I said, my voice a little too loud. They both glanced at me as if they'd forgotten I was there.

"Okay," Paige said, coming in with the charcuterie somewhat arranged and setting it on the table.

"We ready to start?" Esme asked.

"Let's do this," Em said, holding up her paperback book.

"Okay, who did not expect that guy to die?" Natalie said.

"I know, right? I was completely surprised," Charli said, and thus started another lively discussion of Non Book Club. Gray and Natalie ended up sort of giving a little talk about some forensic stuff, and I realized that my friends were both incredibly weird, and incredibly cool. Esme talked about a historical murder that had inspired the author and Paige read some interviews with the author where he talked about some of his inspiration and writing process.

"He still has a home in Maine. We should definitely go on a field trip for our final meeting," Paige said.

"Road trip!" Natalie said, and Em groaned. They'd gotten back together when Em had agreed to fly across the country to pick up Natalie from college and drive her back to Castleton.

"As long as I don't have to drive a moving truck," Em said. "Never again."

"Aw, you did so good. You've got amazing skills," Natalie said, kissing Em on the cheek.

"Never. Again," Em reiterated.

Natalie just laughed.

"I can drive a few of us," Alivia said.

"What if he calls the cops on us for trespassing?" Charli said.

"I'm sure people go there all the time," Paige said. "We're not going to try to break in. We'll just stand outside and take some pictures or something."

It sounded like a fun trip to me. I was totally in. It sounded like a kind of fun trip that Jax might like, but she wasn't going to be coming with us.

A few people ended up looking up where the house was and found several blog posts of other fans who had gone and taken pictures outside. Apparently, he had a huge metal gate with a sign on it out front to keep people from trespassing. Very spooky for a horror author.

The charcuterie was consumed, and I felt bad for being late, so I stayed to help clean up with Paige and Esme.

"How's everything going with your sister?" Esme asked, and I told her about Lizzie going to school, and how much Gray had helped her make some connections at the hospital.

"So I'm going to be on Luna duty for a while," I said.

"How long is her program?" Paige asked.

"Two years," I said. "But I'm not sticking around here that long." I laughed, but Paige and Esme didn't laugh with me.

"You could stay," Paige said.

"Definitely not. I'm not a small-town girl," I said, shuddering.

"You were born in a small town," Paige pointed out.

"Yes, and I left as soon as I could. This is just not for me. It's fine if it works for other people." I didn't want to insult my friends and say that their lives were bad or wrong for living here. We could want different things and still be cool with one another.

"I think this town might surprise you," Esme said.

"Can I order Lo Mein at two in the morning and get it delivered to my house?" I asked.

"No," Esme said, shaking her head. "But if you ever need Lo Mein at two in the morning, you have at least six people you can call that would drop everything and bring it to you."

I shook my head. "It's not the same."

We weren't going to agree, so I decided to drop it. I left soon after, and I had an uncomfortable feeling in my chest all the way home.

"How was it?" Lizzie asked.

"Good," I said, frowning.

"You okay?" Lizzie asked, looking up from her laptop. She was on her computer constantly now, either working on applications, checking email, or doing her financial aid applications. Applying to school was more work than she'd actually be doing once she got in. Hopefully by next week she'd have some answers. The whole family was on edge and waiting.

"No, I'm good," I said, putting on a smile. "Want a drink?" I was in the mood for something to warm me up on the inside.

"Yes, please," she said.

I ended up making both of us an Old Fashioned. Esme had taught me how to mix them, and I was still practicing. I kept telling her she needed to start a cocktail class to teach people basic cocktails.

"Thank you very much," Lizzie said, sipping the drink. "This one is better."

"I think so too." I had it almost right.

"So, I need to talk to you about something," Lizzie said, setting her drink down and closing her laptop.

"Yeah?" I said, my stomach sinking.

"I've done the math and, even if I get aid, school is going to be really expensive. My shifts just aren't going to cover it. I know you've offered to pay rent in the past and I told you not to, but I was wondering if…" she trailed off, unable to say it. Her face was red with humiliation.

"I can absolutely help," I said. "Don't feel bad for asking, at all. I offered, so this isn't coming out of the blue. I've got some money saved, so if you need anything, like for groceries or whatever, I can help." It would mean cutting into my moving fund, but this was more important. I could always work more hours or take on another temporary client to build myself back up again.

"Thank you," Lizzie said, a few tears running down her cheeks. "You have no idea what it's like to have to ask your little sister for money."

"Don't even worry about it," I said, giving her a hug. "We'll get through this. We always do."

She sighed and sniffled.

"And then you'll meet a hot doctor at the hospital that will fall madly in love with you, and then move into his mansion by the beach," I said.

Lizzie laughed. "That sounds like a perfect plan. And you? Going to find a hot doctor too?"

I shook my head. "No, I think maybe an heiress is more my speed." That made me think of Jax. She did come from family money.

"What about royalty?" Lizzie asked.

"Even better. Money and a crown." We both burst out laughing and collapsed against each other on the couch.

We both sat up when a little voice said something.

"Oh, hey baby, did we wake you up?" Lizzie asked, going to pick up a sleepy Luna who had clearly woken up.

"I had a accident," Luna said, and I noticed the dark spot on her pajamas.

"Oh, baby, that's okay. Come on."

Lizzie got Luna in the tub while I stripped the bed and threw her pajamas and blankets in the wash and put on a new set.

"Thanks," Lizzie said, carrying a sleeping Luna back into the room. We settled her into the fresh bed and tucked her in.

Lizzie and I went back out to the living room and finished our drinks.

"I'm glad you're my sister," Lizzie said after a while.

"Me too," I said, holding out my glass toward her. She tapped hers against it.

Chapter Fifteen

I was a jittery ball of nerves on Saturday morning, and it was really silly. I'd already cleared everything with Lizzie and Luna, but what they didn't know was that I wasn't leaving Castleton. The plan was to go pick up Jax and then drive her back. Alivia had hidden a key for me for the side door of the inn and told me which room was mine. It was all very covert and I kind of liked it.

Jax looked annoyed when I showed up.

"Everything okay?" I asked as she picked up her bag and grabbed a scarf. The weather had gotten chillier overnight.

"Yes, but I didn't know what to pack because I didn't know where we'd be going, so I had to bring everything," she said, pointing to the suitcase. It was pretty big. She didn't need that much crap for one night away.

"Let me get that for you," I said, grabbing the suitcase and then nearly falling over.

"What the hell is in here?" I asked.

"Everything in case of emergency," Jax said. "This is what you asked for. This is what you get." It was true. I knew her well enough to expect this was how she'd handle a surprise overnight.

"Okay, how about we both carry it?" I asked. We both stumbled down the stairs and Jax helped me heave the suitcase into the trunk of my car.

"Okay then," I said, getting in the driver's side. "Are you ready?"

"No," Jax said. "But let's go anyway."

～

I THOUGHT about taking a less-direct route to the inn, but I wanted to get there sooner rather than later to maximize my time with Jax, so I drove straight there.

"We're in Castleton," Jax said with surprise. "I thought we weren't supposed to be seen together?"

"We won't be," I said, taking the back way around downtown.

I parked in the back of the lot at the inn and Jax looked up at the large white building.

"This is lovely," she said. The inn was decked out for fall, with pumpkins and wreaths made of autumn leaves and hay bales and everything.

"I have a connection with the manager," I said as we got out of the car. Jax started to walk around the front where the entrance was, but I steered her toward the side door.

"We have to go in this way," I said. She gave me a look but followed.

"Oh, we forgot the bags," I said. We went back to the car and hauled out my backpack and Jax's suitcase.

"Okay," I said, looking around. "She said the key was… there it is," I said, locating a rock that Alivia had told me about. Under it was the key for the outside, along with our room key.

"Ready?" I asked Jax.

"Ready," she said, not sounding confident.

THE FIRST CHALLENGE was hauling her suitcase up the back stairs. I was ready for a nap when that was done, but we finally made it to the main hallway of the inn.

"Let me go first," I said, glancing up and down so no one would see us. Sounds of people having dinner drifted up from the downstairs.

"Okay," Jax said, leaning against her suitcase.

"It's that one at the end," I said, pointing to our room number.

"Got it," Jax said. She seemed a little amused at my insistence on being sneaky.

I strolled down the hall and unlocked the door as quickly as I could before looking back and motioning for Jax to come. She dragged her suitcase along the floor, struggling a little. I heard someone on the stairs below saying they were going to get something from their room, so I waved at Jax to hurry.

She did her best and I got her in the room just as the person reached the top of the stairs.

"That was close," I said, breathing a little heavily.

"You really are too much sometimes," Jax said, panting from hauling the bag.

"Too much? Or just enough?" I asked, pushing her up against the door and pressing my hips into hers.

"Mmm, just enough."

I kissed her and we forgot all about heavy bags and sneaking around.

"Can we at least look at the room first?" Jax asked between kisses.

"Fine," I said, stepping away from her and actually looking at the room. "Oh."

"This is gorgeous," Jax said, pushing her suitcase to the side.

Not only was the room huge, but there was also an ice bucket with a bottle of champagne, and a note that Alivia must have left.

"That's so sweet," Jax said. "Looks like you have friends in high places." I'd rather have family in high places, but I didn't say that.

I read the note. Alivia said to call down to the front desk when we ordered dinner and mention her name and we'd be comped.

I thought Jax would go immediately to the bed, but she was still wrestling with the suitcase.

The room was filled with light from several huge windows that looked out over the sparkling afternoon ocean. The sun was setting earlier and earlier this time of year. Much too early for my taste.

"What are you doing over there?" I asked Jax as she started pulling items out of the suitcase.

"Unpacking," she said, as if that was obvious.

"We're only here for a night. Why unpack?" I was just going to pull stuff out of my bag as I needed it and leave my dirty clothes on a chair until it was time to shove them in my bag again.

Jax and I were very different people.

"Oh my god, did you bring every vibrator you own?" I asked as she pulled out her toys from in between her perfectly folded clothes. She also pulled out a few cloth bags that contained several pairs of shoes.

"Not all of them. Just my favorites. And lube. Can't forget the lube." She held up several bottles.

"You are the most prepared person I've ever met," I said in awe.

She turned around and grinned at me. "Thank you."

My heart stopped. The combination of her organization, the way she looked as the sunlight kissed her skin from the setting sun and the fact that I had her to myself for an entire night was a combination that I almost couldn't handle.

"What is it?" she asked.

"Nothing," I said, shaking my head. She really did put me under a spell without even trying.

I found the room service menu and sat on the bed with it. Jax finished her organizing by laying her toys and lube in a row on the dresser and putting her clothes in the drawers.

Who knew organization could be so sexy?

"So, what do you want?" I asked, scanning down the menu.

A hand pulled it out of my grip, and I turned to find Jax looking at me, her eyes sparkling

"You. Right now, I want you."

"Take me," I blurted out, and she laughed as I blushed.

She reached toward the headboard and tried to shake it.

"What are you doing?" I asked.

"Just testing," she said.

"Testing for what?" I asked.

"How do you feel about being tied up?" she asked, a sexy grin on her lips.

"As long as there is a way to get out of it, so we don't have to call for help, I'm in," I said.

Jax laughed. "Don't worry, my dad taught me how to tie really good knots."

She hopped off the bed and pulled something else out of the suitcase: a length of red rope.

Any hunger for dinner immediately vanished.

I'd never been tied up before, with the exception of one pair of fuzzy handcuffs I'd worn once before they'd broken because they were so cheap. It hadn't done much for me, but the idea of Jax tying me up with elegant knots in this room was…yeah, I was into that.

Jax was nothing if not a teacher. While she worked, she told me what she was doing, describing each knot and making sure nothing was too tight or uncomfortable.

"You know, if you ever decide you don't want to teach kids anymore, you'd be really good at this," I said.

"I don't want to share my skills with anyone but you," she said, leaning down and kissing me, nipping at my bottom lip. I tried to reach for her but was limited by the restraints.

"I'm not going to lie, seeing you like this is really doing it for me," Jax said, stepping back to admire her work.

I quivered with need, waiting to see what her next move would be. The anticipation was almost as intense as an orgasm and I knew that when I came, it was going to be explosive.

"Now, which toy should I use first?" she asked, going to her selection.

"Yes," I said.

～

"HOW WAS IT?" Jax asked, after I'd had three mind-destroying orgasms in a row.

I looked at the subtle red marks on my skin the rope had left behind. They were already fading, and I was almost disappointed.

"Your turn now?" I asked, but she shook her head.

"All that rope work has made me hungry. I can wait. Builds anticipation." She slipped her hand down her front and stroked herself just once.

Fuck. She was so sexy.

My own hunger won out against my need to fuck her. We had all night.

~

SOMEONE DELIVERED a tray of food and left it outside our room. I wondered if it was Alivia as I retrieved the tray, hoping I wasn't going to drop it. Jax had to move a bunch of the sex toys off the dresser so I had room to set it down.

She popped open the champagne and we sat down in two soft chairs with a little table between them that was tucked into a corner of the room.

"This room is pretty great," I said, digging into my baked haddock. I hadn't seen any of the other rooms, but this one had a lovely garden vibe with green toile wallpaper on one of the walls, and soft green linens as well as framed watercolors of daisies on the wall.

"It is lovely. Makes me think of The Secret Garden."

"Love that book," I said.

"Same," she agreed, smiling at me over her salmon.

I asked her how school was going, and she asked me how Lizzie was doing with her college applications, and we didn't talk about the future.

There had been moments when I'd heard her stop herself from asking something that might lead to any kind of "so, what are we doing?" talk.

I knew this couldn't continue forever without a definitive talk. "Let's just have fun" was a temporary solution.

Like it or not, this thing with Jax wasn't just fucking. It hadn't been that from the beginning. The sex was absolutely incredible, but so was laughing with her. So was watching her organize every single corner of her life until it behaved the way she wanted it to. So was seeing her eyes light up when she talked about her students. I couldn't separate the sex from the person, and I'd been foolish to even try.

Paige had warned me, and I hadn't listened. Guess I needed to work a little on my stubbornness.

I could pretend that I was going to leave Castleton in my dust without a care, but that was a lie. Thinking about not seeing Jax again? I hated it. Everything about the city didn't seem as great anymore. Sure, I couldn't get pizza delivered in the middle of the night, but I got to eat pizza that I made with my niece who loved me. I couldn't just walk down the street to a bar, but I could call any number of people who would invite me to have a drink and sit on their couch. I couldn't find pages and pages of women online to swipe right on, but I had the most beautiful woman I'd ever seen spending the night with me.

What was I really running toward? And what would I be leaving behind?

"You're quiet," Jax pointed out. She missed nothing.

"It's nothing," I said, finishing my glass of champagne and pouring another.

"You can talk to me about things, you know," she said.

"I know. I just… I've never been that great with plans, you know? I was a complete mess in school. It's a wonder I even graduated. Somehow, I managed to get through college by the skin of my teeth, but I just sort of wandered around. So many people were so sure of who they were going to be, and I never was." I was rambling, but she sat and listened.

"I guess I'm just reevaluating some shit, and it's throwing me for a loop. How's that for sexy dinner talk?"

Jax smiled and reached out to take my hand across the little table.

"It's okay to change your mind," she said. "Everyone does. It's part of being a human, and it's not a bad thing to admit that you don't want the same things you thought you did. It's brave."

I didn't feel brave. I felt like a failure.

Jax squeezed my hand and I sighed.

"I don't want to talk about that shit. I want to get you naked."

Jax nodded and put her fork down. We both knew I was going to use sex to distract myself, but we also knew that she was going to let me.

"Come here," I said, pushing my chair back from the table. She got up and walked over to me, straddling me with her sexy legs.

"I don't know how to tie you up," I said.

"That's okay. I don't enjoy it anyway," she said, looking down at me and holding my face between her hands.

"How about if I just fuck you until you can't come anymore?" I asked.

"That works for me," she said before placing a searing kiss on my lips.

"DO you want to see the gardens?" I asked a while later as we lay naked in bed. The sheets weren't as nice as the ones in Jax's house, but most things weren't as nice as she had.

"It's the middle of the night," Jax said, rolling onto her side.

"I know, but the moon is out." It was nearly full, so bright it cast pools of light on the floor through a crack in the curtains.

Jax sat up and pushed her hair over her shoulder.

"Okay," she said.

The one downside of a midnight walk in the garden was that we had to put our clothes on to do it.

The rest of the inn was quiet, the lights left on low. We didn't have to worry about seeing anyone else, so we went down the main stairs, through the dining room and then out the back door.

Jax slipped her hand in mine as we walked down the porch

steps and onto the grass. If it wasn't so cold, I would have taken my shoes off to feel the grass between my toes.

Wedding season had wound down, so the lawn where they normally set up the big reception tent was empty.

I led Jax toward the garden with the little pond and a bridge that arched over it and the gazebo.

"There aren't as many flowers now, but it's still pretty," I said, stopping to lean down and smell some roses. When I looked up, Jax was watching me.

"You're really beautiful, you know," she said in a soft voice.

"Thank you," I said, reaching to pull her close. "I think you're really beautiful."

She kissed me softly. Not the kind of hard, brutal kiss that led directly to sex. This kiss was soft and spoke of promises. I should have pulled back, but I didn't.

I just kept kissing her.

⁓

EVENTUALLY WE GOT cold and had to go back inside, but not before Jax twirled me around a few times, both of us laughing, and me trying not to fall over on the uneven ground.

"You know, Alivia said to help myself to anything," I said as we walked back up the porch and back to our room.

"And?" Jax said, raising one eyebrow.

"And I have a craving for something sweet." I walked toward the kitchen instead of toward the stairs. There was something naughty about sneaking around to get a midnight snack.

"Your friend won't get mad?" Jax asked in a hushed voice.

"No, I think she'd be mad if I didn't raid the fridge, honestly," I said. Underneath her very professional exterior, Alivia did have fun, especially when she was around Charli.

The kitchen was mostly dark, so I found a light switch and turned it on. The only sound was the hum of the appliances.

"Okay, let's see what we have here," I said, going to the fridge and pulling it open. Most of the shelves had raw ingredients, or large containers with food that had been prepped.

"Okay, nothing in there," I said, closing it.

Jax had checked out the walk-in freezer but had no luck there.

"If I were treats, where would I be…" I said, looking around the space.

I started opening storage cabinets and hit the jackpot.

"Here we go." I found a box of whoopie pies in various flavors.

"Which one do you want?" I asked.

"Classic, always," Jax said, taking the chocolate pie with vanilla frosting sandwiched between. Whoopie pies were like cake and a cookie got married and had a delicious baby. I selected a chocolate with peanut butter frosting and closed the cabinet.

"Let's go have these with champagne," I said, and we scampered back upstairs, trying not to giggle too much and wake up the rest of the inn.

"I haven't eaten one of these in years," Jax said as we lay in bed with the whoopie pies and passing the champagne bottle back and forth.

"You've been missing out," I said. "Whoopie pies are essential."

"I'm doing all kinds of things with you, Sasha. Whoopie pies, midnight garden walks."

"Good things, I hope?" I said, reaching for the bottle.

"Only good things," she said, licking frosting from her fingers.

~

I HAD to fight the urge to stay up with Jax all night. I might have reveled in how comfortable the bed was compared to the one I had at my sister's house, but Jax's bed was nicer.

"We should sleep," she whispered in a tired voice.

"We should," I agreed. My eyes finally fluttered closed just after hers did.

I AWOKE the next morning to sunlight all over the pillows. Well, part of it was sunlight and part of it was Jax's hair glowing in the light.

"Good morning," she said in a soft voice.

"Good morning," I said, unable to stop smiling at her.

"This has been a really great date," she said.

"It has, hasn't it?"

"I wish we didn't have to leave," she said. "Although, my sheets are nicer."

I laughed. "They are."

She stretched her arms out and ran a hand through her hair.

"Should we shower and then order breakfast?"

I nodded.

JAX and I soaped each other up with the special complimentary soap in the bathroom and then wrapped ourselves in thick towels to wait for our food.

"I have to admit, I do like eating a breakfast I didn't have to cook sometimes," she said, and just a few minutes later, there was a knock at the door and our food arrived.

We ate in bed, with the tray between us.

"I should plan more dates," I said, shoving hash browns in

my mouth. "Although, I can't promise that they'll be as fancy as this one."

"I don't need our dates to be fancy, Sasha. They just have to be with you."

I was still skeptical.

"So, you'd be fine with spending the night in my full-size bed and probably being interrupted by my niece wanting me to read her the same book for the five thousandth time, or my sister being nosy?" All of our dates had been so far outside of my normal life. I'd compartmentalized Jax away from my life. Intentionally and unintentionally.

Would she still like me if she saw it all?

"I'm not afraid of those things, Jax, and it's a little insulting to me that you thought I'd run away because of that. I know your niece. I literally teach her five days a week. I'm not isolated from the bad things in life just because my parents gave me a lot of money."

Shit. I shouldn't have said a damn thing. This was why I should have kept it at just sex. To avoid this exact situation.

"Let's not talk about it," I said.

Jax was quiet for a little while and then mentioned that she saw a bird outside, and we chatted about mundane things until we were finished.

Jax didn't say much as we packed up our stuff and made sure I left the key in the room, along with the key to the side door.

"I'll go first," I said, reaching for her suitcase. Getting it down the stairs was going to be a whole lot easier than getting it up.

"No, I can take it," she said, grabbing the handle. I could tell she was still irritated from our conversation earlier, but I didn't want to get into it again, so I was just going to wait for her to cool off. I couldn't use sex to get out of this one.

I went down the steps and didn't encounter anyone but

kept my eye out as I waited for Jax at the car. The parking lot was somewhat empty, with most of the people staying at the inn having gone out for the day.

After what felt like an eternity, Jax appeared, sweaty and red-faced with the suitcase.

"Next time you can put some stuff in my bag," I said as we heaved the suitcase back into my car.

"Right," Jax said as I slammed the trunk and we got in the car.

It looked like she was going to stay mad for a while.

"I'm sorry," I said. "I shouldn't have brought that stuff up."

"It's not that you brought it up. It's that you just assume all these things about me."

I didn't point out that there were a lot of things she didn't like to talk about, so there was nothing for me to do but assume.

No, I kept my damn mouth shut, because I didn't want to ruin this.

"I'm sorry," I said again.

"It's okay," she said with a sigh.

I sensed she was warming up, so I suggested that we didn't go back to her place right away.

"Did you plan this part of the date?" she asked.

"Nope, this is spontaneous," I said. "You're going to have to go with it."

She pursed her lips and stared out the window.

"I don't know about that."

Her consternation was always so funny to me.

"You can't be in charge of everything, Jax," I said.

"I can try," she mumbled.

Chapter Sixteen

I TOOK us out of Castleton and turned onto the highway.

"You're not taking me out of the state, are you?" she asked.

"Nope. Just a little bit south."

Jax didn't stop asking questions until I finally took an exit.

"You're worse than Luna," I said as she looked around, probably looking for signs or something.

"Are we eating somewhere?" she asked.

"Nope," I said, turning down a quiet street that I'd driven hundreds, if not thousands of times.

I finally pulled into the parking lot of the Summerton Elementary School.

"What are we doing here?" Jax asked, looking at me as I turned off the car.

"This was my school. Come on." I got out and she followed me, concern on her face.

"We're not here to break in," I said. "I would never. Plus, this place has security cameras everywhere. There was a huge vandalism problem a few years ago. Someone wouldn't stop spray-painting squirting penises all over the place." I couldn't get the words out without laughing. "I mean, vandalism is bad, but it was also really funny."

Jax laughed too as I walked around the back of the school and toward the grassy playground. The place was deserted, the swings swaying gently from the breeze, the rusty chains clinking softly.

"Come on," I said, reaching for her hand and taking her toward the swings.

"I was on recess duty last week, but I can't remember the last time I actually sat on a swing," Jax said with a smile as we both sat on the swings.

"This is all new from when I was here," I said, backing my feet up in the cedar chips that still smelled fresh. "Once upon a time, there was a teeter-totter that I think a few kids lost teeth on."

Jax shook her head and started swinging back and forth, pumping her legs to go higher.

"My school had a tire swing that would spin, and we'd get the oldest and biggest boy in the school to would whip us around until at least one kid puked. Pretty sure they wouldn't allow that now," Jax said with a laugh as she swung higher and higher.

"Remember when we thought if we swung high enough, we could go all the way around the swing set?" I asked.

I panted a little. Swinging was hard work. Or I was out of shape.

"Everything seemed possible when we were younger," Jax said.

Deep thoughts for what I hoped would be a lighthearted end to the date.

We swung for a while, smiling as we passed each other before I decided to launch myself off the swing. I stuck the landing, but it jarred my whole body, and I was afraid I'd pulled something.

"Are you alive?" Jax asked, letting the swing slow to a stop and getting off in a much more dignified way.

"I'm good," I said, shooting her a thumbs up sign as I tested my knees to make sure they were still working.

Jax laughed and we walked together over to the play area that had a plastic tube slide, and elevated platforms that kids could run on.

I got in the slide and went down, disappointed by the short ride.

"That was less fun than I thought it would be," Jax said when she came down after me. Both of our hair was all staticky from the slide, and I chuckled as I tried to fix it.

"You look like you've been electrocuted," I said.

We climbed back up again but ended up just sitting on the edge of one of the platforms, our legs dangling down.

"I'm not hating this spontaneous part of the date," Jax said. Our legs touched and kept bumping as we swung them back and forth.

"See? Spontaneity can be a good thing. You don't have to plan everything within an inch of your life." I bumped her shoulder with mine.

"I don't plan everything, you know," she said. "I've done some spontaneous things."

"What's the last spontaneous thing you did?" I asked.

"Kiss you," she said. Right. That was true.

"That was definitely a good choice," I said.

"It was."

"I have a random question about that night that I've been wondering," I said.

"Yeah?"

"Did you have an entire second dress in your purse that you changed into?" I'd been dying to know.

Jax burst out laughing. "Yes, obviously. I always have extra clothes with me."

I put my arm around her and pulled her close.

"Jax Hardy: always prepared."

"That's me," she said, and I kissed her.

I HELPED Jax haul her suitcase into the house, but she told me to just drop it by the door.

"I can unpack it later," she said.

I raised my eyebrows. "Really? You don't seem like the kind of person who unpacks a suitcase later."

"I've got something more interesting to do with my time," she said, taking a step toward me and putting her arms around my waist.

"Oh, what's that?"

"You," she said before she kissed me.

"I'm really glad that I'm more interesting than unpacking a suitcase. That's a real ego stroke," I said, but I was teasing.

"You are far more interesting. You up for taking a bath?" That sounded perfect.

Jax made up some quick sandwiches and drinks and I set the mood in the bathroom.

"You have a candle drawer," I said, pulling several out to test the scent of before I set them up around the room. It was the middle of the day, but that didn't mean we couldn't have ambience. The sun had slid behind the clouds, so candles were perfect for this gloomy afternoon.

Jax put on some soft music. "I like candles, what can I say?"

I also lit a bunch of unscented pillar candles before adding a few in warm fall scents that filled the room with cinnamon and clove and mulled wine.

"You like?" I asked as Jax set up the tray with our food and drinks.

"Very nice," she said.

"That could be my new side hustle. Candle arranger. Mood-setter."

I put the lighter away and slipped out of my clothes and into the bath that was already full of frothy bubbles that were supposed to smell like champagne.

I sunk into the water first with a deep sigh. "Oh, yeah, this is the stuff."

Jax slid in after me, and I moved to give her room.

"You know, I'm going to have a lot of time during winter break," she said. "There will be workdays, but I was hoping we could spend some time together. I know it's a ways off, but I'd really like to see you," she said.

"Yeah, that would be awesome. Lizzie and I are just going to be by ourselves with Luna. We take her to see Skippy's parents so they can get some time with her. He might be a shitty father, but his parents are wonderful, and they love Luna." At least the kid had one decent set of grandparents if she couldn't have a decent father.

"I'm going to my parents. They do a huge party every year, it's a whole production. My mother is obsessed with Christmas. If my father let her, I think she would just keep rotating the decorations all year."

It was nice to hear her talk about her family. Every new bit of information felt like a victory.

"That sounds really nice," I said. I assumed her parent's house was similar to hers. I pictured several Christmas trees covered in red ribbons and glass ornaments, with subtle sparkling lights. Definitely no tinsel. Tinsel would be too tacky.

"I bet you can do a lot for Christmas here," I said.

Jax laughed. "Yeah, that's why I haven't let you see the basement. Half of it is filled with my Christmas stuff. I also do fall decor, but Christmas is my favorite."

"Like mother, like daughter," I said.

"That's what my dad says," she said.

I told her what Christmas was like with Luna, and how we did matching pajamas for Christmas Eve, and our tradition of getting each other a book to read before we went to bed on Christmas Eve, like they did in Norway.

"I love that," Jax said. "Maybe I'll have to do that this year."

"My parents didn't really do holidays for some reason, so now Lizzie and I try to make things extra magical for Luna."

"You're a good aunt," Jax said. "She talks about you all the time."

"She does? I hope she doesn't say anything embarrassing." Leave it to my niece to tell Jax all of the weird shit I did when I thought no one was watching.

"I usually stop her before she does," Jax said casually.

"Oh god, what has she told you?" I asked, wanting to slide underneath the bubbles and head down the drain.

Jax laughed. "Nothing serious. Just that you sing pop songs in an operatic voice when you're in the shower."

Oh, well that wasn't too bad. Who didn't sing in the shower?

"Did she tell you that I can't carry a tune?" I asked.

"She may have mentioned that."

"Betrayed by my own family," I said, shaking my fist at the ceiling.

I leaned back on the edge of the tub and Jax turned the jets on.

"Oh yeah, that's it," I said, closing my eyes.

"I love watching you enjoy things," Jax said in a soft voice. I opened my eyes and found her watching me.

"I'm happy I can be of service," I said, but it was not lost on me that she'd used that four-letter word. The one that began with the letter L. No, she hadn't said she loved me, but she'd said she loved something about me and that was freaking me out.

I hadn't had enough time to process my own changing and overwhelming feelings about her, and this on top of it was making me panic a little.

"Are you okay?" she asked.

"Yeah," I said, trying to make my face look relaxed.

"Okay," she said, as if she didn't believe me.

I grabbed some cheese and shoved it in my face, hoping she'd get distracted.

Then I heard my phone ringing. I'd set it on the counter in the bathroom, just in case.

I got out of the tub and wrapped myself a towel and saw it was my sister before I picked up.

"Hey," I said.

"Hey, sorry to interrupt your date, but Luna started running a fever last night and now she's coughing up a storm, so we're heading to the Urgent Care. I have no idea how I got an appointment, but they can squeeze us in. I just wanted you to know in case you came home and we weren't there."

"Is she okay? Do you need me to come with you?" I asked.

"No, no, she's fine. Just feeling yucky." I heard Luna coughing in the background. Poor baby.

"Do you need me to pick up anything for you?" I asked and Lizzie listed a few things.

"Okay, I'll stop on my way back."

"You don't have to hurry, seriously."

"Give her a kiss for me and tell her that we'll watch whatever movies she wants when I get back."

"I will," Lizzie said, and I hung up, making sure that I immediately made a list so I didn't forget anything.

"Everything okay?" Jax asked, leaning over the tub.

"Yeah, just a sick niece. Lizzie is taking her to the doctor. I hope it's not strep." Please, just a garden variety cold.

"Oh, poor kid. It's fine if you need to go," she said.

"I don't know how long the doctor is going to take, but I need to stop and get some supplies, so…" I trailed off.

What an abrupt end to our date.

Jax stood up, and I was momentarily distracted from my sick niece by the water and bubbles sliding down her incredible body.

"You don't have to get out," I said.

"It's fine," she said, pulling the stopper on the tub.

I handed her a robe and went to put my clothes back on.

"Sorry everything got cut short, but I had an amazing time with you," I said as she walked me downstairs.

"If you have some time next week, let me know. I can always meet you somewhere," Jax said. "And tell Luna that I hope she feels better."

"How would you know she was sick?" I pointed out.

She frowned. "Right. Well, then you tell her for me, but you don't have to say it's me."

All of this secret relationship stuff was starting to wear on me.

"I'll give you updates," I said, kissing her softly.

There was never enough time with her. The hours just melted away and then I had to go back to my mundane life that felt so separate from our time together.

"Bye, Sasha," she said, and it was so hard to walk to my car and drive away.

LUNA DIDN'T HAVE STREP, thank goodness, but she had a nasty cold and required lots of fluids and popsicles and cuddles on the couch.

"I didn't mean to invade your date," Lizzie said.

"You didn't. It's fine. Family comes first," I said, wiping Luna's sweaty forehead. She was laying across both of our laps on the couch.

"Are you ever going to tell me who you're dating? It seems like you're getting serious. You talk to her all the time, and I can see how you feel about her."

How could she? She'd never seen me with Jax.

"It's just a casual thing," I said, lying through my teeth. It wasn't. It absolutely wasn't, at least on my side.

"And she hasn't brought up being more either. This works for both of us," I said, packing on another lie. Leaving Jax today had given me clarity for the first time: I wanted to see her. All the time. I wanted more than weekends. I wanted weeknights and weekday mornings when we woke up and I made her late for work. I wanted to be the person she talked to when she'd had a bad day. I wanted my shoulder to be the pillow she laid on when she cried. I wanted to see her face light up when she decorated for Christmas. I wanted to meet her parents and make awkward conversation with them. I wanted to attempt to make her breakfast and fail but have her laugh and say she appreciated the effort.

I wanted to fight with her and fuck her and everything in between.

"You look like you're having all the emotions at once," Lizzie said.

"I think I am," I said, my voice sounding distant to my own ears.

"Are you having an epiphany?" she asked.

"Just a little bit," I said, staring at the wall. "What the fuck do I do now?"

"Hey, be careful with the cursing."

I checked to make sure Luna was still passed out and snoring softly in my lap.

"She didn't hear me," I said.

"Do you want to talk to me about it?" Lizzie asked.

"I think I just need to…sit with it. I'll let you know."

"I'm here for you, Sash," she said.

"I know," I said.

Holy shit.

I was absolutely, completely, and wildly in love with Jax Hardy.

What the FUCK.

AS SOON AS Lizzie and I got Luna to bed, I called Hollis.

"Whoa, you okay?" I realized that she was in bed and she was naked.

"Uh, are you in the middle of something?" I asked.

"No, she just left, we're good."

I took a breath and then said the words out loud.

"I think I might have fallen in love. A little bit."

"I don't think you can fall in love a little bit, babe," Hollis said, sitting up, the blanket slipping and revealing one of her boobs. She didn't notice or care. I mean, I didn't either. I'd seen Hollis's boobs plenty of times in a friendship context.

"Okay, fine, I think I've fallen in love a lot," I said.

"I'm guessing this is with the teacher?" she asked.

"Yup. I just… I don't know how it happened. One minute I was looking at her and the next I was picturing her in matching Christmas jammies with my family. I was keeping things casual!"

Hollis tried not to laugh.

"I'm so sorry. It's not funny. But it's a little funny. You know the second you try to put a lid on feelings, that's when your feelings sense your weakness."

That was how it felt. I hadn't fallen in love. I'd been ambushed by it.

"How do you not fall in love?" I asked.

"I don't know. Maybe my love bone is broken," she joked.

"I know you've been in love before," I said.

"Yeah, we're not talking about me. We're talking about you." If there was one thing Hollis didn't like talking about, it was that one time she'd fallen in love and gotten burned.

"What the hell am I supposed to do now?" I asked.

"You have two options: tell her or don't tell her. Both have implications. How does she feel about you?"

"I don't know because we never talk about that shit. Both of us do our best to stay away from most serious stuff." She had literally just started giving me a few sparse details about her family. How could she be serious with me if she didn't even want me to know about her family situation.

"So, I don't think she's that deep with me. I don't know," I said. "This is awful."

"Love usually is," Hollis said.

I TALKED to Hollis for another hour, and didn't really figure anything out, but she did tell me about how flexible her latest hookup was, and I got more details than I wanted to know.

I always felt better after I talked with Hollis, but then when I was alone with my thoughts after hanging up, all of the emotions came roaring back at once.

Was it possible to overdose on emotions? I felt like I was close.

Hollis was right about one thing: I could tell Jax, or I could decide to not tell her.

If I told her, then she might say that she didn't feel the same way and I'd end up rejected. Or I could not tell her and see what happened and maybe get some more clarity about how she felt. I didn't need to tell her right now. I could wait and see. Waiting and seeing seemed like the best course of action. Many times in my life, I'd fucked up by making rash decisions. That changed now. I was going to be sensible. To be calm. I was going to be mature about this.

Chapter Seventeen

"Being mature" involved a lot of looking through my old messages with Jax and trying to figure out how she felt about me. Extremely time-consuming and frustrating. It also didn't yield any definitive answers. Jax and I continued to text back and forth, and I was doing my best not to spew my feelings all over her. I didn't want her to figure me out before I had a chance to figure her out.

You want to come over for dinner? She asked on Tuesday, and I said that I couldn't, because Lizzie had taken a shift at the Grille and I had to stay with a sick Luna. Lizzie tried not to work nights, but with school coming up, she was taking as many shifts as she could. She'd gotten an email this week that she'd been accepted into a program that started in January, so she was banking as much cash as she could before then. Fortunately, her student loan package was generous, so she was going to be able to make it happen, but it was still going to be tight.

How about Friday night? She tried again.

I said I was free, and that we could just hang out at her house, if that was cool with her.

She said it was, and I intended to spend the entire date playing Sherlock Holmes.

IT WAS nice that I didn't have to have an elaborate outfit on hand for this date, but I still wanted to look nice, so I ended up pulling out these wide-leg pants that I'd found at a vintage shop on a trip with Hollis, and a ribbed turtleneck. It made me feel like I was going to an opening at an art gallery or something.

When I got to Jax's house, there were pumpkins on the porch and an autumn wreath on the door. Guess she'd been busy this week.

"Hello," she said with a huge smile as she opened the door. A waft of cinnamon and apple-scented air also greeted me.

She wore white turtleneck and a plaid wool skirt, and we almost, almost, looked like we belonged together.

"Turtleneck twins," she said, pointing to my shirt.

"Great minds," I said as I dropped my bag.

"Wow, it looks beautiful in here," I said. The hall table had glass pumpkins and fake leaves scattered on it, and there were additional pumpkins arranged on the floor, but I assumed those were fake.

"I told you I liked to decorate for the holidays. This is nothing compared to what my mother has going on."

I almost asked her if I could see pictures, but I didn't.

Jax walked back through the house and toward the kitchen, just as the chime on her oven went off.

"I made a galette," she said, as if I knew what that meant. "I went and got some more apples and had to figure out what to do with them." She laughed and I noticed the enormous bowl on the counter that was usually filled with various decor now was filled with all kinds of apples.

"My goal tomorrow is to make a big batch of applesauce," she said.

"Is there anything you can't do?" I asked, leaning against the counter as she pulled the galette out of the oven and set it on a rack to cool.

"I can't parallel park," she said.

"Who cares, neither can I," I said with a laugh as she pulled off her oven mitts.

"Isn't that kind of a queer cliché anyway?" she asked as she came over to me and pulled me closer, calling out to her house robot to put on a song.

"I've been thinking about you all week," she said as we softly swayed back and forth.

Thinking about me all week was a good sign. I spent very few moments not thinking about her.

"You did now?" I teased.

"Mmm, yes." Her hands drifted from my hips to grab my ass. Okay, so she'd been thinking about sex with me, which was different. I couldn't separate sex from love, but was Jax that kind of person? I needed to find out.

"What in particular have you been thinking about?" I asked.

She nipped at my earlobe and shivers went down my spine.

"Well, I've been thinking about this," she said, squeezing my ass again. "And this." She kissed my neck, and then slid one hand between us to cup me. "And this."

Things were leaning in a lusty direction.

"And this." She kissed the tip of my nose. "You've got an adorable nose." That was sweeter, more something you'd say about someone you loved.

"And your eyes. I was thinking a lot about your eyes." That was definitely another one for the love column.

I crossed said eyes and made her laugh and then she kissed me again. It was all soft and warm, and she tasted like apples. She must have eaten one while she was making the galette.

"You hungry?" she asked.

"Yeah," I said, stepping away from her.

"I've got vanilla bean ice cream," she said as she got out some plates.

I got the silverware out of the drawer and she handed me a disposable napkin that had a silver leaf embossed on it.

"This is a little bit extra," I said, holding up the napkin.

"I'm a little bit extra, sometimes," she said, cutting me a piece and putting the ice cream on the side.

We ate together in the den. The pie was still hot, so it was a race to get it all eaten before the ice cream melted.

"What else have you done this week?" I asked.

"Besides trainings and trying to get ahead on lesson plans, obviously I decorated, and read, and finally got caught up on some TV shows."

"That sounds perfect," I said. I'd love a week of watching TV and reading books and eating baked goods. I wouldn't want to make them, except if they were from a box. It was so much easier to call Linley or Charli and have them set something from the bakery aside for me.

"One of these days I'm going to have to bring you stuff from Sweet's. Not that your baking isn't good, because it is," I said. This apple tart thing was completely delicious.

"I'm not insulted. I know I'm not a professional baker. It's just a hobby for me, I definitely wouldn't enjoy doing it as a job." Phew, I knew all about that. People assumed a lot that my job involved reading books for money, and yes, I did get to read sometimes, but it wasn't like I could read for enjoyment and that was it. There was a lot of work involved.

"My friend, Em, turned her hobby into her business and she still loves it, but she said she's under so much more pressure now."

"What kind of business?" I told her about Low Tide Creations, and how Natalie helped her, and about Sweet's, and how Alivia and Charli had hooked up. I told her all about my friends and how Paige and I worked together at the café, and how stressful freelancing was. I unloaded on her and she sat there and listened.

I didn't mean to do it. I absolutely meant to hold all of that back, and then my mouth had other ideas.

I was showing her my heart. Pulling back the layers and exposing soft parts. I should have canceled this date.

"Teaching wasn't my first choice," she said, when I'd finished blathering.

"What was your first choice?" I asked.

"English," she said.

"Oh, that makes sense. Did you want to be a writer?" I asked.

"I thought about it," she said. "The plan was to get my degree in English and then an MFA."

Wow, intense.

"Why didn't you?" I asked.

She looked down at her empty plate. "Just changed my mind. Want some tea?"

As it had so many times before, tea led straight to sex. My plan to pull back had completely blown up in my face.

There was no resisting Jax Hardy and her overwhelming charm. Plus, you know, there was the fact that I was desperately in love with her and trying to hide it.

"How about I make you dinner?" I said as we lay next to each other on top of the sex towels on her bed.

"I'd love that," she said. There was that word again.

I got up and, instead of putting my date clothes on again, I put on one of Jax's robes.

"I'm about to blow your mind," I said as she got up and did the same.

"I'm ready," she said, nodding.

∼

WHEN I GOT to the kitchen and started looking through her fridge and pantry, I was starting to feel like I might have overestimated my own cooking abilities. I was used to making pizza for my niece.

Jax watched me as she leaned on the counter, and I could tell she was enjoying herself.

I found some sourdough in the bread box, and a bunch of fancy cheese in the fridge. She also had some cans of crushed tomatoes, fresh tomatoes, heavy cream, garlic, and other spices. She even had fresh herbs in the fridge. I never bought fresh herbs because I could never remember use them before they went bad.

"Okay, I've got this," I said, piling the ingredients on the kitchen island. "Is it okay if I make a mess?"

"Be my guest," she said, and pulled an apron out of a drawer and held it out to me.

I put it on over my robe.

"This is a strange outfit, but I'm going with it," I said.

Jax's knives were much nicer and sharper than the ones I had to work with at home, and I was actually having a good time watching them slide effortlessly through the tomatoes. Jax started some music and kept watching.

"Are you silently critiquing my tomato-cutting in your head?" I asked, keeping my focus on the tomatoes so I didn't slice off my finger. That wouldn't be very romantic.

"No, you're doing a fine job."

"Fine?"

Jax laughed. "I'm not as much of a control freak as you think I am."

But then she came over to me and adjusted my fingers so they were curled around the tomato.

"So you don't cut your fingers," she said.

"Control freak," I whispered.

I THREW ALL the tomatoes in a pot with onions and garlic and basil and salt and pepper and chicken broth. As that was doing its thing and cooking down, I prepped the sandwiches.

"You know, I have a portable grill, if you want to use it," she said. Of course she did. She had everything.

"No way. We're doing this in the pan like commoners," I said with a laugh, but the joke didn't seem to land with Jax.

"That wasn't a very nice thing to say," she said, and the mood instantly shifted from playful to awkward.

"Shit, I'm sorry. I didn't mean it like that."

"This isn't going to work if you keep making little digs like that," she said.

"I'm sorry. I didn't mean it," I said, putting the knife down I'd been using to slice the cheese.

"I know, but on some level you did. Sasha, I don't know." Great. I'd absolutely blown everything up with one comment. Guess that meant she didn't love me, and this was definitely a more casual thing for her.

"I should go," I said, taking the apron off, and then slipping the robe off too. That was my answer. She didn't want this. She didn't want me. It was fine. I'd deal with the fallout later. Right now, I just needed to leave.

I walked, naked, upstairs, put my clothes on and came back down to grab my bag.

"Sasha…" she said, trailing off, but then she didn't say anything else. If she loved me, she would be fighting. If she loved me, we would be sitting down and having a conversation. Instead, I got silence. That was the answer.

"I had a really good time," I said, choking down the tears. I had to hold them off until I got in the car. I needed to get home.

She opened her mouth, but then closed it.

"Okay," she said, and that was the last word I heard before I opened the door and stumbled to my car.

I managed to shut the car door before the tears flooded down my cheeks.

IT WAS a miracle I could see well enough through my tears to get home in one piece.

I was still sobbing as I walked through the door.

"What's wrong?" Lizzie said, coming to me immediately as my legs gave out and I crumpled into a heap right next to the couch.

"Sashie, Sashie!" Luna said, trying to pull my hair back and see my face.

"What happened?" Lizzie said, and I looked up into her frantic eyes.

"It's over," I got out before I started sobbing again.

"Sweetie, can you go get Auntie Sasha some tissues?"

I heard Luna's little feet running down the hall to the bathroom and she came back and shoved a box of tissues in my face.

"Can you go get her a glass of water too? Just be careful."

Since Luna was five, she tried to be careful, but ended up slopping water all over the floor.

I tried to say thank you, but the words wouldn't come out.

"She's okay, baby, she's just really sad. You know how you

get really sad?" Great, now my niece was crying because I was crying. This was the shittiest day.

"I'm okay," I managed to get out as Lizzie picked me up and got me onto the couch. I wasn't okay, but I didn't want my niece to be scared.

"It's okay," Lizzie said, holding me and rubbing my back. "It's going to be okay."

I didn't think that it was, honestly.

MY TEARS LASTED for what felt like forever. I didn't know where I got them all, but I kept managing to find more to pour out.

Luna stopped crying and started petting my head and murmuring "it's okay, it's okay" like Lizzie until I finally started to come out of it.

There was snot everywhere and my cheeks were salty. My eyes had puffed up so much that I felt like I was squinting through them.

"Do you want to talk about it?" Lizzie asked.

"No," I said.

"Can you at least let me know that she didn't hurt you?" She had, but not in the way Lizzie was asking.

"We had a fight, and I left. It wasn't even a fight. She didn't want to fight. She just gave up and I knew she didn't feel the same way. So I left." I'd said I didn't want to talk about it, but here I was.

"What did you fight about?" Lizzie asked.

"She has money. And I made a joke about it and I knew that was a sensitive thing for her, but I wasn't thinking. I apologized, but she just said she was done. So here I am."

Lizzie shook her head.

"That's so shitty, I'm sorry."

"Swear jar!" Luna yelled.

"Yes, I'll put money in the swear jar, baby," Lizzie said, and turned her attention back to me.

"You're going to get through this," she said. "You're gonna cry, and you're going to feel awful, and I'm going to make sure you eat, and then one day it's going to hurt a little less, and a little less, and you'll just keep going, okay? I'm here for you."

She hugged me tight and I tried not to get snot all over her shirt.

I went to the bathroom and washed my face with cold water and tried not to look at how wrecked I was in the mirror. I blew my nose and took a deep breath before walking out again and finding Lizzie pulling a frozen pizza out of the freezer.

"Right now, we need melted cheese and ice cream," Lizzie said.

"Yay!" Luna said, cheering and then running to hug my legs.

"You okay, Sashie?" she asked, looking up at me.

"I'm sad right now," I said. "And I might be sad for a little while."

"I get sad too," she said, nodding. "It's okay to be sad."

"That's right," Lizzie said, shoving the pizza in the oven. "Your phone has been going off."

Shit.

I pulled it out of my bag and found a text from Jax.

I'm sorry it ended this way was all she said.

Fine. It was ended. Over, done, finished. It had only been a casual thing for her, which was fair. That had been the expectation when we first started. I was the one who had to go and mess it up by falling in love with her even though she didn't love me back. And really, what shot did I have any way? Jax could have anyone she wanted. I'd been a fling. A blip. A moment in time. Fun for a little while.

I deleted the message.

~

I ALSO UNFOLLOWED her social pages the next day, and deleted any pictures I had of us, even the ones we'd taken on the mountain. First part of getting her out of my heart was getting her out of my phone.

I stayed on the couch on Sunday with Luna, who had taken it upon herself to try and nurse me. She kept "checking my heart" with a plastic stethoscope.

"My heart is a little broken, Luna Moon," I said.

She listened intently with the plastic ear pieces.

"Yes, I can hear it," she said.

I bet she could.

~

THE NEXT WEEK WAS AWFUL. Truly awful. I had work deadlines, but it was a monumental task to get up the energy to do any of them. I told Paige that I had caught Luna's cold so I couldn't work at the café. I stayed in the house, not even going outside.

The week after that, Lizzie forced me to go outside with Luna and take a short walk. I couldn't use the cold excuse anymore, so I returned to my work dates with Paige, and I told her I'd broken up with the girl I'd been seeing, and no, I didn't want to talk about it. She absolutely respected that, even though I could tell she was itching to ask more questions. She made me go to the Grille and get a free drink from Esme at the bar and watch drunk karaoke. Esme didn't try to give me advice, so I assumed Paige told her I didn't want it. I appreciated that as well.

Halloween came and I went out with Luna, and it did lift

my mood a little bit, as did the Castleton Fall Festival. I tried to eat enough apple cider cookies to drown my sorrows, but it didn't work.

I heard nothing from Jax.

Then a third week passed. I still woke up crying every day, but I was getting better at hiding it.

Hollis had been amazing the whole time, even though she was absolutely allergic to love. She let me cry through our chats and sent me funny things to try and make me laugh.

My friends were so good, and their support, coupled with the fact that Lizzie had two years of school ahead of her and needed my help, cemented the decision that I was staying in Castleton, at least for now. Plus, I knew I wasn't going to bump into Jax. I never had to see her again, as long as I could avoid her whenever I picked Luna up from school.

I'd made a clean break, or at least I thought.

Chapter Eighteen

EM AND NATALIE finally moved into their house and had a housewarming before Christmas. I was thrilled for them and ended up buying them a knife set like the one Jax had. I mean, not a full set because I wasn't made of money. I still saw her everywhere. I saw her in the sunsets and whenever I chopped anything. I saw her in movies and songs and moments. She was gone, but she was everywhere. I just wanted it to stop. I just wanted to get through one entire minute without thinking about her. Maybe next year.

I showed up late to the housewarming and I didn't really care anymore. My friends expected me to be late. They knew who I was.

There I was trying to make small talk with various people, and then she walked in. The air left the room, and I had to clutch the wall so I didn't fall over.

There she was, with another teacher I recognized from school that was friends with Natalie. She must have come as a plus one.

Seeing her again brought everything back, all at once. Every smile. Every kiss. Every laugh.

She was just so fucking beautiful and she didn't want me anymore and I could never be in her orbit again. She wasn't mine, and she never had been.

I walked over to where Charli and Alivia stood, trying to get my bearings. The room was so crammed with people, but I knew she knew I was here without looking directly at me.

"Who's that?" Charli asked Alivia.

"I don't know. She looks kind of familiar, but I don't know where from."

"Jax," I said before I could think better of speaking.

"Sorry?" Charli said.

"Jax. Her name is Jaqueline." Saying her name was like being stabbed in the chest, and I was trying not to cry again.

"Oh, you know her?" Charli asked as I stared at my plate.

"Never mind," I said. "I'm going to get a drink." I hurried away to hide in the kitchen.

I made myself scarce for a little while longer and literally snuck out the back door to leave.

I almost expected her to run after me and call out my name, but she didn't.

What we had was dead and buried.

FROM THEN ON I just kind of walked around with a destroyed heart in my chest, and I spent my nights crying and berating myself for ever getting involved with her in the first place. It could only end badly between us and I'd been fooling myself the whole time thinking I could get out with an intact heart.

I never said I made the best decisions, but that was one of my worst.

I filled my time in between tears and telling myself how much of an idiot I was with work. I took on another client and threw myself completely into my business with an intensity that bordered on manic. It wasn't healthy, and I knew it.

Lizzie finally sat down with me just before Christmas.

"You've got to ease up on work," she said, taking one of my hands that was shaking due to overconsumption of caffeine. I hadn't been sleeping much in weeks, so I'd been drinking twice as much coffee as I usually did, and it was taking a toll.

"I'm really, really worried about you," she said.

"I know," I said. "But I'm going to be fine." I didn't have a ballpark of when that would happen, but I hoped it would be soon. That I'd wake up with optimism instead of dread.

"You really loved her, didn't you?" she said.

"Yeah, I really did." Do. Present tense. Because even after everything that had gone down, I was still in love with Jax, broken heart or not.

"You took care of me when everything happened with *him*," Lizzie said, not using Skippy's name. She didn't like to talk about him around Luna. "So, I'm going to take care of you. Whatever you need."

"You've been taking care of me," I said. She really had been. It was like we'd reversed roles or something. Lizzie's phone sounded with an incoming text message.

"Oh, Anna wants to do a play date," she said. She'd finally reached out to Anna and they'd struck up a friendship in the past few weeks. I was thrilled for Lizzie, and happy for Luna that she and Jackson got to see each other outside of school. We'd had him here at the house and he was just such a sweetheart, and the politest kid I'd met in my life.

"You need more ice cream?" Lizzie asked, responding to the message and then getting up.

"No, I'm good."

We were lounging on the couch, as we always did. I really needed to get another hobby that actually got me out of the house. I was beginning to be one with the couch. Soon we would combine to be one entity. I shut my laptop and rubbed my eyes. What I needed was a soak in the bathtub.

"I'm going to take a bath," I said.

"Enjoy," Lizzie said, corralling Luna so she didn't race in after me and try to hop in with me.

Lizzie's tub was clean, but it didn't have any jets, or candles, and it didn't have Jax.

I tossed in a bath bomb and watched it fizz while the tub filled the rest of the way.

I put on my sad breakup playlist that I'd had on a loop for weeks and sunk into the water, laying back and trying to ease the tension in my body.

Now that I was staying in Castleton, I could make plans. I could figure out what my next steps were. I'd thought about getting my own place, but I wasn't sure. As much as I'd like some privacy, I also loved Luna bouncing into my room and waking me up to make pancakes and watch cartoons on Saturday mornings.

I liked having Lizzie here to talk about work stuff or friend stuff or life stuff. I was afraid if I lived alone I'd just shut the blinds and never go out again and get completely lost in work. If I was living unhealthily now, living alone would make things so much worse. I'd have no one to keep me on track.

The caffeine was still coursing through my system. I should have splurged on that expensive CBD bath bomb I saw online. That would help me chill out.

My relaxing bath was cut short by Luna coming in to pee twice, and then Lizzie calling me for dinner.

So much for that.

I PUT on a happy face for Christmas, and I did have a good time with Lizzie and Luna. We wore our matching pajamas, and I set up my phone to take group pictures and Luna got exactly everything she asked for, and more. Her screams as she unwrapped the life-size skeleton she'd been begging for warmed my heart, even if they hurt my eardrums. We had a huge brunch with pastries we'd ordered ahead from Sweet's, and I make a huge batch of crockpot hot cocoa that we drowned in marshmallows.

Luna ran around while she was hopped up on sugar and her new toys singing Christmas carols at the top of her lungs. Lizzie ended up putting in ear plugs just to get some quiet as we both cleaned up the carnage of wrapping paper and gift bags and bows.

I had lots of messages from my friends wishing me a Merry Christmas, and in a few days, we were having our final Non Book Club meeting in which we would be traveling a few hours away to Jack Hill's house, just to see it. That would also be our own sort of post-Christmas, final party of the year before December 31st, when there was a New Year's Party at Em and Natalie's place, since it was the biggest. No, I didn't have anyone to kiss at midnight, but did that matter? I'd had plenty of good years without a midnight kiss. Still, it would have been nice to have that this year.

Why did everything make me sad? Why did everything remind me of her? It was probably just the holiday season. Made you think about the people you cared about.

Jax had probably moved on. Found someone in that bar to kiss and hook up with. Someone new to show her sex toy collection, and to make post-coital breakfasts for.

Hollis called me on Christmas Evening when Luna had finally crashed and fallen asleep in a puddle of new stuffed animals on the floor under the tree. I put a blanket on her and made sure she was still breathing.

"Hey, Merry Christmas," I said.

"Yeah, yeah, Merry Christmas to you too. Guess what," she said, unusually brusque.

"What?"

"So, remember I told you I had a great-aunt who died last year and had a house in Castleton?" I vaguely remembered the mention.

"Yeah, why?"

"Well, her will finally made it through probate, and it turns out my mom is getting the house. It's a complete dump, but since she retired, she's looking for a project, so she's moving. And, my sister just happened to get a job at a preschool in Castleton, so she's moving too. Can you believe that?" I honestly couldn't. What were the chances? How small was this planet?

"Wow. Which house is it?" I asked, pulling out my laptop.

"It's on Bluebird Lane," she told me, and I looked up the street view.

"Oh, yeah, that is a dump."

The house had probably been beautiful once. It was a lovely farmhouse with a pretty red barn just behind the house, but the paint was peeling, and weeds had overtaken the lawn and even creeped up to cover the porch. There was a rusted-out station wagon parked on what I assumed was the driveway. A mess. It was a complete mess.

"That's going to be a huge project. Is your mom up for that?" Hollis's mom was just as intense as her daughter. When Amanda Carr put her mind to something, those things ended up happening.

"She's already been in touch with an appraiser and a contractor and I wouldn't be surprised if it gets done in like, a month." I laughed.

"Wow, so that means I can visit with her. That's nice." Hollis's mom and sister didn't live that far away, and I'd gone and had tea with them a few times since I'd come here, but I definitely needed to see them more often. I loved her mom, and her sister was a total sweetheart. Whereas Hollis got all her mother's sass, Ellie had gotten all the gentle softness.

"And you can check on them and make sure they're not lying to me about how bad the house is. I'm going to come up and see it, but I'll need you to be my spy when I'm not there."

"You got it," I said, saluting her. "I miss you."

"I miss you too. But I'm literally going to see you tomorrow. And I'm going to give you the biggest hug."

Since Hollis was at her mom's house just an hour north of Castleton, it only made sense to see her while we were both in the same state. Plus, I'd get to eat all the Norwegian butter cookies and drink eggnog that was so thick you could eat it with a spoon.

Lizzie was coming with me, and no doubt Luna would get even more presents from Amanda and Ellie.

The holidays were a marathon, not a sprint.

SEEING Hollis again was so great, and I melted into her hug.

"I like this," I said, touching the fresh undercut on one side of her head, just above her ear. She'd left the rest of her dark hair long, and she looked so cool I couldn't stand it.

Amanda shoved a cup of eggnog in my hand and gave me a hug so tight that I couldn't breathe. Luna bounced around and chattered to Ellie.

"Did you ask them not to talk about anything?" I asked Hollis.

"Don't worry," she said, threading her arm through mine and drawing me through the warm house and toward the fire roaring in the stove.

"Thanks," I said, resting my head on her shoulder. "You're the best friend."

"I don't know about that, but I try."

The afternoon was spent with laughter and plenty of food and drinks and warm conversation. No one mentioned my breakup or asked me about my broken heart. It was such a relief, and I almost forgot about it. Almost.

Thinking about Jax never went completely away.

"You have a good time?" Lizzie asked as we drove back home with a sleeping Luna and a massive box of cookies in the backseat.

"Yeah, I did. It was nice to sort of stop thinking about stuff for a while."

"What kind of stuff?" Lizzie asked.

"You know what stuff," I said.

"But it seems like you're doing better?" Lizzie asked, fishing.

"Yeah, definitely," I said, lying. I'd cut my daily crying time down by a few minutes, so that was progress, right? I wasn't completely devastated every time I saw something that reminded me of Jax. Now I could hold it in long enough to wait until I was alone to completely fall apart. If that was better, then I was doing better.

"ARE WE READY FOR THIS?" Paige asked as we gathered at Em and Natalie's to make the drive to Jack Hill's house. Charli had wanted us all to wear coordinating shirts, but no one else wanted to, so we'd all just put on our regular clothes. We did have snacks, though. And we'd all bought physical copies of the book and pens for him to sign them, just in case.

"We're not going to get arrested, are we?" Linley asked as we all loaded up the cars.

"It's not a crime to stand on a public sidewalk, which is

where we will be outside his house. Plus, people do this all the time, I guarantee you," Esme said.

Alivia was driving her SUV since it had the best seating, and Gray was driving the other car. I'd elected to go with Alivia, along with Charli, Em, and Natalie. We had a planned pit stop about halfway there, but I was already breaking into the box of snacks that Paige had put together, with Linley's help.

"This is exciting. What if he's there?" Charli said.

"He's not going to let a bunch of random people in his house," Em said.

"Definitely not," I said. "But we can take pictures."

That led to a discussion of other random celebrity encounters, which took us most of the way to the pit stop, which was a diner that Jack Hill had mentioned in the book we'd read.

"Wow, it looks exactly like he described," Alivia said when we walked in. There was all kinds of Jack Hill memorabilia around, even signed books you could buy at the counter next to a basket of fresh-baked muffins.

A signed picture of Jack Hill hung on the wall just above the cash register.

"He really does look familiar. I know I've seen him before," I said as a waitress led us to a large table that would fit all of us.

The diner specialized in huge sandwiches, everything fried, and slabs of cake the size of your head.

I ordered the fried chicken with curly fries and a vanilla milkshake.

"Jack Hill fans?" The waitress asked as she delivered our food.

"Do we look like fans?" I asked her.

"Yes," she said. "We get all kinds of people in here because of his book. Real nice of him to include us." Yeah, it was. Jack Hill had also highlighted other Maine businesses and there was even a Jack Hill Tour you could do, hitting all of them in one day.

I couldn't stop thinking about Jax and how much she'd like this. How she would have gotten the double chocolate shake and devoured the sticky chocolate cake that was so big, you had to share it.

"Everything okay?" Paige asked, touching my arm.

"Yeah," I said. "Just thinking about things."

She squeezed my arm.

"It'll get better. I promise."

That's what everyone said. I was still waiting to believe them.

WE ARRIVED outside of Jack Hill's house in the early afternoon. The sun shone off the freshly fallen snow.

"Oh, shit," Em said as we got out of the car. We'd parked in the lot of a convenience store down the street, but the house was easy to spot. Tall and imposing, it looked like a gothic Victorian dream. Luna would absolutely lose her mind. Surrounding the house on all sides was a black wrought-iron fence that was topped with flying bats. Of course.

"This is so cool," Paige said as we crossed the street and slowly approached the house.

The gates were closed, of course, but there were three cars parked in front of the garage.

"Look at this," Linley said, walking over to a metal plaque that was affixed to part of the fence.

Yes, this is the home of award-winning writer, Jack Hill. Feel free to take pictures outside of the fence. All trespassers will be prosecuted (or disemboweled).

"Huh, funny," I said. There was also a sign from the security company that said his home was protected by their business.

"Cameras," Gray pointed out. I didn't know how he'd seen them, but yup, those were definitely security cameras.

"Should we wave?" Charli asked, and then looked up toward one and beamed as she waved.

"Hello, Jack Hill!"

"Pinky, I don't think he can hear you," Alivia said with a smile as she put her arms around Charli and kissed her cotton-candy pink hair.

"You never know," Charli said.

"Okay, well, he might be home, but he's definitely not coming out. Should we take some pictures?" Esme said, and then we all spent way too long taking hilarious selfies pretending to try and break through the gate.

"Wait, someone's coming out," Natalie said, and the front door opened.

"Hide!" someone yelled, and we all tried to find somewhere to crouch behind. The house was situated on the corner of a street, so most of us went to the street side and ducked down behind some bushes. Someone on the sidewalk could clearly see us, but anyone coming from the house couldn't.

"We're going to get in trouble," Linley said, worrying.

"We'll be fine," Gray said, rubbing her shoulders.

We all waited for a car to leave the driveway or something else, but what I did hear was someone walking down the gravel driveway. Step, by step. The crunching just added to the ominous feel of the whole situation.

"Jack Hill is coming to murder us," Natalie whispered, and Em shushed her while trying not to laugh.

From the outside, we probably looked like complete weirdos, hiding on a public street.

The footsteps grew closer and closer and my heart started beating louder and louder.

"They're going to see us," Linley hissed.

"Then we say hello, we love your books," Paige whispered back.

There was a metallic sound and then the gate started to open. Guess it was on a motor.

"It's happening," Paige said. "Oh my god, it's happening."

And then I heard the last voice in the world I thought I would hear.

"Sasha? Is that you?"

Chapter Nineteen

I FELL RIGHT over from my crouched position and onto the cold and icy sidewalk. Fortunately, I had a thick coat and gloves on, and I didn't have far to go, so I didn't do too much damage. Plus, there were several sets of hands to pull me up and ask if I was okay.

"Sasha?" Everyone was staring at me

"What do I do?" I asked, and then Jax walked around the corner and I almost fell over again.

"What the fuck are you doing here?!" I blurted out. What was happening?

"I saw you on the security camera," she said, as if that answered my question.

"Why were you in Jack Hill's house?" I asked.

She inhaled once before she answered. "Because he's my dad."

"Jack Hill is your *dad*?" The words just didn't make sense.

"Yeah, he's my dad. I'm here visiting."

I blinked a few times, trying to process.

"Jack Hill is your dad, and you didn't tell me."

"No, I didn't. People get weird when they find out who my

dad is. I liked being without all of *this*." She motioned to the fence and the house.

I stood full upright and realized that my friends had retreated down the street to give us some privacy, even though they must have been even more confused than I was.

I took a step toward Jax.

"Jack Hill is your dad," I said again.

"Jack Hill is a pen name," she said. "His real name is James Hardy."

Oh. That answered my first question.

"Are you still mad at me?" was my second question.

"No," she said. "I'm so sorry for overreacting. I just… I was feeling shitty about lying to you and I took that out on you." She hadn't put a coat on and was shivering. I pulled mine off and offered it to her.

"No, I'm fine," she said.

Seeing her again made me want to cry, to kiss her, to yell at her for breaking my heart, all at the same time.

"Well, I'm not fine. I'm really shitty, actually," I said, folding my coat over my arm instead of putting it on. If she was going to be cold, then I was going to be cold.

"Me too," she said. "These past weeks have been horrible. I kept trying to figure out how to reach out to you, but I didn't know if you wanted me to. I didn't want to hurt you further, so I just… didn't."

"I wanted you to. I was waiting for it," I said. I would have jumped the second she sent me a message. "Things ended so abruptly, and I figured you just didn't feel the same way, so you wanted a clean break."

She shook her head. "I didn't want things to end."

"Well, I didn't want them to end either. I'm staying in Castleton, by the way. My sister has two years of school, and my niece needs me. I'm not going back to Boston. At least not for a long time."

"Oh," she said, the word just an exhale.

Silence fell between us.

"I got you a Christmas present," she blurted out uncharacteristically.

"You did?" I asked.

"Do you want it?" she asked.

"Yes," I said.

"It's in the house," she said, looking toward the imposing figure. "Your friends are probably freezing. Why don't you come inside and we can talk?"

I looked toward my friends and motioned for them to come over. They were all huddled together, their breath steaming in the air.

"Hi, everyone," Jax said, waving. "I'm Jax. Jack Hill is my dad and he'd love to meet some fans, if you want to come inside?"

Every single one of them looked shocked.

"So, you two…" Em said, pointing to Jax and then to me.

"Is this your mystery woman?" Paige asked.

"Uh, yeah," I said and Jax nodded.

"Well, this is an interesting turn of events," Gray said. What an understatement.

Jax led all of us up the driveway and into the house, which was so warm that I almost sighed in relief. The foyer smelled like warm mulled wine. Just like I thought it would. Soft piano music piped throughout the house and I was having a little bit of déjà vu.

"Just give me a second to explain," Jax said, touching my arm and then walking from the massive foyer and down the hall. My friends admired the staircase and the fully bedecked Christmas tree that had to be at least twelve feet high.

"Holy shit, we are in Jack Hill's house," Paige said. "What is even happening right now?"

Jax came out a few moments later with the man whose face

I'd seen on the book jacket, and a lovely woman with honey-blonde hair who could be none other than Jax's mother.

"This is my father, Jack Hill, and this is my mother, Elizabeth," Jax said, pointing to her parents.

"It's Betty, please," Elizabeth said. "You all look cold. Please come in and have some tea."

"We're happy to have you here," Jack Hill said, putting his arm around his daughter. With the two of them side by side, it was hard to believe I didn't see it. Jax was a carbon copy of her father, minus the hair that she'd gotten from her mother.

"Thank you so much for inviting us in, sir," Linley said.

"Please, you can call me James."

I watched as my bewildered friends walked down the hall in Jack Hill's—excuse me—James Hardy's, house, all of them looking around in awe.

"It's not as spooky as I thought it would be," I said to Jax when they were gone.

"Yeah, that's my mother's influence, but my dad does get to have his study however he wants, and he's in charge of Halloween every year." She led me up the stairs and down to a bedroom that was almost as large as the master in her house. This room also had a Christmas tree.

"Oh wow, you weren't kidding about your mom being extra about decorating," I said.

Jax smiled as I looked at the tree. This one was obviously artificial, since it was white and sparkly, and covered in silver ornaments and lights that looked like flickering candles.

Jax dug around in her suitcase and pulled out a small box that was wrapped in red paper with a white bow on it.

"I've had this for a while and I've just been carrying it around. I don't know why. But since you're here…" She trailed off and handed me the gift. I sat in one of the soft chairs that was placed in front of the fireplace to make a cozy seating area away from the large four-poster bed.

"Did you bring your dildo collection?" I asked, and she shushed me.

"Not all of them," she said, sitting in the other chair with a wink.

I opened the present carefully, instead of just tearing off the paper like I normally would.

I pulled the top off the jewelry box and found a necklace sitting on a little velvet pillow inside.

"Oh, wow," I said. It was a teardrop emerald on a rose gold chain.

"It was my grandmother's, but I got a new chain for it. I just... It looked like you," she said. I touched the emerald that sparkled on the pillow. Not only was it perfectly cut, it was also huge. I knew emeralds weren't as expensive as other stones, but something told me this one was more than a few carats.

"It's so beautiful," I said, picking it up.

"Let me help you," she said, and I pulled my hair forward so she could fasten the clasp for me before settling the chain around my neck.

I stood up and looked at myself in the mirror above the fireplace.

"It's lovely," I said.

"I got you a present too, but I don't have it with me," I said, getting my phone out. I went to my email and found the order I'd placed after I logged in to the site.

"But you'll get part of it, uh, next week," I said.

"What is it?" she asked.

"You'll have to wait and see," I said, looking up to find her scowling at me.

"I love how much you hate surprises," I said, laughing.

Jax leaned back in her chair.

"It's weird seeing you here," she said.

"I know. This was the last place I expected to find Jax

Hardy. You're going to have to tell me all about how it was to grow up with a famous horror author as your dad."

Jax rolled her eyes.

"It's not really that interesting. He'd camp out in his office, and sometimes he'd go on trips and bring me back fun things from the various places he visited. For the most part, it was probably like having any other kind of dad."

"I'm not so sure about that. I'm guessing your Halloweens were very different than mine."

"Okay, that's definitely true," she said and then she sighed. "I missed you, Sasha. Everything's been really shitty without you, to be honest."

"I haven't exactly been having a good time either." She didn't need to know just how badly I'd been doing without her.

"I shouldn't have let that comment get to me so much. And after you left, I realized that I didn't want to lose you. I went to that party hoping to see you, but then you disappeared."

Wait, was she saying what I thought she was saying?

"I love you," I said, just completely cutting her off. "Sorry, I just had to say that. I've been holding it in, and I couldn't anymore. Continue." I gestured to her to keep speaking.

"What did you just say?" She stood up and fell to her knees in front of my chair, grabbing both my hands.

"Did you say that you love me?"

"Yes, I did. Sorry."

She stared at me. "Why are you apologizing?"

"I'm not really sure," I said. "I'm not really sure what I'm doing or saying right now. Everything feels completely surreal." She squeezed my hands.

"It's real. I'm real. And I love you, Sasha. I wanted to tell you for so long, but we said this was a casual thing and I didn't want to hold you back from your dream of moving back to Boston. I didn't want to hold you back in a life you didn't want."

I clutched her hands, using her to hold me in the moment so I didn't float away.

"Boston isn't my dream anymore. You are."

She started to cry, and I couldn't have that, so I pulled her up so I could kiss her.

"I'm really hoping those are happy tears," I said, holding her face between my hands.

"They are," she said, laughing a little.

"I love you," I said again, just for the joy of saying it.

"I love you, too," she said, kissing me, and pushing me back into the chair.

I had no idea how it was going to work between us. How we would find the hours in the day to see each other, how we would tell my sister, how to do a relationship between us. All I did know was that I loved her, and I had to have her in my life.

"I want you to meet my sister, not as Luna's teacher, but as my girlfriend," I said. If she wanted, I'd take her to my house right now.

"I want that too. I know it's a little complicated. And we'll definitely have to keep things kind of on the down low for a little while," she said. "Just until Luna isn't my student anymore."

Right.

"I'm okay with that. I mean, we've sort of gotten good at this covert thing. It's kinda sexy."

"Is it now?"

"Mmm, very," I said, pulling her so she was standing up with me, and running my hands down her back until I squeezed her ass.

"I missed this, too," I said.

"I missed your everything," she said.

"Aw, I was making it dirty and you turned it cute again."

She laughed. "There's no reason that cute and dirty can't coexist."

"That is a true statement," I said and kissed her again.

JAX and I made out in her childhood bedroom until we remembered that my friends were downstairs with her parents, and we should probably see what the hell was going on.

"Finding out you love me and meeting your parents in the same day? That's a lot, Jax," I said. She slipped her hand into mine.

"It'll be okay, I promise."

I took a deep breath.

"I trust you."

Jax led me out of her room and down the stairs, never letting go of my hand.

We found all of my friends sitting in the den of the house, which was massive and had four couches and numerous chairs. Plenty of room for everyone.

Jax's dad, James, was holding court and telling a story that was making everyone laugh while Betty passed around plates of cookies and refilled cups from a teakettle.

It was all very cozy.

"Not having too much fun, are you?" Jax said, making our presence known.

Everyone looked up, and I watched everyone realize that I was holding hands with Jax, so I figured I should just break the silence. I held our hands up.

"Yeah, this happened," I said. "Mr. and Mrs. Hardy, I love your daughter."

"Oh, so you're just going for it," Jax said, staring at me.

"Yeah, why not. Go big," I said, smiling at her.

She grinned back at me and she was so pretty that I couldn't stop myself from kissing her.

"I think that deserves a round of applause," Paige said, and a few people clapped as Jax broke the kiss and laughed. I could feel myself blushing.

James walked over and held out his hand.

"Well, Sasha, it's so nice to finally meet you. I feel like I know you already."

I shook his hand.

"I've talked about you a little bit," Jax said, blushing even harder.

"Can I give you a hug?" Betty asked, coming over and holding her arms out.

"Yeah, sure," I said, and she enveloped me, and her hug smelled like expensive perfume and gingerbread cookies.

Betty pulled back and her eyes flicked down to the necklace that rested against my chest.

"That looks absolutely beautiful on you, dear."

I took a shaky breath and my friends moved over on one of the couches so Jax and I could sit down. I felt like I was on stage for an audience, but Betty said that she could take everyone on a tour of the house, including the library, so soon it was just me and Jax and James. Or Mr. Hardy? I wasn't sure what to call him.

"It's so nice to see Jax smiling. She's been pretty morose lately," James said, sitting back in his chair and studying me behind the rim of his glasses.

"Dad," Jax said. "I wasn't that bad."

"There is no chocolate to be had in this house. You even found my secret stash," he said to Jax.

"Only because the code on your safe is literally my birthday. Get a more secure password," Jax said, and I watched the back and forth between them with amusement. Something told me she and her dad were two peas in a pod.

James's attention turned to me, and he asked me a few questions about myself. I tried my best to answer, holding onto Jax's hand. I just wanted him to like me.

"What a coincidence that your book club would pick my book," he said, musing.

"I know. Out of all the books," I said.

"Out of all the classrooms in all the schools in all the world, she had to walk into mine," Jax said, emulating a quote from a famous movie.

"Dork," I whispered to her, bumping her shoulder with mine.

I glanced over to find James watching us.

"It really is so nice to meet you, Sasha."

I HUNG out a little bit longer with Jax and James, and then the group came back.

"So, uh, we're going to head out, if that's okay," Paige said. "Do you want to come with us, or..." She left it open ended.

"I'm going to stay," I said as Jax put her arm around me.

"I'll make sure she gets back to Castleton in one piece," she said. "It was really nice to meet all of you. I'm sorry for crashing your Non Book Club."

"Oh, it's more than okay," Charli said, winking at me.

Someone ran to the cars and got all the books for James to sign, which he did, and then gave everyone extra copies of some of his other books, also signed.

My friends were sent off with piles of books and smiles on their faces.

The door closed and the house was quiet except for the music.

"I'm so happy you're staying for dinner," Betty said, putting her arm around me. "I've got to get to know this woman that has my daughter so entranced."

"Entranced?" I asked, looking at Jax, who rolled her eyes.

Looks like her parents liked to wind her up as much as I did.

We all headed for the kitchen, which was even more elaborate than the one at Jax's.

"How do you feel about chicken tikka masala with rice and saag paneer and naan?"

"That sounds amazing," I said. I used to order Indian food whenever I had a bad day in Boston, which means I ate it at least several times a week. I'd attempted to copycat some of my favorite dishes at home, but I just didn't have the right touch.

I watched Jax and her mom cook while her dad stood by and offered suggestions that neither of them took. I liked their family dynamic. It felt like the one I had with Lizzie and Luna.

I ended up sending Lizzie a message trying to explain what had happened, but she had so many questions that I said I would explain when I got back. Right now, I just wanted to be with Jax. The time for questions and introductions would come tomorrow. Too much had already happened today.

I started asking James about his writing process and he was more than happy to talk about it, and ended up asking me questions about my work.

"You know, I've been meaning to hire another member for my team for a while. Someone younger who knows more about social media than I do," he said with a chuckle.

"You don't have to hire me just because I'm in love with your daughter," I said.

"I know. But I'd still like to see some of your work. See if we might be a good fit." He gave me his email, and I really hoped he didn't hire me just to make Jax happy, but only time would tell.

We sat down on one end of an absolutely enormous dining table. The food was incredible, and I ate so much I could barely move.

"That was wonderful, thank you," I said, pushing my plate away when I absolutely could not eat any more.

"I hoped you saved room for dessert," Betty said, getting up to take my plate. I protested, but she said I was a guest.

Jax and James brought me back into the den and we sat while Betty passed out little glasses of port and even more cookies. I guess I knew where Jax got her cooking skills from.

When I'd thought about meeting Jax's parents, I'd pictured cold people, very WASP-y, who wouldn't talk about emotions and wouldn't laugh.

James and Betty were warm and charming and every bit as wonderful as their daughter. How could they not be? I relaxed in the opulent house, and even though I was still nervous about spilling on the furniture, I wasn't afraid to talk with them anymore.

"I want to show you the library," Jax said in my ear.

"Okay," I said. I thanked James and Betty for everything and went upstairs with Jax.

"So, you come by your book collection honestly," I said as she took me to a room that was across from her bedroom.

"Oh, shit," I said.

The library was two stories, and even had a balcony to get to the second floor of books. And ladders. Multiple.

"Holy shit," I said, looking around. "This is a lot of books."

"Yeah, I don't like to think how much they weigh," Jax said. "I make sure that my parents have someone come out to make sure the foundation is stable every year or so," Jax said with a laugh. "I spent more time here than I did in my room."

"I can see why," I said.

"I used to make my dad push those two desks together and put blankets over them and then I'd crawl under it and read," Jax said.

"We make forts with Luna in the living room," I said. Luna would love this place.

Jax showed me around the room, the rarest books, and the ones that were from her personal childhood collection.

Then she took me back to her room and closed the door, making sure it was locked.

"I missed you," she said, leaning against the door.

"I know, I missed you," I said.

"I think it's time we reunited," she said, stepping toward me, and I figured out what she missed. As soon as she touched me, I almost moaned in relief. It felt like we'd been apart for years, not weeks. Her touch was both familiar and intense, lighting me up from the inside.

"How many toys did you bring?" I asked her as we stumbled toward the bed, trying to get our clothes off as quickly as possible.

"Enough," she said, laughing as she reached down to her suitcase. "Let me show you."

Epilogue

"I CALL this meeting of Non Book Club to order," Paige said, pretending to strike a gavel.

"I thought we weren't doing that," Esme said.

"Well, I just did," Paige countered, looking at us.

"Okay, carry on," Esme said, smiling at Paige.

"So, we're starting our newest Jack Hill book tonight, does everyone have their copy?"

All my friends, and Jax, held up their hardcover copies.

"He really didn't have to send so many," Jax grumbled.

"It was very nice of him," I said, nudging her.

Our book club was still going strong, two months after we'd started with that first Jack Hill book. Now it was spring and we were reading his latest. During our last meeting, we'd got a visit from the author himself, which was a rare treat as he didn't do appearances like that. I had connections.

Jax had joined our club and managed to have incredible insights that I loved to hear for hours. Her mind fascinated and enthralled me every single day. I still wasn't officially living in her house, but I might as well have been. I usually spent most of the week there, going back to Lizzie's on the weekends to have time with Luna. She'd taken the transition surprisingly well, and actually loved that I was dating her teacher. Lizzie had been surprised, of course, but when she saw us together, she said she couldn't imagine me with anyone else. I felt the same way.

"That was fun," Jax said, on the way back to her house from Em and Natalie's after Non Book Club.

"I'm glad you like it. And I'm glad you like my friends. That would have been a disaster if you didn't."

"Your friends like you, I love you, ergo, I like your friends," she said.

"I can't wait until Hollis gets here," I said.

In completely shocking news, Hollis had announced to me that she, too, was moving to Castleton. Her mom had somehow gotten the crumbling farmhouse livable, and had even fixed up the barn to be a cozy little apartment. I wouldn't call it bribery, exactly, but she did know how to get Hollis to move out of the city she promised she would never move out of.

"She sounded like she was sick of the city," Jax said. She often jumped in to chat with Hollis, and the two of them got along surprisingly well.

"Yeah, I have no idea what that's about, but I just can't picture her here. She's going to be climbing up the walls." If I had suffered without 2 a.m. takeout, Hollis was really going to suffer. It was going to be interesting to see, I'd say that much.

"How about we take Luna to the beach this weekend?" Jax asked. "It's supposed to be gorgeous."

"Yeah, we can give Lizzie a break." Lizzie was absolutely killing it in her online program, but it did mean that she needed more help with Luna. It was a good thing that she and Anna had formed a quick and tight bond that mirrored that of their children. Anna was more than happy to grab Luna from school or watch her for a few hours so Lizzie could get work done. We'd also found an excellent babysitter for emergencies.

All of those problems that I thought would crop up ended up being no big deal. They all fell away in the face of my fierce love for Jax. The two of us made a team that could take on anything.

"How do you feel about Tuscany?" she asked out of the blue.

"I don't know, why are you asking?" I asked. She knew I had always wanted to go there.

"I was thinking, since we have all this wonderful time together, that we should take a trip. You said you wanted to go to Tuscany, but if you prefer somewhere else, we can go somewhere else."

She said it so casually.

"Oh, wow. A trip." I had been on very few trips in my life, so there were dozens of places I wanted to go.

"You'll love it. We can tour the vineyards and get tipsy and silly and eat too much bread and fuck in a villa," she said.

I was in favor of all of those things.

"Until then, how about we go home, have some bread, and then fuck in *our* villa?" I asked.

Jax laughed. "I love this plan. Especially the fucking. And the bread, to be honest. We have that new loaf of challah from Sweet's."

Now that Sweet's Sweets had expanded, I was never in want of baked goods. I picked up an order every time I came back to Castleton.

"I love bread," I said.

"And me?" Jax asked.

"Oh yeah, I love you. But the bread…"

"So, you're saying you love bread more than me, I see how it is," she said, pretending to be offended.

"Oh, Jax, I love bread, but I love you more. You know that.

Bread doesn't cuddle me in the middle of the night. Bread doesn't wake me up with a beautiful breakfast every morning. Bread doesn't make me laugh so hard that my stomach hurts. Bread doesn't have those incredible boobs." The last part made her laugh.

"You could make bread boobs," she pointed out.

"Not as pretty as yours," I said as she pulled into the driveway and turned the car off.

"I love you," she said, reaching for me.

"I love you so much more than bread," I said, and she kissed me.

About Just One Date

Hollis Carr never expected her city-loving self moving to Castleton, Maine, and living in a converted barn. She's not totally hating the slower pace of life in Castleton, but one thing she can't handle is the pressure from her mother and her sister to find a nice person to settle down with. Hollis doesn't do love, period.

Only after immense pressure does she agree to go out with Julia Williams, her sister Ellie's co-worker. Julia is petite and bright and shiny in a way that Hollis finds completely irresistible, not to mention she's not as innocent as she seems. Hollis can't believe her luck when Julia says that she only agreed to the date to get a persistent suitor off her back. She proposes an arrangement that will benefit them both: pretend to date for the summer, then have a massively public breakup, and go their separate ways.

One small, very tiny problem: Hollis has fallen utterly in love with sweet, bubbly Julia. She closed off her heart many years ago and was convinced that no one could make her feel that way again. Will Hollis risk everything for love? Or will she slam the door and walk away forever?

When my alarm went off and I opened my eyes, for a second I thought I'd been kidnapped. I looked up at the wood beams above my head and remembered that no, I did not live in a tiny Boston apartment with popcorn ceilings anymore. I now lived in a converted barn that I swore still smelled like horses.

"Another day in paradise," I said to myself as I got up and walked down the steps from the converted hayloft, where I slept, to the downstairs area. What had once housed livestock had been converted into a living room, kitchen, and decently sized bathroom. When my mother had showed me the plans, I hadn't known that she'd been building the place with me in mind, but I should have. One of her main goals in life had been to get her two chicks (me and my sister Ellie) back under her roof so she could meddle in our lives like a mother hen. In a loving way, of course. Ellie was easier to convince than I was.

I got dressed and, even though I had my own kitchen, I stumbled across the yard and made my way to the main house.

"Good morning," I called, coming in the side door. The farmhouse was bright and full of sunshine and still smelled slightly of fresh paint.

"Come and have some breakfast, my love," my mother called back as I walked into the kitchen, which was at the back of the house.

"Ellie already left for work, but I've been keeping a plate warm for you, sleepyhead," Mom said, beaming at me. She was already dressed and had probably been up for hours.

"Thanks, Mom," I said, sitting down on one of the stools at the island as she heated up a plate of blueberry pancakes, bacon, and potatoes. Yes, I was a grown-ass woman, but I'd tried to fight her making me breakfast every morning. That had resulted in her knocking on my door and barging in with food anyway, so it was easier to just let her do her thing. She needed hobbies in her retirement, and cooking was one of them.

She also poured me a cup of coffee and frothed some almond milk as well. We were very high class at the Carr house.

"There you go, angel," Mom said, giving me my latte.

"Thank you," I said as I poured syrup on my pancakes. Mom leaned on the counter and stared at me.

"I know you're absolutely dying to talk to me, but I'm gonna need a few minutes." Both my mom and sister woke up like hyper birds, chattering away as soon as their eyes opened. It was a lot to take, which was why some mornings I waited until my sister left for work before I walked into the house. Two of them at once was just too much.

"What are your plans for today?" Mom asked, mere seconds later, as if she hadn't heard me.

"Work, Mom. Lots of work." I absolutely loved my job as a freelance book cover and graphic designer. I got to make an image that would speak the thousands of words my authors had so carefully written. Best job ever.

"Any plans this weekend?" she asked, leaning in a little bit closer as I crunched on my bacon.

"Trying to get into trouble, probably," I said. Since my move, my weekend plans had become decidedly less exciting. At least Castleton had a bar.

"Maybe you could go on a date?" Mom said hopefully. I shouldn't have come over for breakfast. I should have locked my doors and hid under the covers.

"Mom, we talked about this yesterday." And the day before that. And the night before that. I swear, there hasn't been a day since I got here a few weeks ago that hasn't involved my mom or my sister asking me about my dating life.

My phone vibrated with a message from my best friend, Sasha. She had excellent timing.

Work date today?

Sasha was also a freelancer like me, and she would meet a few days a week with her friend Paige, another freelancer, at the Castleton Cafe to have coffee, work, and use their excellent wi-fi.

Meet you in an hour? I sent back to her. I needed some more time to wake my brain up.

"I just want you to be happy," Mom said, tears in her eyes. She was really laying it on thick.

"Mom, I am happy. I'm fine."

Her only answer was a sigh. That sigh said she didn't believe me.

What did "happy" mean, anyway? No one was happy all the time. That wasn't realistic.

I finished my breakfast while listening to disapproving noises from my mother, and then gave her a kiss and headed back to the barn to get ready to meet Sasha.

~

"We finally booked our tickets to Tuscany for the fall," Sasha told me excitedly, when I sat down with her and Paige at the café with an iced tea. Sasha's girlfriend, Jax, just happened to be the daughter of bestselling (and extremely wealthy) horror author Jack Hill, a fact that had stunned all of us because she'd hidden it so well. They claimed they weren't living together, but Sasha was at Jax's house about ninety percent of the time, so I didn't know what else you'd call it. Sasha was happy, and Jax spoiled her, which thrilled me and gave Jax bonus points in my book.

"Are you nervous?" I asked Sasha.

She shook her head. "I'm going with the most prepared woman in the world." The smile on her face was soft. Sasha was so in love, and it was so cute.

"You'll have to give me all your travel tips," Paige said, sipping her mystery drink and cringing. "Oh, that's not my favorite." Blue, one of the baristas of the Castleton Cafe, liked to test out wacky flavor combinations, and Paige was often a willing sacrifice.

"I'm trying to plan the honeymoon with Esme and we're having a lot of disagreements about where we want to go," she said. Paige was marrying Esme, the bartender from the Pine State Bar and Grille, this summer. Since I was so new to town,

I hadn't expected to even be invited, but an invitation had shown up in my mom's mailbox. *Hollis Carr and Guest.*

"What are you disagreeing about?" I asked. Paige rolled her huge brown eyes.

"Well, I want to go to Iceland, and Esme wants to go to Hawaii. So we're kind of at an impasse." I laughed. Talk about opposites attracting.

"Is there some kind of compromise?" Sasha asked. "What about like, Ireland?"

"How is Ireland a compromise between Iceland and Hawaii?" I asked her.

"Well, it's a middle ground, in terms of climate, and they have all the whiskey places there. Esme would love that," Sasha said, as if this was completely obvious.

"Oh!" Paige said. "That actually isn't a bad idea. Thanks, Sasha!" Sasha blushed from her cheeks to the tips of her ears. As a redhead, she couldn't exactly hide any of her feelings. Her sincerity was one of the things I adored about her.

"Okay, enough about my honeymoon," Paige said. "We should probably work."

Each of us used our headphones or earbuds of choice, cracked open our laptops, and started working. We might have been sitting at the same table, but we were each in our own worlds.

I checked my daily spreadsheet to figure out what deadlines I had coming up, and what tasks I needed to get done sooner rather than later. I had edits that I needed to complete on a fantasy cover for an author, I needed to search stock images for a romance cover, and I had to format a paperback cover and hardcover for a third author. Then there were the endless emails, the website updating, the invoice sending, and all the other nonsense that I had to deal with owning my own business.

It wasn't until Sasha tapped me on the shoulder that I realized I was absolutely starving. The three of us took a break to eat fresh chicken salad sandwiches and refuel our caffeine stores.

I found that I'd missed a text from my sister, Ellie. She'd gotten a job at a daycare in Castleton called Magic Castle Daycare, and she'd often send me funny videos of the kids throughout my day.

What are you doing this weekend? she asked, and I frowned at the message. I'd been hoping one of the daycare kids had said something cute.

Why are you asking? I responded to her. I knew why she was asking. She and my mom had a mission to set me up with one of Ellie's coworkers. No idea why, but they were persistent.

No reason. Are you at the café today? Oh she definitely had a reason. Neither my mother nor my sister was sneaky. A lot like Sasha, actually. Maybe that's why she was my best friend.

Yeah, I'm here, why?

I still had my radar of suspicion up.

Just checking. Thought I might come say hi after work if you're still there.

That didn't make any sense. I'd just see her at home later. Something was afoot and I wasn't pleased.

"Everything okay?" Sasha asked.

"Swell," I said. "Just my meddling family doing the most."

"Still trying to get you to date that girl?" Sasha asked.

"Yup. I'm really hoping they don't stoop to kidnapping me, but I wouldn't put it past them." Both Paige and Sasha laughed.

"They sound like Linley's mom, Martha. Now that she's gotten her daughter married, she's concentrated her efforts on becoming a grandmother," Paige said, speaking of another one of her friends. Sasha referred to them as the Castleton Crew. Linley's parents owned Sweet's Sweets Bakery, which was just two shops away from the café. They also had recently finished a huge commercial kitchen and now shipped their delicious baked goods all over the US. From what I'd heard, the matriarch of the Sweet family, Martha, was a force to behold. Sounded like my own mother when she set her mind to something.

"She has my sympathies," I said. Sasha had been bugging me to join their book club, but I'd been resistant. I was still trying to find my groove in Castleton. It was just so different from Boston that I was really having issues adjusting. I needed to figure out my place here before I jumped in with a huge already established group. Sasha and my family were more than enough for now.

Eventually, we all went back to work and I was completely immersed when Sasha tapped on my shoulder.

"Your sister's here," she said, nodding toward the door. Ellie waved to me, a huge smile on her face. Ellie and my mom were carbon copies of each other, with full smiles and rounded cheeks. Unfortunately, I'd taken after my dipshit dad with weird angles and a strong nose that I'd been made fun of for in school, but the bullies had stopped when they realized I didn't care what they said. My nose made a statement.

Ellie, my mom, and I all shared dark hair, which was nice.

But it wasn't my sister that I was looking at. Oh no. It was the creature beside her with the reddish-brown hair and the dark green cat-eye glasses. She was petite; I didn't think she'd top 5'3". And, oh, she had curves not only for days, but for lifetimes. I swore my mouth immediately started watering.

"Who is that?" I breathed as Ellie walked over with the stranger. I couldn't take my eyes off her as she moved.

"Hey, Hollis, fancy seeing you here," my sister said, pretending to be shocked to see me. "I just thought I would swing by and grab a few treats for everyone at work and Julia volunteered to come with me." She gestured at the beautiful woman beside her.

"Hi," Julia said, waving at all three of us.

"*You're* Julia?" I asked.

"I'm Julia," she said, blushing and pushing her glasses up her nose.

About the Author

Chelsea M. Cameron is a New York Times/USA Today/Internationally Bestselling author from Maine who now lives and works in Boston. She's a red velvet cake enthusiast, obsessive tea drinker, former cheerleader, and world's worst video gamer. When not writing, she enjoys watching infomercials, eating brunch in bed, tweeting, and playing fetch with her cat, Sassenach. She has a degree in journalism from the University of Maine, Orono that she promptly abandoned to write about the people in her own head. More often than not, these people turn out to be just as weird as she is.

Connect with her on Twitter, Facebook, Instagram, Bookbub, Goodreads, and her website.

If you liked this book, please take a few moments to **leave a review**. Authors really appreciate this and it helps new readers find books they might enjoy. Thank you!

Also by Chelsea M. Cameron

The Noctalis Chronicles

Fall and Rise Series

My Favorite Mistake Series

The Surrender Saga

Rules of Love Series

UnWritten

Behind Your Back Series

OTP Series

Brooks (The Benson Brothers)

The Violet Hill Series

Unveiled Attraction

Anyone but You

Didn't Stay in Vegas

Wicked Sweet

Christmas Inn Maine

Bring Her On

The Girl Next Door

Who We Could Be

Castleton Hearts

Mainely Books Club

Love in Vacationland

Made in the USA
Columbia, SC
27 September 2023

23485397R00150